Tessa

Tessa

From Fear to Faith

Melissa Wiltrout

Melissa Wiltrout 12/20/13

LIFE SENTENCE
Publishing, LLC

www.lifesentencepublishing.com

TESSA – Melissa Wiltrout

Scripture quotations taken from the New American Standard Bible®, Copyright © 1960, 1962, 1963, 1968, 1971, 1972, 1973, 1975, 1977, 1995 by The Lockman Foundation

Used by permission. (www.Lockman.org)

First edition published 2013

LIFE SENTENCE Publishing books are available at discounted prices for ministries and other outreach. Find out more by contacting info@lifesentencepublishing.com

LIFE SENTENCE Publishing and its logo are trademarks of

LIFE SENTENCE Publishing, LLC
P.O. BOX 652
Abbotsford, WI 54405

Paperback ISBN: 978-1-62245-087-9

Ebook ISBN: 978-1-62245-088-6

10 9 8 7 6 5 4 3 2 1

This book is available from www.lifesentencepublishing.com, www.amazon.com, Barnes & Noble, and your local Christian Bookstore

Cover Designer: Amber Burger

Editor: Sheila Wilkinson

Share this book on Facebook

Contents

Acknowledgements

First of all, thank you to Mom and Dad for putting up with the inconveniences of living with a writer. Thanks for believing in me, even when you couldn't fathom my compulsion to rewrite and re-edit everything *ad nauseam*. Thanks for listening, critiquing, and encouraging me.

Thank you to my critique group partners at Western Wisconsin Christian Writers Guild for teaching me to sharpen my writing. I'd still be muddling around on lined paper without that!

Thank you to the talented people at Life Sentence Publishing for turning my manuscript into a book. I especially wish to thank Sheila for patiently answering my endless barrage of punctuation questions.

Most of all, I want to thank my Savior, Jesus, who wrote the true redemption story and signed it in His own blood. My story is but a dim echo of the one He wrote. Thank you, Lord, for your gifts of inspiration, imagination, and language!

1

Stop! Thief!"

Fear stabbed my chest. I dodged in front of a loaded shopping cart and shoved through the outer set of glass doors at Allen's Super Foods. The plastic bag of hot dogs and bread knocked against my leg as I took a sharp left and sprinted down the dark sidewalk.

"Stop, you punk!" Footsteps pounded close behind me. I could hear heavy breathing. I ran faster, willing all my energy into my legs. My breath came in ragged gasps. I kept my eyes fixed on the lights of the busy street half a block ahead. *I sure hope there's a break in the traffic. There's no way I'm gonna be able to stop if there isn't...*

I had cleared the far end of the building and was racing across the final stretch of parking lot when the clerk caught up with me. He grabbed my shoulders and kicked me in the legs, slamming me to the pavement. I screamed as pain ripped through my right ankle and leg. He threw himself on top of me, closing huge hands around my neck and shoulders. "I got you now, you punk."

His sudden weight on my back left me breathless. I struggled to roll him off, but he tightened his grip. His knee pressed into my back and his fingernails dug into my shoulder like claws. "Oh no you don't."

"I . . . can't breathe," I gasped. "Get . . . off of me."

"That's what you all say. I'll get off of you all right – when the police get here." As he spoke, he shifted his weight higher on my back. My chest began to hurt.

"No," I pleaded. "Stop. You're . . . killing me."

"Shut up," he said. I heard a faint beep, beep as he pressed the buttons on his cell phone. I was crying. Sharp pains shot up my leg from my twisted ankle, and I was helpless to relieve them. Cold pavement bit into my chin. I tasted blood where I'd cut my lip falling. I made one more attempt to free myself, but it was no use. The guy must've weighed two hundred pounds. At last a police cruiser pulled up with its lights flashing, and an officer stepped out.

"You Bruce Sommerfeld?" he said to the clerk.

"I am."

"You can let go now. I've got her."

Bruce surrendered his grip on me reluctantly. "I caught this little punk red-handed. And it's not the first time she's pulled this. I can prove it."

I took a breath and started to push myself up, but the officer stopped me, pulling my hands behind my back. Cold metal clamped around my left wrist, then my right. What on earth was he doing? Handcuffing me? I hoped nobody was watching.

Fresh pain shot through my ankle as the officer pulled me to my feet. "So you were shoplifting, huh?" he said.

It wasn't a dream this time. I was being arrested.

"I didn't do nothin'. I swear!" Frantically I tried to wrench free of the steel cuffs. "He's lying. He hates me. You all hate me!"

"That's enough. Settle down." A second officer, a woman, stepped close and took my other arm. She began steering me toward the black and white car. "My name's Pat. And you are . . . ?"

I didn't answer. My wrists stung from my fight with the cuffs. I had never felt so helpless and humiliated in my life.

Pat opened the rear door of the cruiser. "Okay, in you go."

I hesitated as my eyes took in the hard black seat, the bars over the window, the mesh divider. This was for criminals, not for somebody like me. Did I have to get in? But the firm pressure on my arm told me I had no choice. I dropped into the seat, my face hot, wincing as my hurt ankle bumped the door frame.

I fit in there – sort of. There wasn't more than eight inches of knee room in front of that seat, and with my hands squashed behind my back, I was miserable to say the least. They didn't really expect me to ride like this, did they?

Tears pricked my eyes. I bit my lip hard to restrain them. Through the barred window, I saw Bruce enter the store with my bag of food. As if he needed it. My stomach growled, reminding me I hadn't eaten since yesterday.

"How old are you, kid?" Pat twisted around to look at me from the driver's seat.

"Old enough."

"Old enough to be on your own?"

In the darkness, I felt my face flush. *Is it that obvious I'm a runaway?* I thought of the stains on my jeans, the long, jagged tear in the sleeve of my purple sweatshirt, and the shiny wire I'd used to reattach the soles of my worn tennis shoes – all things I had convinced myself no one would notice. I must've been crazy.

Heat blew into the back of the car, raising a smell of sweat and dirty clothes. I tried to flip back the tangled locks of dark hair that kept falling across my face. My teeth chattered, but not from cold. I was scared of being put in jail.

The ride to the Northford Police Station was short. Pat pulled into the garage. From there, she marched me into a long narrow room. I squinted against the glare of fluorescent lights. Pat removed the handcuffs and directed me to one of the plastic chairs at a small table.

I sank into the chair, glad to get off my hurt ankle. By now it had swollen to the size of a small grapefruit. The pain was agonizing. Had I broken it? I leaned forward and with one hand loosened my shoelaces. Even that was a painful operation. Making it all the way back to the garage where I was staying would be impossible.

"Did you hurt your ankle?" Pat asked. She pulled the other chair around to sit facing me.

I stiffened. "It'll be okay." Did she have to sit so close to me?

"You sure? You were limping on the way in."

I hesitated, torn by the sympathy in her voice. But did I dare confide in a cop?

"It's nothing, really. I-I got a charley horse."

"I see. How long has it been since you left home?"

"Awhile." My eyes traced the green and white tiles at my feet. If only I could get rid of that lump in my throat that threatened to make me cry.

"Like a week? Ten days?"

"Yeah, maybe." It had been longer, but she didn't need to know that.

"That's a long time. Have you been stealing food this whole time?"

"Some of it."

"Yes?" she pressed. "How much is some?"

"Most of it, I guess."

"You know stealing is a crime, don't you? You can be fined and even imprisoned for it. If you need food, there are better ways to get it."

"Well yeah, but –"

"No buts. Maybe no one's ever told you this, but stealing is wrong. It's serious. You ought to be ashamed of yourself."

I could feel the heat rising in my cheeks. What did Pat know? She'd never gone hungry or spent the night under a deck in the drizzling rain. It wasn't like I'd hurt somebody. The store would never miss what little I'd taken.

Pat shuffled a few papers on her lap. "I understand the store is not pressing charges this time. However…" She paused for emphasis. "If this sort of thing happens again, you will be charged with retail theft. You'll have to go to court and pay the consequences. Plus it will get on your record. Do you understand?"

"Yeah." I felt a tiny glimmer of hope. "Does this mean you're gonna let me go?"

"It means your parents will have to come get you. I take it you're not on the best terms with them just now. Am I right?"

I exhaled slowly. My sweaty hands clenched in my lap. I should've known they'd call my parents.

I felt Pat eyeing me. "It's that bad, huh? Want to talk about it?"

My mind raced. For a second I considered it, but then I shook my head. Talking would only make things worse. Much worse.

Pat was still watching me. "I've got the time," she said.

I shook my head harder. "Can't you just let me go? It's not like I'm gonna do this again or something."

"Sorry, but it's not my call. Rules are rules." Pat laid her papers on the table. "You're Tessa Miner, am I right? And your parents are Walter and Julie Miner?"

I gulped. How did she know that?

"Is this phone number correct?"

I had to stop her somehow. "Look, you don't hafta call them, okay? I-I'll just walk home."

Pat stood up.

"Can't I? I'll go right home, I promise. It's not that far, and…"

"Ten miles with a hurt ankle isn't far, huh?" There was sarcasm in her voice now. She shook her head. "It doesn't work that way, Tessa."

I was trapped. There was no way out. Even supposing the doors weren't locked, I'd never escape with this ankle. The muscles in my chest constricted, suffocating me. I leaned my elbows on the table and forced myself to breathe. I needed to be at my best to face Walter.

Walter. The name dredged up images I didn't want to remember. I could see my father standing there, his hands on his hips as he screamed at me.

"You idiot, what'd you do that for!"

"You're coming if I gotta drag you there! Now get out here!"

"Guess you didn't listen, did you. Well, this time I'll make you!"

I could see the home place – the shabby white house with its sagging porch, the huge junk heap in the back yard, and my dad's green, almost-brand-new pickup truck parked in the driveway. I could smell the cigarette smoke and the coffee. I could see, too, the secret garden by the back fence that was my dad's special concern. He allowed Mom to plant hibiscus and hollyhocks along the edge, but the rest was off limits. I learned this the day I tried to capture a baby rabbit that was trapped inside the fence. Walter caught me in there and beat me bloody, even though I hadn't damaged anything.

I could see the old shed near the garden, where Walter had locked me up for two days after my last attempt at running away. I recalled the torture of spending a night leaning up against the lawnmower, my back aching like fire while I tried to ignore the rodents scurrying and chewing in the walls around me. I'd be lucky if that was all I had to face this time.

A sudden noise in the room caused me to start in fear. Had my father come already? But it was only Pat dropping a pen. I sank back, my heart still pounding. If only I could awaken from this nightmare. But try as I did, I could not suppress the memories which played like a bad movie across my mind.

I felt a hand on my shoulder. "Tessa, your father's here."

2

*W*alter was standing, arms folded, in the lobby of the police station. He looked the same as always – stained zip-front jacket, oversized pair of dirty Levis, scuffed boots. Stubble covered his chin. A crumpled baseball cap, more pink than red after a summer of wear, topped a tangle of curly hair that should have been trimmed weeks ago. His eyes hardened when he saw me.

"So here's the tramp." He clamped a heavy hand on my shoulder. "Told you I'd find you." His steel blue eyes bored right through me.

I couldn't breathe.

Walter wasted no time. "Well, come on. You're needed at home." Grasping me by the arm, he walked me out to the pickup. I fought to conceal the agony of each step. If he found out about my ankle, he'd take advantage of it somehow.

The familiar odor of smoke and stale mouse nests greeted me as I swung up into the warm cab. Walter slammed the door behind me and walked around to the driver's side. The radio burst to life when he turned the key – the same disgusting rock station he always listened to.

I hunched in the seat, picking at the hole in my jeans as Walter pulled the truck away from the curb. He drove in silence, his lips pressed into a thin line, his jaw set. Wasn't he going to yell at me? Threaten me? Tell me how much trouble I'd be in when I got home?

Buildings slipped past my window – the bakery, the print shop, the senior center, the public library – all of them closed and dark. A knot of dread tightened in my stomach. Why was Walter driving up through the east end of town? He should have turned on Main Street, a block from the police station, and taken the bridge out of town.

I tried to quiet my fears. No doubt he was planning to stop at one of the taverns along the river. But when he turned on Washington Avenue and crossed the river, leaving the city behind, I knew I was in trouble.

"Where are we going?" I ventured.

Walter didn't reply. The road snaked through a large industrial development and bumped over three sets of railroad tracks before taking us out into the country. Fearfully I stared into the passing woods. Not only did I have no idea where we were, but the occasional houses were separated by long stretches of forest. I was alone in the middle of nowhere with a man I knew would hurt me.

I kept trying to think of a way to escape. But I had no weapon of any kind, and even if I managed to get out of the truck, I wouldn't be able to run on account of my stupid ankle. Briefly I wondered if it would do any good to pray.

Rounding one of the curves, Walter braked and turned down a rutted dirt lane. Trees arched overhead and branches slashed the sides of the truck as we careened ahead. I gripped the seat with both hands and held my breath, too scared to ask what he was doing.

Maybe I should have talked to Pat. The thought haunted me. It was too late now.

Walter kept driving and soon turned onto a one-lane gravel road. I strained my eyes through the darkness for a road sign, but could find none. My fear increased as I realized Walter could do anything to me here, even kill me, and get away with it. I contemplated jumping from the truck, but at fifty miles an hour, I couldn't bring myself to do it. If only I'd had the sense to escape while we were yet in town.

A short distance down the road, the trees gave way to grassland. Moonlight shimmered off a wide creek. Here Walter pulled partly off the narrow road and jammed on the brakes.

I had my door unlatched even before the truck came to a stop. Hurt ankle or not, I was determined to run. But my door wouldn't open. I pushed harder, but to no avail. Walter had parked against a guardrail.

I had no time to react. Walter reached over and shoved me, slamming my head into the door frame. Then he began dragging me across the seat. I grabbed the steering wheel and we wrestled for a moment, but I was no match for his two hundred pounds of muscle.

He pulled me from the truck and threw me to the ground. "This'll teach you to rat on me!" he yelled. "Nobody pulls that on me and gets away with it!"

What? Too shaken and terrified to argue, I started screaming.

If anything, that seemed to fuel Walter's rage. He grabbed me by the hair and began to smash my face into the hard-packed gravel. I could feel the sharp edges cutting into my skin. I quickly put up my hand to cushion the blows. Blood streamed from my nose and down into my mouth, gagging me.

Walter yanked me upright and shook me, then slammed me down again, this time on my back. I heard a sickening crunch as my head struck the rocks. I tried to roll over, but Walter grabbed my shoulders and slammed me down again.

As the beating continued, I realized he was going to kill me if I didn't do something. But what?

Play dead. The thought came automatically, as if it was programmed into me for situations like this. I stopped screaming and went limp.

It worked. Walter slammed me down one more time and stopped. I lay motionless on the ground, in great pain, too scared to breathe. Would he leave me for dead? Or was he waiting for me to revive so he could beat me some more?

A slight chill passed over me, like a night breeze or maybe a warning. I inched my eyes open. What I saw made me gasp. Walter's big .45 pistol was pressed into my forehead.

Terror constricted my throat so tightly I couldn't scream. The gun stared unmoving, the smooth metal gleaming in the moonlight. I felt sick to my stomach. My vision blurred. Then, through a sort of haze, I saw Walter lower the gun and step back.

"All right, get up. Quit that stupid crying and start walking. You got a long ways to go."

I just stared, unable to process what was happening.

"Come on, move!" He jerked me to my feet, then followed up with a shove which sent me sprawling.

"Move!" he screamed.

Somehow I managed to get to my feet. I stumbled a few dozen yards before I fell again, twisting my injured ankle worse than ever. I began sobbing uncontrollably.

Walter was unrelenting. He grabbed my arm and hauled me to my feet. "Shut up and get going. You're walking home. And stay on the road! Any more trouble, and you know what you got coming." He rested a hand on the gun stuck under his belt.

I couldn't stop crying. The tears stung as they ran down my battered face. I was still bleeding from my nose, and my face and hands and shirt were sticky with blood. Each faltering step was torture. I knew I could not make it very far in my condition, much less all the way home. I also knew if I didn't, Walter would feel justified in punishing me further.

Gravel crunched behind me as Walter pulled the truck up. I could feel the hot breath of the engine on my back. For one awful moment, I thought he was going to run right over me.

"Can't you go any faster?" he yelled.

His cruel words only brought on more sobs. Did he have to make sport of me too? He was so evil. I wished I could just drop dead there in the road and not give him the pleasure of tormenting me further.

Time dragged. The night air was cold, and shivering made my injuries hurt even more. Each agonizing step further cemented my despair. Ahead of me stretched a never-ending tunnel of misery. Why keep going? No one was going to rescue me. I might as well give up.

I wondered if it hurt to die. Even if it did, at least then it would all be over. Walter could never beat me or make fun of me again. The pain and fear and misery would be ended forever. In my thoughts

I found myself pleading with a God I wasn't sure existed. *Please. Don't make me stay in this hell and suffer anymore. Let me die. Please!*

In a daze, I felt myself falling. Then, *whump!* I hit the ground hard. Shivers of pain reverberated throughout my entire body. Had I tripped over something? I tried to get up, but the earth under me heaved and rocked. Dizzy, I sank back to a half-sitting position.

The next thing I knew, Walter was standing over me with a thick wooden stake. "I said move! If you can't walk no more, then you better crawl!"

I tried to move away from him, but my body wouldn't respond. My legs felt like cast iron. Instinctively I ducked, shielding my head with my hand as Walter brought the stake down in a smashing blow. Everything went black, and I remembered no more.

3

In the fog of half consciousness, I thought it all just a horrible nightmare. Surely when I opened my eyes, I'd be back in the garage of the empty house on Spruce Street, lying on the pile of tarps I'd been using as a bed.

I'd had my share of bad dreams since I'd run away. Most involved Walter, but none of them had been quite this real. I felt the pain even in my sleep.

It was the pain that finally roused me. I felt like I'd been run over with Walter's truck. Fire raged in my ankle. I had an excruciating headache and chills, and the harder I shook, the worse everything hurt.

I opened my eyes, but saw nothing but blackness. The stench of gasoline and fermented grass gagged me. From the smell, I knew I was in the shed out back of our house, where Walter had locked me up last time I ran away. I touched a hand to my face. It was caked with dried blood and dirt.

Nausea twisted in my stomach, then burst upward. With effort, I raised myself up on my elbows. Hot tears trickled down my cheeks. Hadn't I been through enough without getting the flu on top of it?

My damp clothes didn't help matters. I had no idea how I had gotten so wet. The fabric felt like ice against my feverish skin. I needed to change, but how?

For what seemed like hours, I lay on the gritty plywood floor, too weak and hurt to look for a more comfortable place even if there had been one. Fear consumed me – fear that I wouldn't be found, fear that Walter would come back and beat me, fear that I was going to die. I didn't dare call out lest I draw Walter's attention. I dozed, only to face terrifying reruns of the beating. I woke up crying and threw up again.

Footsteps crunched in the dry leaves outside the shed, then paused. My heart lurched. What would Walter do to me now? The hinges creaked, splashing sunlight into the room. I froze. Maybe he would think me still unconscious and leave.

"Tess?" It was my mother's voice. "Tess, are you in here?"

Relief surged through me. "I'm over here." My voice was little more than a hoarse whisper.

Mom hurried toward me. I tried to sit up, ashamed to be seen lying on the filthy floor, but sharp pains in my neck stopped me. Mom crouched on the floor beside me and tried to brush the matted hair from my face. "Are you all right?"

It was a dumb question, and she knew it. Compassion warmed her gray eyes and softened the lines twenty-five years of anxiety and cigarettes had etched on her face. For a minute, I thought she was going to cry.

"Oh, honey. I've been looking everywhere for you! Walter didn't tell me you'd been found." She shook her head. "I'm so sorry. What hurts?"

"Everything. Especially . . . my ankle."

Mom dragged the heavy lawnmower back a few feet and knelt down to take a closer look at my ankle. "Ooh. Not good."

I drew a sharp breath as her fingers prodded the injury.

"Just a bad sprain, I think, though it's pretty swollen. You're not gonna be walking on this for a while."

"It's not broken?"

"Don't think so." Her fingers kneaded my ankle once more, harder this time. I was sorry I'd asked.

"We've got to get you back to the house," she said. "Can you walk at all? Maybe if I help you up..." She reached to place her hands under my armpits.

"No. Please." As much pain as I was in, the thought of trying to walk filled me with dread.

"Well, you're not gonna get better out here. Either you let me help you, or I'll have to get Walter."

I let my eyes close, putting off the impossible decision. How could she suggest such a thing, after the way he'd treated me?

Mom sighed. "Let me see if he's still around." She turned abruptly and walked out, latching the door behind her as if she thought I might escape.

I cried when she was gone. Couldn't she show me some tenderness? The thought of facing Walter turned my stomach, but I couldn't muster the strength to get up.

Quite some time passed before Walter arrived. By the way he kicked the door open, I knew he was annoyed. Mom was right behind him; but even so, the sound of his heavy boots clumping across the floor filled me with panic. I knew it was going to hurt when he picked me up.

Hurt it did, a lot worse than I expected. Not only was I bruised all over, but my neck was so stiff and sore that every tiny jolt caused excruciating pain. I was terrified Walter would drop me or slam my injured ankle on the door frame. Somehow, he didn't.

Walter carried me to the house and down the hall to my bedroom, where he dumped me on the bed. Then he left.

Mom rolled me onto an old blanket. Then she brought a dishpan of hot water and a big bath towel.

"What are you gonna do?" I asked, apprehensive.

"Get those wet clothes off of you and clean you up a bit. I can't believe Walter let you lie out there all day without telling me. No wonder you're sick." As she spoke, she worked at the knots in my shoelaces. "Good grief, Tess, even your shoes are soaked. Did Walter drag you through the swamp or something?"

"No. Maybe. I don't know." My voice choked.

Mom didn't pursue the question. I wished she would. I needed to tell someone what he had done! But it was no use telling her unless she wanted to hear.

Mom talked of other things as she peeled off my damp clothes and sponged the blood and dirt from my cuts. It hurt, but I tried my best not to complain, knowing she'd get impatient and be less careful. At last she helped me into a clean nightgown and tucked me into bed with two ice packs bound in a towel around my hurt ankle.

"There, how's that?" she said.

I nodded gratefully. Already I felt warmer.

"Are you up to eating something? I've got some chicken soup in the fridge that I can heat up."

"That'd be good," I said.

Minutes later, she returned with a steaming bowl. The soup tasted good, but my hand shook from the fever and I kept spilling. Mom finally took the bowl and spoon-fed me.

When the soup was gone, she gathered my wet clothes from the floor. "Well, I'm gonna let you rest. If you need anything, just call."

She was going to shut the door and leave, and still she hadn't asked what happened. I couldn't hold the pain inside any longer.

"Mom?"

"Yeah?"

"Don't you even care what Walter does to me?"

A look of puzzlement flickered over her face. "Why, of course I do. You know I do."

"You don't even know what he does." Tears slipped down my face.

"Well, I don't see much point in hashing it over. I'm just glad you're okay." Her hand moved to the doorknob.

I couldn't believe it. Didn't she care about me even a little? Sure, she had addressed the cuts and bruises. But the real agony – the devastating fear and pain I would carry inside for the rest of my life – that she didn't want to hear about. I would have to bear it alone.

The thought was too much for me. I broke down sobbing. Mom dropped the bundle of clothes and sat on the bed, rubbing my shoulder in an awkward attempt to soothe me. "I know. It's been pretty bad, hasn't it."

More sobs shook me. "He . . . he's evil." I couldn't say anything more.

Mom didn't counter me. She just kept rubbing my neck and shoulders in slow, gentle circles until I stopped crying. Then she turned my pillow and slipped away, leaving me to rest.

***

I had contracted a bad case of the flu in addition to my injuries, and I spent the next week in bed. Mom faithfully applied cold packs to my swollen ankle and provided plenty of soup and tea. She was an excellent nurse and never grumbled. But whenever I brought up the events of that night, she'd go quiet and change the subject. As the days passed, I became increasingly frustrated. Every time I fell asleep, I had nightmares. I spent my waking hours brooding, unable even to concentrate on the novels Mom had brought me from the library. Constantly I berated myself for my carelessness in getting caught at the store that night.

But one thing kept puzzling me. I had never given Pat my name, yet she had known who I was and where I lived. There was only one way that could have happened.

I cornered Mom one evening while she was changing my sheets. "So, Walter actually called the cops on me, huh?"

Mom smoothed the sheet, tucked it in at the bottom, and spread a blanket over it.

"No," she said, without looking at me. "I did."

"You? But Mom!"

"Do you have any idea how worried I was about you?" She straightened and faced me. "You're too young to be on your own, you haven't got any friends, anything could've happened. I hope you've learned your lesson this time." She folded back the bedspread and plumped up the pillow. "There, your bed is ready."

"Are you mad at me?" I persisted.

"Mad at you for what?"

I rubbed a hand across my forehead. "For running away." I felt silly saying the words.

Mom sat down on the foot of the bed. "Well, I'd have to say I was. You caused me a lot of worry, and when the police showed up . . . you can imagine the scene that was. But Walter was pretty hard on you. I don't approve of his punishment, and I guess I'm not really mad anymore, only I hope you don't try it again."

I wanted to protest that I had never planned to run away; I'd only done it to escape Walter. But I knew Mom would just tune me out as she had so many times before. So instead, I said, "Why is Walter so mean?"

She shook her head. "When something upsets him, he gets that way. You have to learn to get along with him."

I nearly choked. But Mom was still talking, so I bit my tongue and waited.

"'Course, he wasn't always mean," she continued. "When your sisters were little, he'd play with them, make them laugh." A half smile crept across her face. "I can remember him playing horse with them, down on his knees, both of them riding on his back. Then he'd pretend he was a bear and go growling and lunging, both of them rolling on the floor and laughing like they were having the best time."

She stopped suddenly, and the half smile vanished. "Let me help you get back to bed."

I knew better than to pry; but as I settled into bed, I could not hold back one final question. "My sisters, how old are they?"

Mom sighed, as if the question bothered her. "I guess they'd be twenty and twenty-two. That's enough questions now, Tess. You need your rest."

That night I could not sleep. For hours I lay awake, thinking and wondering. Mom rarely spoke of my sisters. I had never seen a photograph of them or even heard their names. I'd always assumed Mom had given them up for adoption. But why the secrecy about it? Why the pain in her eyes whenever she mentioned them?

Maybe, I thought, *maybe Walter had something to do with their disappearance. Maybe they ran away, like I did, and Walter shot them dead on some back road. The thought chilled me. Next time I leave, I've got to have a plan. Some way to make sure he can't find me again.*

My thoughts turned to Mom's account of Walter playing with my sisters. I knew it couldn't be true; nevertheless, the story fascinated me. I wondered what it would be like to have a father who did those things. The more I thought about it, the bigger the ache inside me became. I wanted to cry, but I couldn't.

4

"T essa!" My mother's voice, sharp with irritation, penetrated the walls of my bedroom. "Get out here and get this stuff put away right now!"

I was sprawled on my stomach across my bed, too depressed to do anything except listen to the radio and munch some corn chips I'd swiped from the kitchen pantry. Physically, I had healed a lot over the last three weeks. Emotionally, I hadn't.

"Tes–sa!"

I swore under my breath and turned up the volume on my radio a few more notches. Mom had been after me all day to take care of some stupid bag of groceries she'd brought home earlier. Never mind that I still couldn't walk without my ankle hurting. As usual, Mom cared more about herself than me. I waited as long as I dared, then tugged a sweatshirt over my pajama top and limped out to the living room.

"What stuff?"

Mom sat on the couch, sewing up a sagging hem on her bathrobe. "You know what I mean."

"What's the big deal? I'm not your slave or something. Don't I get any time to myself around here?"

She gave me a look and pointed to the kitchen. I complied, but resentfully, trailing my sore leg behind me in an exaggerated limp. Next to the stove were three paper bags of groceries. I grabbed them and dumped them out on the counter, making a tremendous clatter. Cans of mushroom soup and green beans tumbled to the floor, drowning Mom's reprimand from the next room. Somehow, nothing broke.

The noise pacified my injured feelings somewhat. I gathered the dented cans and stuffed them into the pantry. Mom could arrange things later if she wanted to.

On the way back to my bedroom, Mom called to me again.

"What now?" I growled, and kept walking.

"Tessa, you've been smoking again, haven't you."

I paused in the doorway. "So? You smoke."

"Don't get smart with me. It's a filthy habit."

"Well, maybe you should quit then."

Mom rose to her feet, her face red. "You sass me one more time, and you're gonna be sorry! There'll be no more smoking for you. If I find any more of my cigarettes missing, I'll see that you pay for it!"

"We'll see about that," I muttered, as I limped down the hallway to my room. I paused in front of the mirror and eyed myself. Inheriting my mother's slender frame was a blessing, mostly. I could eat what I liked and still be the envy of the girls at school. But at five foot three and ninety-four pounds, I would never pass for eighteen at the convenience store. Not that I had the means to get there anyway.

Mom is so mean. The springs in my mattress creaked as I threw myself onto the bed. *How am I supposed to survive without a smoke when she can't?* Grabbing my radio, I turned the dial until I hit a hard rock station, the kind Mom used to scold Walter for playing when I was around. This time, I didn't care what she thought.

Another hour passed before the slam of the back door alerted me that Walter had come home. My heart rate kicked up and the muscles in my neck tightened. I hadn't seen Walter since he beat me up. I made sure to stay in my room when he was around, and so far he hadn't bothered me. But I knew my luck was running out. Any day now, Walter could demand that I start working for him again.

Clicking my radio off, I slipped from the bed and pressed an ear up to my door. Weary as I was of my parents' constant fighting, I felt safer when I knew what was going on.

"Where have you been?" Mom greeted Walter.

"What do you mean, where've I been?" he shot back. "I'm not your kid." Then he thought better of it. "I was out in the shop doing some varnishing. Told Jeff I'd have that desk done by next week. So, when's supper? We gotta get going."

Dread coiled in my stomach. I knew all too well what it meant when he used the plural pronoun. Out in the kitchen, Mom caught the word as well.

"We?" There was a scrape as she pulled out a fry pan. "Who's we?"

Walter began to whistle, ignoring the question.

"Don't you dare, Walter. She's not going anywhere with you. She can barely walk."

"Oh yeah? Then how come you been bugging me to send her to school?"

"Look. She can't stay out forever. She's a spoiled brat. She won't listen to me, she's smoking again, and she doesn't get out of bed until noon."

Walter laughed. "Sounds like you'd have a heck of a time getting her there at all, much less on time. I wouldn't bother."

"I can get her there just fine! Provided you don't start working her til some ungodly hour again."

"Forget it, Julie. I need the help."

A fist slammed on the counter, rattling the dishes. "I will not allow my daughter to grow up to be the idiot that you are!" Mom yelled. "I insist she goes to school!"

"Hey. I'm earning the money around here, just in case you forgot."

"You think that proves you're smart, huh? Look at yourself! You can't even read your own traffic tickets!"

"Why, do I want to?"

"You're impossible. Tessa is going to school if I hafta drag her there in her pajamas. And if you get in my way, I'll call the cops."

"Yeah? That'd be the day. You take one look at a cop, and you freak out."

I withdrew from my door with a sigh. My parents had been sparring on this topic ever since I'd recovered enough to crawl out of bed. Nothing ever seemed to come of it. Personally, I hoped nothing would. Going to school after Walter had worked me til two or three in the morning was a total nightmare. Last spring, my grades had slipped to the point I had to attend summer school just to pass. The opening week of school, before I'd run away, had been equally miserable.

In the kitchen, I could hear the rise and fall of Walter's voice as he made the usual assortment of phone calls that preceded a work night. I groaned and pressed my hands over my ears, trying to block out his voice. How I hated working for him! Not only was the job detestable, but I had to endure his company the whole time as well.

Mom came down the hall and rapped on my door. In a surprisingly cheerful voice, she said, "Supper's ready."

Like I'm going out there. I rolled my eyes in disgust. Mom knew full well what Walter was doing, yet she pretended we were just a normal family coming together to enjoy dinner. This make-believe of hers could get so convincing at times that I'd question my own perceptions. But tonight I wasn't buying it.

Out in the kitchen, Walter was still on the phone. Who knew if he'd bother to eat before he left? As I had done many times before, I glanced around my room for something heavy enough to barricade my door. And once again, I discarded the idea as too dangerous and ineffective. The only thing that ever worked was running away.

I rose and limped to the window, then returned to the bed and sat down again. I tore off my sweatshirt because I was hot, but put it on again because I started shaking with cold. My ankle began to ache. I rubbed it, wishing I could get a fresh ice pack from the freezer. *Come on, Walter. Just leave already.*

The clatter of silverware on plates drifted in from the kitchen, mixing with TV commercials from the next room. My mouth watered as I caught a whiff of fried potatoes. I was hungry. Too bad I'd finished off the bag of corn chips earlier.

A chair scraped the floor in the kitchen, and I heard heavy footsteps coming down the hallway. I leaped up, my heart racing.

Walter shoved my door open without so much as a knock. "C'mon, kid. Let's go. We got work to do."

I stammered as I tried to protest. "I . . . ah . . . can't I eat something first?"

"Supper's done. Now move it; we're already late for an appointment in town."

I wasted as much time as I dared tying my shoes and getting my coat. I hated going to town with Walter. He'd stop at the convenience store for a case or two of beer, then hang out with his friends at the bar for a couple of hours. Often it was midnight or later by the time we started working.

Tonight, however, the bar stop was strictly business. Walter left the truck idling at the curb while he talked to a couple of guys in the side alley. Minutes later he was back, fuming.

"Guess who didn't show up. Again. I am not putting up with this. I'll take you out there, and you can get started while I track him down." He jammed the truck in gear and pulled out into the traffic.

Get started . . . by myself? I swallowed the protest, but my head spun. This was asking too much. One tiny mistake, and the whole building would explode in a giant fireball. Or so Walter liked to tell me.

The truck careened around a corner and sped down Second Street, heading toward the bridge. I hunched in the passenger seat, too preoccupied to notice how fast he was going. As he rounded the next corner, a flash of red and blue lights caught the back window. Ice touched my heart. Last I heard, Walter didn't have a driver's license anymore.

Walter saw the lights as well. He swore and made a quick left in front of several oncoming cars. The police car followed. Cursing, Walter knocked a small newspaper-wrapped bundle onto the floor and kicked it under the seat before pulling to the curb.

"What do you want?" he demanded of the officer who tapped on the window. "I'm in a hurry."

"I noticed that. I'll need your license and proof of insurance."

"What for?"

"License and insurance, sir."

With an oath, Walter pulled out his billfold and began digging through it. "I ain't got the money to pay your stupid fines," he grumbled. With two grimy fingers, he extracted his license and thrust it at the officer.

The officer studied it a moment, as if making sure it was valid. "Do you still live at 16187 Vance Road, Northford?" he asked.

"Most of the time; why?"

"Is this truck titled in your name?"

"It's my truck, so it better be."

"Walter, I stopped you for going 40 in a 25-mile-per-hour zone and not wearing a seat belt. I'm going to run a check on your license before I write you a ticket." The officer walked back to his car.

I sank back in the seat and closed my eyes. *Please, don't find anything wrong,* I pleaded silently. The thought of another ride in the back of a police car, followed by another long wait in the booking room under the stern gaze of an officer, was more than I could bear.

Walter smoked part of a cigarette; then muttering that this was taking too long, he opened the door and got out of the truck. A second officer quickly intercepted him.

"Get right back in that truck," she said. It was too dark to see her clearly, but I recognized her voice. It was Pat.

"Oh yeah? I don't have to listen to you," Walter scoffed, and let loose a string of obscenities.

I drew a sharp breath. What was he doing – trying to get arrested?

Walter must have had the same thought, for he stopped in the middle of his rant and got into the truck. He slammed the door and sat revving the engine, muttering unrepeatable things until the other officer returned with his license and ticket.

5

The dilapidated two-story farmhouse where Walter had set up shop loomed up against the night sky like a huge dead thing. Overgrown lilacs, taller than a man could reach, choked the boarded-up front windows and the little decaying porch that led to the door. Giant trees stretched their heavy arms above the steeply pitched roof, groaning slightly with the wind. The empty blackness of broken windows stared back at me from the second story.

I had to force myself to step out of the truck. I was shaking all over. Entering an abandoned property alone, after dark, was enough to frighten anyone. Never mind that what I would be doing was blatantly illegal, or that I could get murdered if one of Walter's deranged friends showed up.

Behind me, the pickup idled as Walter waited for me to slam the door and start toward the house. "What're you waiting for?" he hissed. "You got your keys, don't you?"

I did have my keys; but I dug a hand into my pocket anyway, stalling for time. "I don't know," I said. "Can't you just get me started?"

With a sigh of disgust, Walter slid from the truck. "What's the matter with you? Scared of the ghosts?" He strode past me onto the porch and undid the heavy padlock.

I followed reluctantly. Even with the fresh breeze blowing, I could smell ammonia. I made a wide circuit around the rusted-out Volkswagen that sat near the corner of the house. Bees nested in the old car during the summer, something I had learned the hard way. One by one, I climbed the creaky steps, careful to keep to the edges where the wood was not as badly rotted. Walter waited at the top with growing impatience.

"Hurry up," he said, and gave me a push through the door. "You know what's gotta be done. Now get at it!"

I held my breath as I entered the dark room, but it didn't help much. The fumes were so strong they stung my eyes. I groped through the darkness until I located the switch on the battery-operated work light on the table. I knew what to do, all right. At least I hoped I did.

The room I was standing in had once been a kitchen. Decayed pink linoleum, heavily tracked with sawdust and mud, covered the floor. Warped wooden cupboards and a narrow counter topped with the same ancient pink linoleum lined the mustard-colored walls. The counter was cluttered with junk – mason jars full of yellowish liquid, empty medicine boxes, dirty rags, old rubber gloves, pie tins, pop bottles, rubber tubing of all sizes and lengths, and some glass measuring cups Mom was probably looking for.

A substance that resembled dried cake batter had dribbled down the front of one cupboard and pooled in a crusty mass on the floor. An ancient refrigerator stood near the boarded-up windows, its rusted door held closed with a brick and a bungee. Piled against the refrigerator and extending most of the way to the door was a huge heap of trash. In the middle of the room stood a battered Formica table and a single-burner stove connected to a propane tank.

The first deep breath I took scalded my throat and set me to coughing. Was it worse than usual in here, or had I forgotten how bad it was? I longed to crack the door for fresh air, but Walter had strictly forbidden that. My best recourse would be to move ahead and get the job over with as quickly as possible.

Taking an empty glass coffeepot from the counter, I wiped it out with a paper towel and set it on the table. Walter usually worked in the sink, but I preferred the table because the lighting was better. I reached over and lifted a gallon-size can of camp fuel down from the cupboard. The can was full and much heavier than I expected. It slipped from my fingers and fell, smashing my left big toe.

The pain was intense. Rage boiled up in me. I could almost hear Walter's caustic laughter. Without thinking, I pulled back my right foot and kicked the can as hard as I could.

Instant pain shattered through my partly healed ankle and leg. I doubled over gasping. *How stupid can I be?*

Over by the refrigerator, the fuel can lay on its side, dented nearly in half and leaking fluid into a growing puddle.

"So sit there!" I hissed at it, as I hobbled around the table to the only chair, a very rusty kitchen stool. "See if I care." I'd have to mop up the mess before Walter returned, but for now, the sight of the ruined can appeased some of my anger.

My ankle, though, was hurting terribly. Within minutes it began to swell. Knowing what would happen if I didn't address this, I retrieved a handful of half-melted ice from the refrigerator and began to massage it.

The rhythmic motion was soothing. I could feel the pain seeping out of my ankle. The anger and anxiety seemed to seep out with it, leaving me relaxed and almost sleepy. Even the smell in the room was less noticeable. I knew I should get back to work, but I delayed, not wanting my ankle to start hurting again.

Time slipped by. I was daydreaming when the soft bump of a car door jerked me to reality. *Walter's back, and I haven't even started. Now what?* Leaping up, I began frantically rearranging the junk on the table so I would look busy. I strained my ears for footsteps on the porch, but all I could hear was a buzzing in my head.

My heart settled back into place. I could have been mistaken. But it was definitely time to get going.

I didn't pause to ask why I was feeling so dizzy. My thoughts revolved around how furious Walter would be if he returned to find nothing had been done.

Hobbling over to the counter, I hoisted down a new can of fuel, pried the cap off, and began pouring the clear liquid into the coffeepot. The pot was brimming before I realized I'd made another stupid mistake. Several inches in the bottom would have been plenty.

"What on earth is wrong with you?" I scolded myself, as I pawed through the junk on the counter for a funnel. My voice sounded distant, drowned by the ever-increasing buzz in my ears. I set the funnel on the can and began pouring the extra back in. Fuel dribbled down the side of the pot as I poured, splashing the table and the front of my jacket. I dabbed at the mess with a wad of dirty paper towels and tried to move on with the next step of the process.

But something was wrong. I had a weird sense of being disconnected from my body and my surroundings. I kept tripping over my feet and dropping things. The buzzing in my head had grown to a steady roar. Why was Walter running the air compressor?

My mind seemed to be full of sticky molasses. I lost all sense of what I was doing. In total confusion, I decided to look at the instructions to see if the place had caught fire yet. With clumsy hands, I pulled the poster-sized sheet off the front of the refrigerator. Why was the room reeling around me? Breathing heavily, I leaned on the table and stared stupidly at the diagrams on the page. The little ink lines seemed miles away. Why could I barely see? Was the light dying?

Air. I've got to get some air. It wasn't even a conscious thought. Raw instinct drove me across the room toward the door. Back at the table, the poster slid to the floor with a slap.

Grasping the knob with both hands, I tugged at the door. It didn't budge. I braced myself and yanked harder, but still no luck. Crazed with panic, I began kicking and beating the steel with my fists. The exertion only intensified my critical need for air. I clung to the slippery knob as the world dissolved into a vibrating blackness. The roar in my ears was deafening. A powerful force seemed to be pressing down upon my ribs, crushing the breath out of me. The roaring grew until it swallowed me up. Underneath it, barely audible, someone was talking very fast in a monotone, or was it the radio?

My thoughts fractured into multiplied thousands of tiny pieces, like shining bits of glass dust. I watched as they continued breaking down into ever smaller particles, then began falling like meteors. Only they were falling ever so slowly.

6

i awoke to the familiar sound of my own coughing. My bedroom was dim, lit only by what little daylight permeated the drawn window shade. Flashes of things from the night before swept my mind like strobe lights. Confused voices, bright lights, someone pounding me on the back. Muffled arguing that droned on and on. And my own desperate attempts to escape an intangible terror. Had it been only last night? It seemed like weeks ago.

Pushing back the covers, I stared bleary-eyed at my denim-clad legs. What was I doing in bed fully dressed? My eyes were watering so profusely I could hardly see. I slid out of bed and managed to stand up, but the room wobbled and turned around me in a slow, drunken motion. I blinked, trying to clear my vision and get my bearings. Hadn't I taken a shower last night? My clothes, my hands, everything was filthy. My eyes locked onto an ugly raw spot on my left hand near my thumb. About the size of a half dollar, the wound had blistered like a burn and was stinging like fire. What on earth had happened?

I collapsed onto the bed as another fit of coughing shook me. Even lying down, the room was spinning. My throat burned as if I had a bad cold. Was I dying? I recalled the strange dizziness of the night before. Maybe the fumes had grown so powerful they'd knocked me out. I pictured Walter returning late and unlocking the door to find me slumped behind it, cold and dead. Maybe that was what had happened. But then how could I still be alive? Was I alive?

I tried to shake off the irrational thoughts that clung like cobwebs in my mind. I had to find a way out of working in that stupid drug lab before it was too late.

But what could I do? I had tried everything – running away, hiding out in the basement, faking illness, outright refusal. I had even tried appealing to Mom, but for whatever reason, she turned a deaf ear to me. I couldn't talk to the police. Walter had made it clear that if I did, we'd both end up in prison, but first he'd kill me. Was suicide the only option I had left?

Tears slipped down my face. *Sure my life sucks, but I don't want to die! There's got to be another way.* But in my weakened state, the only thing I could think of was to talk to Mom again. Somehow I had to make her understand.

It took me several hours to muster enough willpower to get out of bed again. I tugged on a cleaner pair of jeans, swiped a damp washcloth across my face, and stumbled out to the kitchen.

I found Mom at the table, dozing over a cold cup of coffee. She stirred and yawned when I entered. "Oh good, you're up. How are you feeling?"

"Okay, I guess." I was scared to say more. Suppose she belittled or laughed off what had happened? Avoiding her gaze, I sank into an empty chair and pulled a banana from the bunch in the center of the table. I pulled back the yellow peel and took a bite, but all I could taste was ammonia.

Mom poured herself a fresh cup of coffee, added a pinch of sugar, and stirred it. "You had me pretty worried last night. You sure you're okay?"

"I'd be a lot more okay if Walter wouldn't keep dragging me off to work in his stupid drug house." The words tumbled out faster than I could think.

"Tessa!" Mom scolded. "Watch what you say. What if somebody heard you?"

"I don't care. I'm sick of pretending." My voice choked. "Maybe we should just get arrested and be done with it." I bent my head and coughed painfully.

"Look, Tess, I'm really sorry this happened. But why in heaven's name didn't you tell me what was going on? I never would've allowed such a thing."

I stared at her, trying to make my eyes focus. "So now it's my fault, huh?"

"No, Tess. I just wish you would've told me." She shook her head and toyed with the corner of the tablecloth. "I figured he was up to something, but I had no idea it was this bad. I'm sorry. I'll see that it doesn't happen anymore."

I was silent. I wanted to scream that it was all her fault for not listening to me, but I couldn't seem to organize my thoughts. Had whatever happened last night damaged my brain?

Mom downed her coffee, then yawned again. "This stuff isn't working. I've got to lie down before this headache kills me. If you're up to it, maybe you could wash some of those dishes."

I couldn't believe it. I was sick and so dizzy I could hardly stand up, and she was putting me to work because she had a headache? But I forced my anger down. I needed to be on Mom's good side when Walter came home.

"I suppose I could work on it," I muttered, "but I'm gonna take a shower first." As bad as I smelled, I wondered that she hadn't mentioned it.

I took a long shower, savoring the feel of the hot water spraying on my back. As I relaxed, some of the weariness and misery of the last twenty-four hours slipped away. If only the dizziness would leave with it. I'd be doing well to get through the dishes without blacking out. Why had I agreed to do them?

By the time I returned to the kitchen, it was almost noon. I made a face at the sink full of dirty dishes submerged in cold gray dishwater. Couldn't Mom at least have let the water out yesterday? I reached in and released the drain, then ran fresh water. But as I was carrying a stack of dishes from the table, I tripped over the vacuum cleaner. A glass serving bowl fell to the floor and smashed.

Sweat broke out on my palms. Mom would be mad if she found out about this. I grabbed the broom and swept up the scattered pieces, then tipped the garbage can and slid the pieces in as quietly as I could. With luck, maybe Mom would blame Walter for the missing bowl.

I had just replaced the lid on the garbage can when I caught movement out of the corner of my eye. I drew a sharp breath and froze. Walter stood blocking the doorway, his hands on his hips.

"Can't you ever keep from breaking things?" he demanded. "What's the matter with you!"

"I-I'm sorry." I took a few steps backward.

"Sorry doesn't fix anything. What the hell were you doing last night? Trying to blow the place up? You had enough fuel spilled in there to burn a whole city!" As he spoke he advanced on me, cornering me in front of the pantry.

I was so terrified I couldn't think. I could smell his foul breath as he yelled at me, his face inches from mine. Black shadows danced on the edges of my vision. My head swam.

"What's going on here?" Clad only in a thin nightgown, her long hair tousled from sleep, Mom pushed in between Walter and me.

Walter gave her a shove. "Get outta here."

She came right back at him. "Suppose you tell me what you're so mad about."

"None of your business! Now bug off!"

"If it's last night, she's had more than enough punishment already. Isn't it enough for you that she could've died?" I felt her arm tighten around my shoulders. "Now leave her alone or you'll be sorry."

"You crazy…" With both hands, Walter grabbed the stack of dirty dishes off the counter and smashed it on her feet.

"Fine. Have it your way!" he screamed. "You can coddle your spoiled little brat all you want. But don't you dare blame me next time, you hear?" He stomped toward the back door.

"There won't be a next time!" she screamed back, as the door slammed behind him. Releasing me, she limped through the mess of broken china to the nearest chair. She removed her right slipper and shook off the tiny shards of glass. There was a purple lump the size of a walnut on top of her foot. "Could be worse, anyway," she muttered, and swore. "He didn't hurt you, did he, Tess?"

I shook my head. I was so dizzy I didn't dare let go of the counter.

"You look terrible. Come on, let's try to get you to the couch."

It felt good to lie down, although it was a long time before I began to relax. Not knowing how long Walter would be gone didn't help. I kept thinking I heard his truck drive in.

Mom called me around four o'clock for an early supper. I felt better than I had that morning, but by the time the meal was over, I was again too dizzy to walk straight. I sprawled out on the couch, letting the warm rays of late-afternoon sun slant across my face. Try as I did, I could not think of a single thing I wanted to do. Even watching TV seemed like too much bother. Maybe I should turn the TV off. It might be pleasant to sit in the quiet.

Suddenly, there was a loud rapping at the front door. I jerked upright. Mom hurried around the corner, her hands still dripping suds. "Get down the basement," she ordered.

7

omething in her tone caused me to obey without hesitation. My heart pounded as I crouched in the dim stairwell. I pressed an ear against the door and listened. If it was the police, I would flee down the steps and hide behind the dryer.

"Good evening," said a man's deep voice. "We're your neighbors down the road there in the yellow house, just moved in a couple weeks ago. We thought we'd stop and say hello. I'm Tom Erickson, and this is my wife, Patty."

Mom's reply was guarded. "Well, it's nice to meet you. I'm Julie. I'd ask you in, but Walter's not here and as you see, the place is kind of a mess."

"That's fine," said Tom. "We just wanted to let you know we're around."

Mom's tone grew friendlier. "That's nice of you. Most people wouldn't bother. You know, why don't you two stay a bit and have some coffee. Never mind the mess."

I blinked in surprise. Had she really said that? As far as I knew, visitors were not allowed into the house under any circumstances. Walter met friends and furniture customers out in his shop, and Mom talked to the occasional seller of dollar candy bars through the screen.

I vividly recalled the lesson I'd learned a few years earlier. I had invited my best friend home with me after school so I could show her my music box. To my ten-year-old mind, it seemed natural –

didn't everybody invite friends over to play? Apparently not. Janet hadn't been in the house two minutes before Mom appeared and tore into me like I'd committed murder. I ran to my room crying, and Janet spent the rest of her short visit sitting on the front steps waiting for her mom. I never tried it again.

Curious what was going on now, I eased the door open and stole around the corner into the kitchen. If I stood behind the table in just the right place, I could see everything that happened in the living room reflected in the glass doors of the china cupboard.

Mom was settled in Walter's easy chair, smoking and talking enthusiastically. Occupying the couch across from her was a well-dressed middle-aged couple. They sipped their coffee and tried to act interested as she carried on about her favorite soap stars, the best way to grow hollyhocks, and why it was a total waste of time to keep tropical fish. I could tell Mom was enjoying the rare opportunity to talk to someone. But after about ten minutes of this one-sided conversation, the visitors began to fidget.

"Well, I suppose you'll be wanting to get home," Mom said, pausing to take a drag on her cigarette.

The visitors exchanged glances. "Actually," said Tom, "as long as we're here, there's something I'd like to ask you. Do you believe in God?"

Mom's face stiffened. She blew out a cloud of smoke, blinked a couple of times, and said, "Sure I do. What did you think I was, an atheist?" She forced a laugh.

"Have you heard how Jesus came to earth and died for our sins?"

Mom interrupted him. "Yes, of course. You're talking about Christmas. Which reminds me. I was gonna tell you, since you're new around here, don't buy a tree from that used-car place on the edge of town. We did two years ago, and the thing was practically dead. Waste of money, not to mention a fire hazard."

"We'll keep that in mind," Tom said. "But you know the whole reason for Christmas is to celebrate the birth of Jesus. He came to forgive our sins and give us a new life. We all need His forgiveness. No one can live pleasing to God or get to heaven without it."

Mom shrugged. "I wouldn't be so sure about that. Maybe you people need it, but don't look at me. I live a pretty good life."

"Would you like to see what the Bible has to say about it?"

"I don't have one."

"That's okay. I've got one here in my coat pocket."

Mom stood up. "Look, it's been nice talking to you guys, but I've got stuff I gotta do."

"Mind if we leave you a tract?"

She shrugged again. "Suit yourself."

Patty unzipped her purse and pulled out a small green booklet. "You'll like it," she said. "It's a testimony of someone who didn't know the Lord and then turned to Him. It's a good story."

Mom stuck the booklet in her back pocket. "Well, thanks. I suppose you'll be leaving now."

"Yes, we'd better go," Tom agreed.

"I forgot your husband's name," Patty said, as she pulled on her coat.

"Walter." Mom stood holding the door open, clearly impatient for them to leave.

"And are you in the phone book in case we ever need to get a hold of you?"

"Last I saw. The name is Miner."

It was with obvious relief that Mom shut the door behind them and returned to finish the dishes. "Some of those crazy religious people," she told me, dumping their leftover coffee down the drain. "If I'd known that, I would've made them bad coffee."

"Bad coffee?" I asked, curious whether this oft-made threat of hers had any real power. "How do you make that?"

"Don't ask." She laughed. "It's my private recipe. All I can say is, I don't even think Walter would drink it."

"What's the booklet they gave you?" If it was a story, I wanted to read it.

"What booklet?" Her voice was sharp now. "If you're well enough to stand there and talk, maybe you can dry some dishes."

"Never mind." I turned and walked out of the kitchen. I could not understand Mom's irritation with religious people. Even if she didn't care to talk about God, why act so threatened at the mere mention of him?

I spent the rest of the evening hiding out in my room in case Walter returned. He had been known to pick me up for work as late as eleven. I lay down, but I couldn't fall asleep. My mind spun in relentless worry. Would Mom keep her promise to stop Walter if he did show up? Could she stop him? What if she didn't? More than once I leaped to my feet in fright, thinking I heard Walter's truck. But each time, it turned out to be just another noisy vehicle on the road.

Eleven o'clock finally came. Water roared in the pipes as Mom filled the tub for a bath. Later I heard the familiar sound of her padding down the hallway to the living room to watch a late show. Could it be Walter wasn't going to come home tonight after all?

I rose and peered out the window one last time, as if to reassure myself that all was clear. I then stretched out on the shaggy white rug beside my bed to do some serious thinking. I needed a plan.

8

*A*t first the knock at my door was so soft I didn't hear it. I was lying
flat on my back on the rug, brainstorming about how to get far
enough away from home that Walter couldn't find me again. I'd read fascinating stories of people jumping freight trains, but the trains I'd seen passing
through Northford were going way too fast for any such stunt to work. There
was hitchhiking, but that idea scared me almost as much as the train idea.

My best plan was to somehow get my hands on a car. Could a
person my age buy a car? I tingled with excitement at the thought.
Walter had taught me how to drive. If I could figure out where to
get a couple hundred dollars, I might be on my way. That was a lot
of money though, more than I could get from raiding Mom's purse.

The knock came again, more forcefully. I scrambled to my feet,
my thoughts shattering like dropped Christmas ornaments. How
had Walter sneaked in without me hearing him?

"Tessa?" It was Mom's voice.

I sank down on the rug in relief. It wasn't Walter. But did she
have to scare me like that?

"What're you doing in here? Sleeping with the lights on?" Mom
pushed the door and sat down on the bed.

"I know it's late, but I wanted to talk to you about going back
to school," she began. "Walter won't like it, but I'm not asking his
opinion. If you're in school, it'll be a lot easier for me to put a stop
to this other stuff."

I was in no mood to have an amicable talk. "Yeah?" I challenged. "How do you figure that?"

"It'll give me a lot more leverage."

"Leverage? Walter don't listen to you no matter what."

For a moment, Mom looked like she wanted to slap me. But instead she folded her arms and said, "Now look. I've known Walter a lot longer than you have, and that means I know some things about him that you don't. Understand?"

I hated it when she used that tone. She made me feel like a five-year-old. "So, how come you suddenly care so much about this? You never did before."

Mom hesitated. "Well, I wasn't going to tell you. But I got a call from Walter last night, must've been about ten thirty. At first I couldn't understand him at all, his words were so slurred. I figured it was some stupid joke. But he sounded desperate, so I kept listening. He was saying, 'What do you do if somebody's not breathing?'"

Shivers ran up my spine. She continued. "I tried to tell him, but he was too drunk. I got in the car and rushed over there as fast as I could. I'll never forget it. The whole way there, all I could think was, 'it's probably too late already.'"

She dabbed her eyes with a wadded tissue. Her voice was thick with emotion. "Tessa, I'm so sorry. I didn't know it was like this, or I would've put a stop to it a long time ago, believe me."

I couldn't speak for the lump in my throat. "Did I . . . was I . . . ?"

She shook her head. "I don't know. Walter was pretty drunk; he could've been wrong. By the time I got there, he had you out on the porch, and you seemed to be breathing. But you were limp as a rag doll. I was scared you wouldn't come out of it, and sat up pretty much all night after I got you home."

An improper question burned in my mind. I hated to ask it, but I had to. "What would you have done, you know . . . well . . . if I hadn't come out of it?"

"I guess I would've called the police, taken you to the hospital, whatever. Walter would be mad, but I guess I don't care what he thinks anymore."

"Yeah, but by the time you got me to the hospital, wouldn't it have been a little late?"

Mom's face reddened. "What're you getting at?" she snapped. "Why I didn't call an ambulance or something? You know why. Walter would kill me."

"So then what you just said about going to the hospital is a bunch of bunk." My voice shook. I'd never dared to confront Mom like this before. But I had to get the truth.

"Well, I'd have to be careful, that's for sure."

"So what you're really saying is it's you, then me."

"What the hell is that supposed to mean?"

"That I better look out for myself and not believe a word you say." I stood to my feet, gripping the windowsill to steady myself. "One of these days I'm gonna leave for good, and you can forget about finding me again, because you won't."

"Tess, please. That's crazy talk. You know what a minefield it is, living with Walter. So maybe I should've called for help last night. But since everything's okay, why make a big fuss about it? It's not gonna happen again, all right?"

I stood silent, staring out the window into the night.

"You know, I'm still limping around from protecting you this morning. I still got bruises on my arm from trying to get Walter to send you to school. Last night I risked my neck driving out to that stupid farmhouse, and then I sat up with you all night. I've still got a headache. Where are you getting this crazy idea that I don't care about you? What more do you want?"

The dizziness was beginning to overwhelm me. I sank down on the opposite side of the bed. She continued. "Now, if you're going to school, there's a few things we have to work out, such as–"

"I'm not going."

"So you'd rather stay here and listen to us fight all winter?"

I rolled my eyes. What a stupid question.

"Seems to me that's about all you do."

"It is not."

"Oh?" She bent and picked up a crumpled sweatshirt off the floor. "Just what do you do in here all day?"

I traced a crack in the wood floor with my shoe. "Maybe I escape from this lousy family for a while."

"And then when you come out, we're still here."

"Unfortunately."

"So I should think you'd be glad to get away from us for a while."

"That's what I'm gonna do."

Mom rose and walked around the bed to stand beside me. "Tessa, I don't know how to put this." Her voice was quiet but intense. "You're the only daughter I've got now. I know things have been tough, and I can't blame you for wanting to find a better life. But Tessa, you don't know what you're talking about. No runaway teenage girl is gonna do well. I don't care how smart you are. It's not gonna work. You might get away from Walter, but you'll end up someplace that's a whole lot worse. There's evil men out there who gather up girls like you and force them into prostitution so they can make money. Once you get into something like that, you never get out." Her voice broke. "Tess, I can't lock you up and force you to stay here; but if you leave, you're doomed. You can ask anybody."

I wouldn't look at her. Why did she have to bring all that up? As if I wasn't doomed if I stayed here. I picked at the two oversized bandages covering the side of my hand. I still had no idea how I'd gotten burned. Of course, it wouldn't have been difficult, considering the caustic chemicals I was handling last night.

Mom spoke again. "So. How about it? You willing to go back to school?"

I hesitated, which she took to mean yes. She told me I'd be going come Monday morning, and then she said goodnight and left.

I felt like punching something. I resented being forced to trust Mom again, when all she ever did was look out for herself. But until I could perfect my escape plan, it looked like I had no choice.

***

In bed that night, my thoughts drifted to my sisters. Try as I did, I could not remember them at all. Still, I missed them. I wondered what it would be like having older siblings to look up to and confide in. Life might still be hard, but at least I wouldn't be alone. I was so tired of being alone. Where were my sisters?

9

onday morning dawned overcast and blustery, a perfect match for my mood. I had barely slept for worrying. Even the mega dose of Nyquil I'd taken before bed didn't help. I was terrified the people at school would be able to tell what I'd been through just by looking at me. I knew this was ridiculous; the bruises from Walter's beating had faded, and I'd showered and thoroughly washed my hair, so I smelled all right. My coughing fits could be explained away. Yet, fear and shame gripped me. I managed to choke down the orange juice Mom poured for me, but I couldn't eat anything.

Mom drove me to school in her car. Despite my anxiety, I felt my spirits lift as I watched the countryside unfold outside my window. Although most of the colored leaves had fallen from the trees, the land still glowed with the rich brown of oak forests and the gold of cornfields not yet ready for harvest. Mom had been right on one thing. I did need to get out of the house more.

But as we crossed the bridge into Northford, my fears returned in force. What if I couldn't do my schoolwork with this fogged-up feeling in my head? What if the office questioned Mom's explanation of my six-week absence? By the time we pulled up in front of the school, my stomach was in knots.

"Well, here we are," Mom said. "You got my note?"

I nodded and stepped out of the car, ducking my head against the biting wind.

"Try to have a good day," she called after me. "I'll be back around three thirty."

I slammed the door without answering. I hoped she felt bad about dumping me off like this. The wind tugged at my coat and spat drizzle in my face as I started toward the sprawling brick building. Could I just walk in unannounced after being gone for so long?

Two students hurried past me up the wet sidewalk. I recognized one of them as Ethan Anderson, my best friend Janet's older brother. With him was a tall blond girl I didn't know. She was laughing as he pretended to shield her from the rain with a battered notebook. I followed them at a distance, walking slowly to conceal my limp.

Colorful posters announcing fall play auditions greeted me as I pushed the door and stepped inside. I tried to project self-confidence as I threaded my way through the sea of students, but I was scared. There were so many unfamiliar faces. Even among my friends, I worried what kind of reception I would get.

Partway down the hall, someone caught my arm. "Tess! Where've you been all this time!" Janet's dark eyes sparkled as she folded me in a bear hug. Her long black hair brushed my cheek, and I caught a whiff of almond shampoo. I hugged her back.

But there was no time to talk. Several other girls crowded around. "Hey, Tess! We heard you were missing. Did you run away? Where were you?"

I laughed and continued walking. "It's a long story. You don't wanna hear it."

"Aww, come on," Lois prodded. "All this time we figured you'd been kidnapped or something."

"You don't know the half. They locked me up in a basement full of rats and demanded ten million in ransom."

Shrieks of horror rose from the girls. I worked the combination on my locker and pulled open the door. Yes, thank goodness, my books were still there.

I managed to make it to lunchtime without any serious questioning. By then the worst of my fears had subsided. Mom's partly true tale about me running away, getting sick, and then having to travel to Texas for my grandmother's funeral must have satisfied everyone. What worried me most was the fog and dizziness building in my head. If it got much worse, I doubted I'd be able to learn anything, much less keep track of all the assignments the teachers were giving me.

Three of my best friends joined me at lunch.

"Have you been sick?" Lois quizzed me, as she consumed macaroni and cheese at a record speed. "You've been coughing something awful."

My heart rate doubled, but I tried to answer calmly. "Yeah, it was pretty bad. I kept thinking I was over it, then – bam – it'd come right back. But I'm feeling a lot better now." I covered my mouth as another burst of coughing erupted. My throat and chest ached from all the coughing.

Sandy looked up from her salad in concern. "You sure you're not contagious?"

"Have you been to a doctor?" added Janet. "Maybe it's whooping cough or something."

"I promise, I'm not contagious," I rasped. "I've just got a tickle in my throat."

"I bet you got sick when you ran away." Lois fixed me with an inquisitive gaze.

My stomach tightened. I did not want to talk about that, especially with Lois. She was the biggest blabbermouth in the world. But Lois kept eyeing me, expecting a reply, and I felt my cheeks beginning to flush.

"So, where'd you get that idea?" I said.

Lois's plump face creased with disbelief. "What, that you ran away? Everybody knows that! Your mom was calling all over the place, trying to find you. She said you'd been gone for a week already."

My face burned. That explained Mom's refusal to leave my misbehavior out of her note. What could I say now? The stupid fuzziness in my head made it hard to think.

"Yeah, well, it was kind of an experiment," I said. "I slept in a garage for a couple nights."

"Was it fun?" Sandy's brown eyes danced with adventure.

I shrugged. "Depends what you call fun. I wouldn't recommend it."

"Why, what happened?" Lois pried.

The stress of answering their questions made my dizziness worse. "Look, can't we talk about something else?"

Lois opened her mouth to protest, but Janet cut in first. "Hey Lois, did you see Caleb Tanner's new wheels? Man, would I love to have a ride in that thing!"

"What, that red Mustang? I hear his dad bought him that for his birthday. Some present!"

"I am so jealous! Looks new, too."

I concentrated on my turkey burger, content to let the laughter and conversation swirl around me. Thanks to Janet's quick thinking, my adventures had been forgotten.

Or so I thought. Even before Lois had finished eating, she began circulating the news that I had indeed run away and had slept in a garage. "And something terrible happened," she added, "something so awful she's afraid to talk about it."

I kept my head ducked as I tried to force down the rest of my food. *Leave it to Lois to do this to me. Why didn't I invent a better story? I guess my head's more messed up than I thought.* I knew I needed to lie down for a while, but how could I?

I didn't notice Janet standing at my elbow until she spoke.

"Tess, you okay?"

I jerked in surprise, upsetting my carton of milk.

"Oh, I'm sorry." Janet grabbed a napkin and helped me mop up the mess. "Are you all right, girl? You seem really out of it."

For a brief second, our eyes met. Had we been alone, I might have told her the truth; instead, I turned away and said, "Yeah. I'll be fine."

Janet squeezed my arm. "It sure is good to see you again. I'm sorry you've had such a rough time."

"Yeah, well, it's nothing, really. I did something stupid. I just hope I'm really over that flu. I feel kind of weird."

"Maybe you better go down and let the nurse check you out."

"Nah. I'll be okay." To prove it, I shoved back my chair and stood up.

Janet picked up her tray and followed me to the trash can. "Well, I'll see you later then, but you take care of yourself. You don't look so good."

Although kindly intended, her words struck panic in my heart. Could Janet tell I wasn't being straight with her? Did she suspect it was more than the flu that had kept me out of school for so long?

In the restroom, the combination of nerves and dizziness proved too much and I lost my lunch. Afterwards, I stood in front of the mirrors, pretending to touch up my makeup while I studied my reflection. My eyes were red and a little glassy, but otherwise I looked okay, didn't I? I frowned at the greenish-yellow mark on my right cheekbone. In this harsh light it was more noticeable than I'd thought. I'd better have an explanation ready in case someone asked me about it.

I washed my hands, careful not to wet the two large bandages on my left hand. Maybe they had prompted Janet's comment. Thinking about Janet, I felt tears trying to come. We'd been best friends since fifth grade. I hated having to lie to her.

The door opened and a group of girls entered, engaged in animated conversation. I recognized the tall blonde as the one I'd seen with Ethan that morning. Watching her, I felt a stab of envy. Not only was she stunningly pretty, but she carried herself with an air of easy confidence I could only dream of.

Some people have everything going for them, I thought, as I shoved the door and stepped into the hallway. *Me? I've got nothing.* The thought stung, but I held onto it as I pushed my way through the crowded hall toward English class. The sooner I accepted my lot in life, the less painful it would be.

When school let out, Janet caught up with me at the locker we shared. Beside her, to my surprise, was the same blond-haired girl.

"This is my cousin Heather," Janet said. "She's staying with her grandparents for a couple months, so she's been coming to our school."

Heather stepped forward with a bright smile. "Hey, Tessa. Nice to meet you. I hope we'll be friends."

I smiled and said something I hoped would sound nice, but I knew someone like Heather would never bother with me. Especially if she found out what a loser I was.

Mom was waiting for me out in the car. "How was school?"

"Okay, I guess." I dropped my heavy knapsack on the floor and settled into the passenger seat.

"Any problems? Did they question you?"

"No, not really." I turned to face her as I spoke, and that's when I saw the ugly purple bruise on the side of her face. Not this again.

"Walter's mad, huh?" I said.

Mom swore. "Yes, but he's not gonna win this. Look here." She reached into a shopping bag and handed me a stainless steel slide bolt about six inches long. The thing was heavy in my hand.

"I got four of these this afternoon," she said. "Cleaned out the tray in the store, in fact. If my carpentry skills are anything like they used to be, I'll put two of them on your bedroom door, and he'll never get in."

I shook the package, eyeing the short screws. If they stripped out...

"We got one thing going for us with that old house," she continued. "The thing's pretty well built. This would never work otherwise."

"Sure; but I don't trust these tiny screws."

"There's any size screws we want out in the shop. I guess the landlord won't like it, but since when does he come around anyway."

"Well, if he does, we can just lock the doors, and he'll never know."

When we got home, Mom set to work installing the bolts, two on my bedroom door and two on the bathroom door. I watched with some trepidation.

"So what's the deal; I'm supposed to hide out in my room all the time, or what?" I asked.

"You have a place to go if Walter bothers you. That's all."

"And when he gets mad and starts shooting holes in the door, then what?"

She looked at me strangely. "Shooting holes in the door?"

"Yeah. He's got a gun, remember?"

"I guess. I haven't seen it around lately. I'm sure he'd never hurt anybody with it."

I stared at her in astonishment. Was she crazy or what? Almost every day now Walter mistreated us, yet she continued to insist we could live peaceably with him. Why didn't she get smart and leave, like I was planning to? The bolts were a good idea, but in reality, I feared they'd only make Walter madder.

I wandered out to the kitchen, where I began pacing. I had to find a way out of here, and soon. The obvious choice was to run off with Mom's car; but knowing her, she'd call the police on me for stealing it. I probably wouldn't even make it out of the state.

From down the hall came the whine of Walter's power drill. I paused in front of the china cupboard and pulled three cigarettes from Mom's half-empty pack, then proceeded to light one.

***

Supper that evening was unbearably tense. Mom had put together a hamburger hot dish, but neither of us could eat as we anticipated Walter's return. Every tiny noise made my heart leap into my throat. Mom carried her plate over to the counter so she could watch the driveway while she ate. I gave up and locked myself in my bedroom. I hunched motionless on the floor in the semidarkness, my back against my bed and my knees pulled up to my chin. Like a piece of a song on a broken record, a single thought played over and over in my mind. *I've got to get out of here. I've got to get out of here. I've got to get out of here.*

Time passed. My legs cramped up and my back ached, but still I sat, numb with silent desperation. It was then I received a most remarkable gift.

Mom tapped at my door. "Tessa? Come on out here. You're not gonna believe this."

She sounded happy – almost excited. I uncurled my stiff limbs and said, "What?"

"Walter's in jail. He's not coming home. I just got the call."

A wild burst of hope sent me scrambling to my feet. I fumbled at the bolts in my haste to open the door. "Really?"

Mom's eyes were wet as she nodded. "Really."

"What happened? How long's he gonna be there?"

"A month, I suppose. That's about all that's left of his sentence."

"Probation violation, huh?"

We both laughed. Walter was constantly in violation, but he was hard to pin down.

"He can just stay there," I said. "Couldn't we call and ask them to keep him?"

Mom laughed again. "That's a good idea. I wish I'd thought of it. But seriously, I don't know how we'd pay the bills without him. It's gonna be tight as it is."

Her concern did nothing to dampen my joy. No Walter meant no fighting, no threats, no trips to the tavern, no late nights working at the old farmhouse. I could sit in the living room and watch TV in the evenings, eat supper in peace, and go to bed at decent hours. Life was going to be awesome!

Little did I know that Walter wasn't the only problem in my life.

10

School days were always a challenge. I was sure if my friends found out what I was like, they'd want nothing to do with me. So I pasted on a smile, laughed at all the jokes, and worked hard in an effort to blend in. I wasn't an exceptional student, but I could pull passing grades if I put in the time. The only subject in which I couldn't was algebra.

I hated algebra. Adding and subtracting letters made no sense to me. I could limp through the daily assignments, but tests were a nightmare. Complicating matters was the fact I had an algebra guru sitting behind me in class.

Gary was a short, fat kid with a pimply face and thin straight hair that was so pale it looked white. Everything came easily to him – math, science, art, even music. Unfortunately, one of his favorite pastimes was picking on people who were less gifted, like me.

On this particular day, I'd just gotten another test back – with red marks all down the front and a "54" marked at the top. It wasn't my fault. I'd tried my best to battle the beastly problems with guesswork, at one point even making up a sample problem with numbers in place of the letters in a desperate attempt to rediscover the rules of algebra. But Mr. Stone didn't care how hard I'd tried; he only cared whether my answers were right. And they weren't.

With the best show of indifference I could muster, I creased the test in half and shoved it between the pages of my notebook. Then I turned to the new chapter and tried to look attentive as Mr. Stone presented the first unit.

When the bell rang, signaling lunch time, I closed my book in relief and joined the general surge toward the door. All of a sudden, I felt the books shift under my arm. I glanced down. My notebook was missing.

What in... I turned in disbelief. A few paces back stood Gary, holding my notebook by the spine. He shook it, and my test and several loose papers slid out into his hand.

I flew at him in a fury. "Give that back!" I demanded, yanking at the papers. With a sharp ripping sound, they tore. Gary laughed and waved his portion over his head as he sauntered off toward the cafeteria.

I lingered in the hall as long as I dared, trying to calm my rage. *It's only Gary. Who cares what he thinks, anyway.* I fingered the mostly empty pack of cigarettes in my pocket as I took my place at the end of the lunch line. If things got unbearable, I could always slip off and have one. But I'd have to be careful.

Shame crept over me as I recalled what had happened a few days before. Unknown to me, Janet had been in the restroom when I sneaked in to smoke, and she had caught me in the act. Janet hadn't said a word, but the look of surprise and hurt on her face had been harder to take than Walter's worst scolding. I had been avoiding her ever since.

I forced the memory aside as I picked up the last ham sandwich, added a scoop of peas and carrots, and started toward the table by the window where Sandy and Lois always sat. At least they still liked me.

Halfway across the room, I felt a rough shove from behind. Laughter erupted as my lunch tray crashed to the floor. Food scattered everywhere. Turning, I came face to face with Gary's infuriating grin.

"You pushed me," I sputtered.

He was still laughing. "You're so cute when you get mad."

I was so angry I couldn't see straight. *He is not going to treat me like this!* I was about to smash a fist into his mocking face when someone grabbed my arm. I jerked free, then realized it was Heather.

"Go sit down," she said. "I'll take care of this mess. You can have some of my food."

I stared at her, certain I had not heard right. But she was serious.

"Go on," she said, giving me a little push.

Still seething, but aware that arguing would only cause further embarrassment, I complied. Heather scooped the worst of the mess onto the tray and tipped it into the trash can. I watched in bewilderment. I didn't even know Heather beyond Janet's introduction a few weeks ago. Yet here she was, smiling as she offered me a generous portion of her lunch. I managed a sincere thank-you.

My friends didn't know what to make of it. "She seems to be some kind of do-gooder," Sandy commented, as Heather walked away, "but she's nice, too. She sure didn't have to do that."

"That Gary is so cruel," said Lois. Then she began to laugh. "Man, but you should've seen the look on your face. Like you were gonna kill him or something. I wish I had a picture. He pushed you, didn't he?"

Her amusement touched off another flare of anger. "Of course he pushed me. He's always trying to make me look like a fool. If he touches me again, I'll bust his head!"

Sandy put a hand on my arm. "Hey girl, settle down. If you hit him, you know he'd just turn it around and get you in trouble. You'd best just forget it and stay away from him."

I didn't answer. She was right, I knew, but revenge would be so sweet!

Lois finished eating first. "I'm going to go ask Heather why she did it," she announced.

She returned a short while later, her eyes gleaming.

"Well?" Sandy asked.

"She's weird. She claims the Bible told her to do it."

Sandy laughed. "Really? The Bible *told* her?"

"Yup. That's what she says."

I shrugged. "Well, it sure was nice of her, whatever her reason. I don't know about the Bible; I've never read it."

"Nobody does anymore," Sandy said. "They just keep it around as a good-luck charm."

"Yeah, can you imagine actually trying to keep all those rules?" Lois wrinkled up her nose. "You'd get stiffer than my uncle Bradley. He looks just like that guy in *American Gothic*."

"Maybe you better warn Heather before it's too late," Sandy joked.

Both of them laughed. I couldn't help joining in, though I felt uncomfortable doing so. Heather was different, all right, but she was also the nicest person I'd ever met.

***

When school let out that afternoon, Sandy and I stepped out into the November rain together. Mom's black Grand Am was already parked at the curb.

"Looks like your mom's here," Sandy commented.

"Yeah, I guess so." Did Sandy think it strange that my mother drove me to and from school every day? Probably not. Sandy had no way of knowing it was twenty minutes one way to my house.

"Make sure to ask if you can go to the mall after school tomorrow."

"Right."

Sandy caught my arm. "Oh Tess, please. I really want you to come. You have to see the prom dresses in that new fashion shop. You'd look fabulous in the little red one."

I laughed. "All right. We've got a lot going on, but I'll sure try." I lifted a hand and hurried down the sidewalk toward the waiting car.

Sandy had invited me to go shopping with her and her friends a full week ago; but fearing what Mom would say, I'd put off asking. Now there was no more time to waste. Dismally I stared out the rain-streaked window at stubbly farm fields. It would be much simpler to just tell Sandy I couldn't go. But the thought caused an aching inside of me. I wanted to go. How could I get Mom to agree to it?

I pondered the problem as I watched the ruler-straight rows of a pine plantation flick past the window. We were getting close to home. It was now or never.

"Say Mom, you know my friend Sandy?"

"Uh-huh."

"Well, she's pretty good in math, and you know how bad my grades are. She says if I come to her place after school tomorrow, she'll help me. That is, if you don't mind."

"This your idea, or hers?"

"Hers, I guess. We were just talking, and she offered to help." I toyed with the zipper on my knapsack, praying Mom would believe me. She could sniff out a lie faster than a terrier dog tracking a rabbit.

"That's real nice of her, but I don't really have time to drive you all over the place."

"You don't have to. The bus goes right past her place. I could get off there, stay a couple hours, and then you could come get me like you always do."

Mom was silent for a minute. "Well... I'd have to talk to her mom about it first."

"Yeah, I know," I said quickly. "But I'm sure she's okay with it. Sandy helps other kids like this all the time."

That seemed to do it. Mom nodded and didn't say anything for a few minutes. I was imagining the fun we'd have at the mall when she said, "So what's your other reason for going?"

"Huh?"

"I've never seen you so keen about math. That can't be what's on your mind."

"So maybe I wanna improve myself. Is that so bad?" My voice rose. "Look. I totally blew my test today. I don't get this number stuff! If you won't let me go to Sandy's, it'll be your fault when I flunk out."

Mom slowed the car as we approached a narrow bridge. Through the raindrops on my window, I caught a glimpse of the tiny creek below.

"Tess, unless Sandy's some kind of magician, a couple hours with her aren't gonna keep you from flunking. If you're serious, you should talk to your teacher about it."

"He don't care."

"You've asked him?"

I shook my head in frustration. "Look, why can't I go? Maybe it won't fix everything, but so what!"

"Tessa, you know what we've said about parties and such."

"It's not a party!" I practically screamed. "Listen, I wanna go, all right?"

"You wanna go to *what?* Her daddy's brother's deer camp in the woods?"

I felt my face growing hot. "Never mind."

"I wish we could let you go, Tess, but rules are rules."

I nearly choked. "Rules! But Mom, I'm almost grown up, come on! We were just gonna go to the mall. Besides, that was Walter's rule, and he's in jail!"

Mom steered the car left onto our road.

"Please, he'll never know. Can't I go, just this once? I won't spend any money. I promise."

"Tessa, you heard me. No."

"You're cruel!"

"That's enough, Tess."

"Fine. If you're gonna be mean about it, I'll find my own way there."

I wished I could carry out my threat. But things weren't pretty when Mom got mad. I turned away, my eyes pricking with angry tears. Why was I such a wimp? Why couldn't I take charge of my life and tell Mom what I was planning to do, the way my friends did, instead of always asking her permission like a kindergartener?

Mom pulled the car up level with the weathered mailbox at the end of our driveway. "Might as well get the mail this way," she said.

Rain blew in the car window as I depressed the button. Reaching out, I yanked open the metal door. The mailbox was empty.

"Nothing? That's odd," Mom said. "Guess he's late today."

"Or else you got it earlier and forgot," I retorted.

Mom pulled in and parked in the usual spot near the back steps. I stepped wide over a puddle as I got out.

"Oops, there's the mail now," Mom said. "Would you run get that for me, Tess? I'll take your knapsack in."

Ignoring her offer, I hitched the heavy bag higher on my shoulder as I started down the muddy driveway. Rain pattered on my coat, then dripped off the hem and soaked into my jeans.

Mom is just plain mean, I fumed. *First she treats me like a five-year-old, then she expects me to run all the way out here in the rain and get her stupid mail for her. And you know it's just a bunch of junk she's gonna throw away anyway. It would help if I got something once in a while. But you can bet that's against the rules too.*

I slid the bundle of mail from the box and slammed the door shut with a clang. Everything was against the rules. Self-pity enveloped me as I reflected on my endless list of disadvantages.

I've never gone on a vacation. I've never even been out of the state, since before I can remember, anyway. I've never gotten to go swimming or camping. I've never once gotten a single piece of mail, not even a birthday card. I can't have a computer, email, or a cell phone. I can't go anyplace, can't talk on the phone, and now I can't even ride the bus. Why? So Walter and Mom can do what they please, that's why.

I kicked fiercely at a loose piece of gravel. Mom treated me well enough; but when it came to the so-called family rules, she was Gibraltar. I could see now how it would be. Until the glorious day when I finally moved out, my parents would just keep holding me down under the same stupid rules they'd made when I was five or six years old. It was crazy; no, cruel. How was I ever supposed to grow up? Or would they rather I didn't?

As I neared the house, the rain began to pick up. I hurried up the wooden steps, then paused, my hand on the door latch. What was that sound? I strained my ears, but the tap of raindrops on my hood kept blotting it out. I thrust my things into the house and then descended the steps to investigate.

11

*A*s I reached the bottom of the steps, I heard it again – a high-pitched squeaking. It seemed to be coming from the lilac bush behind the landing. I peered into the dense branches but saw nothing. Still the insistent squeaking continued. I knelt on the soggy ground and shoved aside the dripping branches. In the dead leaves at the base of the bush, under the remains of an old robin nest, I found the source – a scruffy little mouse no bigger than my thumb.

"You poor thing." I scooped it up. Its tiny body felt cold in my hand. I stroked its damp fur with the tip of one finger, and it curled its long tail around itself and emitted a series of pitiful squeaks that shook its whole frame. That sealed it. Slipping the little creature into my pocket, I turned back to the house.

Mom looked up from folding laundry when I walked in. "What'd you do with the mail?"

"It's right there." I jabbed a thumb toward the scattered pile under the desk, then stripped off my dripping coat and hurried to my room.

"You're an orphan, aren't you," I murmured, as I blotted my new pet dry with a tissue. "What happened to your mama?" The mouse was quiet now, except for a slight trembling, but it seemed unable to open its eyes. I held it up, admiring its dainty pink feet and white bib. Such a pretty mouse deserved a name. I would have to think of something. I wrapped it in a dry tissue, then tucked its cold little body close to mine.

By now the rain had progressed to a heavy downpour that roared on the roof and slapped against my window. I leaned my elbows on the sill and watched the storm, all the while contemplating my new responsibility. The little mouse had to be hungry. I knew nothing about how to feed it, but I didn't dare ask for help raising an animal most people considered a pest. Besides, it was probably against the rules to have it.

With careful planning, I managed to sneak some milk and a bit of cheese into my bedroom. Sitting cross-legged on my bed, I poured a bit of the milk into a plastic bottle cap and held it in front of the mouse so it could drink.

The mouse dipped its nose into the liquid, choked, and then pawed wildly, spilling the milk down its belly and onto my bedspread. I dabbed at the mess with my last tissue and headed to the bathroom for more. On the way, I met Mom coming from the kitchen, her arms full of folded clothes.

"What have you got?" she asked.

"Nothing." I slipped my hand into my pocket and ducked around the corner into the bathroom.

Mom followed right behind me. "You were getting milk for some reason. What have you got, a kitten?"

My heart lurched. She hadn't even been in the kitchen when I got the milk. What did she have, X-ray vision?

"You better show me," she said. "I can't guess."

I was caught. I withdrew the tiny mouse from my pocket, cupping my hand over it so that all Mom could see was a whiskery little nose.

"Oh dear. A baby mouse." There was a note of disgust in her voice.

"She's an orphan. Her name's Genevieve."

"Where'd you get it?"

"Outside. I rescued her from the rain. Isn't she cute?"

Mom looked unconvinced. "Tessa, I don't think…"

"I'm gonna take care of her. She won't be no trouble. You'll see."

"But Tessa, you haven't got time, with school and all…" Her voice trailed off.

"It is kind of cute," she conceded. "I guess you can try, but as little as it is, I wouldn't rate your chances of success very highly."

"Don't worry, Mom." I tucked the mouse back into my pocket, grabbed the box of tissues, and returned to my room. It couldn't be that hard to raise a mouse.

But eight capfuls of milk and a dozen tissues later, I was about to give up. Either the mouse choked and blew bubbles out of her nose, or she spilled the milk all over herself and me. And she kept spitting out the cheese.

"The way you're going, you're gonna starve, you stupid thing," I scolded. I plopped her down on the bed. "And it won't be my fault. What's the matter with you?" The mouse sat still for a moment, then began creeping toward the edge of the bed.

"Supper," Mom called from the kitchen.

With a sigh of resignation, I tucked the mouse back into my pocket. "Be quiet," I warned. I had a feeling Mom would not appreciate the mouse coming to supper.

"So how was school today?" Mom asked, as she passed the meatballs my way. "You didn't say anything about it on the way home."

I shrugged. "Nothing new. Just Gary acting like a moron again." I paused and poured spaghetti sauce over my meatballs. "I guess there's some kind of special event tomorrow."

"Oh? What's happening?"

"I'm not quite sure." I could feel a tickling sensation as the mouse burrowed around in my pocket. What if she crawled out?

"They didn't tell you what it was?"

I reached down and pushed Genevieve back into my pocket, then plugged the opening with my hand. "Well, they did . . . but I don't remember. It's nothing important."

Mom studied my face, but she didn't inquire further. I was glad. I didn't want her to know there was still a slight fuzziness in my head. Sometimes I had trouble remembering things.

Later that evening, after she had cleaned up the dishes, Mom stopped by my bedroom. I was sitting on the floor in front of the open closet door, putting the finishing touches on a tiny box I'd made from a margarine carton. A faint odor of sour milk hung in the air.

"How's the critter?" Mom asked.

"She's sleeping."

"You need to get started on your homework."

I shrugged. Opening one end of the box, I began filling it with fine shreds of tissue.

"You can't take the mouse to school with you tomorrow," Mom said.

"Yes I can. I'm gonna put her in this box so she can't escape. Nobody will know."

"You're not taking it," she repeated. "I will personally see to that."

I twisted around to face her. "But, Mom! I can't leave her here. She'll die."

"I guess you'll have to find her a babysitter, then." A slight smile played across her lips. Was she making me some kind of offer?

I hesitated. "Well . . . you gotta be awfully careful with her, you know. She's so little, and..."

"Stop your worrying. I've raised three babies; I guess I can babysit a fourth."

"You mean you really would? You'd feed her and everything?" I couldn't contain my delight.

Mom laughed. "I don't think I have any choice, do I? Now you get after that homework; and when you're done, we'll see what we can do with the little critter."

***

I worked on homework at the kitchen table until almost nine o'clock. By then, the mouse had set up a persistent squeaking inside my pocket. Mom unglued herself from the TV, warmed a cupful of milk in the microwave, and brought it over to the table.

"Before you feed her, you should check the temperature of the milk on your wrist, like this," she said. "This feels just about right."

Following her example, I dipped a finger in the milk and sprinkled my wrist. I couldn't even feel the drops. "I didn't think about heating it," I said.

"It's a good idea. It'll keep her from getting chilled and make it easier to digest too."

I dipped a bottle cap into the milk and tried once more to feed the mouse, with the usual results. Mom watched, her face thoughtful.

"I have an idea," she said. She disappeared down the hall toward the bathroom, returning a moment later with a cotton swab. "Here. Dip this in the milk and let her suck it."

After one or two false starts, the mouse began sucking vigorously on the swab. Mom helped me add drops of milk one by one.

"This works pretty good," I said after a while. "Where'd you learn all this?"

"Oh, it's just mothers' instinct. But I think she's had enough for now. If you overfeed her, she'll get sick." Mom stood up and stretched. "Wipe her all over, especially on the bottom. I'll get a bed ready for her."

I watched as Mom laid an old dishrag in the bottom of a shoebox and built a nest of torn tissues in the corner. Then she set the box on my dresser, bending the gooseneck lamp down close to the nest.

"That should do it," she said. "She'll move away from the light if it gets too hot. Now you better hurry and get to bed, because you've got about four hours, if that, before she's gonna want to eat again."

I wanted to thank Mom for helping, but I knew she'd just brush it off. So I whispered goodnight to little Genevieve, who was already asleep, and then put on my pajamas and crawled into bed. Briefly my thoughts shifted to the mall trip I had wanted so badly. It still stung that I couldn't go, but the arrival of the tiny mouse helped. Maybe this hadn't been such a bad day after all.

12

i awoke before dawn to the sound of the mouse rustling around in her box. I glanced at the clock and groaned. *She can't need anything yet.* Hardly three hours had passed since her last feeding, a nocturnal affair during which I'd managed to spill a half cup of hot milk down the front of my pajamas. Pulling a pillow over my head, I tried to go back to sleep, but the rustling noises increased. Soon a pitiful squeaking began.

"All right, all right," I muttered as I dragged my weary body out of bed. I could feel the muscles tightening in the back of my neck, bringing on a headache. But I could not hold back a smile when I reached into the box and Genevieve climbed right into my hand.

"You're getting strong," I murmured. Her eyes, which had been sealed yesterday, were now little shining slits. I warmed some milk and carried it back to my bedroom, glad that Walter wasn't around. I knew what he would say if he found out I was raising a mouse.

I fed the mouse, then watched in amusement as she sat up on wobbly hind legs and tried to wash her face. Next she set about burrowing up my pajama sleeve. I left her loose on the bed while I brushed out my hair in front of the mirror.

No tests today, I thought in satisfaction. *But I wish I could remember what that special event is.*

"How's the critter this morning?" Mom asked me at breakfast.

"Kind of demanding. Already she thinks I'm her mama."

"Is she eating okay?"

"Yeah, I think so. She woke me up because she was hungry." I spread raspberry jam on my toast and took a bite. "So . . . are you still gonna feed her for me while I'm gone?"

"I said I would."

"I figure she'll want to eat again around ten."

"All right." Mom sounded resigned.

Later, Mom dropped me off at school with the usual farewell: "Bye, have a good day." I nodded and hurried inside, making a wide circuit around where Lois stood gossiping with her friends.

At my locker I met Janet. "Isn't there something going on today?" I asked, as I pulled off my coat and stuffed it through the narrow opening.

"Sure, it's Good Citizens' Day. You and I get to skip English class. How could you forget something as important as that?" She swatted me playfully.

"I don't know." I laughed at how foolish it sounded.

Good Citizens' Day was a creation of the Northford school system. Every year, on the first Thursday in November, we were given a special forty-five-minute presentation in place of one of our regular class periods. Once a lady from the Red Cross did a slide show and handed out pamphlets on volunteer opportunities; another time, Janet's grandfather spoke about his experiences as a soldier in the Korean War. As I gathered my books and headed toward my first class, I wondered what they had come up with this year.

"Hey, Tess." Lois caught up with me, her face flushed with excitement. "You'll never guess what happened last night."

"To you? I'm not even gonna try."

"Well, me and Andrea…" She paused to catch her breath. "Me and Andrea were watching a movie last night when this police car turns into our driveway. He had his lights on and everything. So my mom grabs her slippers and runs to the door and guess what?"

"Your roof was on fire."

"No!" She was giggling almost too hard to talk. "He said somebody had dialed 911. Mom told him that was silly, but afterwards she went down the basement and guess what? That crazy cat of ours had knocked the phone onto the couch and was standing there, kneading the pillows and rubbing on it. Apparently she hit the buttons and called them."

"Seriously?" Although Lois had a history of grand exaggeration, still I laughed at the image of a befuddled dispatcher trying to decipher the sounds of purring and kneading.

"I'm telling you. There isn't anything she can't do."

"Guess not."

It was one of the few laughs I had that day.

Right after lunch, I joined the throng of students headed down to the auditorium for the presentation. Not far ahead of me walked Janet and Heather.

"Let's sit up front," I heard Heather say to Janet as they entered through the double doors. "Nobody ever does, for some weird reason." With that, she grabbed Janet's hands and began prancing up the aisle, towing Janet along behind like a trailer.

"Oh, stop!" Janet screeched, and both of them broke into gales of laughter.

Loneliness swelled in my throat as I watched them. Janet and I used to get along like that, back before Heather showed up. *Back before Janet caught me smoking that one day,* I quickly amended. *She tries to be friendly and act like it never happened, but things aren't the same.*

Lois spotted me and gestured frantically for me to join her and Sandy. I pretended not to notice. That constant chatter of hers could drive a squirrel crazy. I kept walking and slipped into an empty seat toward the front, several rows behind Janet and Heather.

Moments later, a touch on my shoulder made me look up. There stood Heather, smiling as always. "Want company?" she asked. Behind her, Janet had already sat down.

"Um, sure," I fumbled. "But you guys were sitting up there."

Heather slipped into the seat next to mine. "Yes, but we'd like to sit here with you, if you don't mind."

I shrugged. "Cool." They were strange, I thought. Why should they want to sit with me? I could smell a touch of perfume on Heather – not overpowering, just pleasant.

I shifted in my seat. All I ever smelled like was smoke. What must Heather think of me? Had Janet told her I smoked? Did she guess how often I sneaked out after lunch to have a cigarette? My face grew hot as the shameful thoughts continued. I chewed my lip, wondering if there was a tactful way to get up and move to another part of the room. But just then the principal walked out on stage.

He cleared his throat. "Good afternoon, everyone," he said. "As you know, today is our Good Citizens' Day. Our goal in setting aside this day is to provide some practical and enjoyable instruction in how to be a good citizen in your community and beyond. We ask that you be respectful and give your full attention to our speaker, who has taken time out of her busy schedule to be here with us today. Also, don't forget to take notes. Your teachers may test you on some of these things.

"This year's presentation will be on community law and order, and I'm delighted to have Officer Pat Bridgers from our local police department here with us to speak on this subject."

No! Was this a joke? But there was Pat, ascending the steps and shaking hands with the principal as if they were old friends. I could feel a slow flush spreading across my face. Would Pat recognize me? I was certain she would.

Pat faced the crowded auditorium with a smile. "Hello," she said. "My name's Pat, and I'm happy to be here with you today. I love doing things like this; it's a lot of fun, and I learn things too. You guys can ask some pretty formidable questions, and sometimes I can't answer them." She laughed a little.

"As a police officer, I get to work with young people who have made some wrong choices and gotten in trouble with the law. I always try to help them as much as I can. My work can be challenging, but it's never boring.

"Today I'd like to talk about our laws – that is, why they're necessary and why you should feel good about yourself when you obey them. Contrary to what some people believe, it is not a mark of courage or bravery to break the law. True courage manifests itself in more positive, constructive ways."

I wasn't listening. What I really wanted to do was get up and leave; but sitting this close to the front, I couldn't do so without attracting attention. I hunched lower in my seat and fixed my gaze on my clenched hands. Maybe if I tried, I could forget about Pat.

My thoughts drifted to my pet mouse. I pictured her the way she'd looked that morning, a silver spray of whiskers framing her face as her tiny pink tongue reached to lap a drop of milk. I could see her exploring my bed on wobbly legs, her ears standing erect when I spoke softly but flattening when I laughed. Was Mom really taking care of her for me? I imagined Genevieve with a checkered bib around her neck, sucking a miniature baby bottle, and almost laughed aloud.

Next to me, Heather was scratching notes on a folded piece of paper. Had someone said we should take notes? I glanced up just as a ripple of laughter spread through the auditorium.

"There's one more reason why we need laws," Pat was saying. "People who are committing crimes need to be punished, and if possible, rehabilitated to become productive members of society. Laws are needed to establish proper penalties for these people, while at the same time ensuring that they are not unjustly punished."

Yeah, right. My mind flashed back to the night I'd been arrested. I could still feel the cold metal of the handcuffs, still recall the shame and the fear. *I didn't deserve it. All I was doing was getting something to eat so I wouldn't starve.*

"There's one crime that's quite prevalent around here, which I'd like to cite as an example of what I've been saying," Pat continued. "That is the production and sale of methamphetamine."

I cringed. *Does she have to talk about that?* I could feel my blush deepening. I sat rigid in my seat, sweating, my fists clenched so tightly my fingernails bit into my palms. I took a deep breath, then another, trying to force my thoughts onto something else. But Pat's words came through in spite of my best efforts.

"Methamphetamine is an illegal drug made by mixing and 'cooking' certain volatile chemicals with cold medicines. The process is extremely dangerous, both to the person doing it and to anyone nearby. Sometimes the chemicals explode, causing uncontrollable fires and serious burns. Even when this doesn't happen, they still emit a host of poisonous vapors which damage one's internal organs and cause serious respiratory problems.

"The manufacture of methamphetamine does significant damage to the environment. Each pound of meth that is produced creates an additional five to seven pounds of toxic waste, which is simply dumped down the drain or thrown into a ditch somewhere. This contaminates the soil and nearby water supplies. As you might guess, cleaning up a mess like that is no small task. It costs thousands of dollars.

"Methamphetamine is an instantly addictive substance that devastates the lives of those who use it. It corrodes their face, rots their teeth, and destroys nerve endings as well as every major organ in their body. In the end, it kills them.

"And that's just one side of the story. Many meth addicts are parents, so their bad choices affect their children as well. Some face permanent developmental and personality problems due to exposure to toxic chemicals. A large number end up in foster care when their parents get arrested, which they usually do, for crimes that range from possession to theft to murder."

Pat paused. "This stuff is bad, any way you look at it. Are you with me?"

I didn't dare raise my head. I was so nervous I was shaking. I had to clench my teeth to stop them from chattering. Luckily, my friends were too absorbed in what Pat was saying to notice.

"Making and selling methamphetamine, or possessing any amount of it, is against the law," Pat continued. "As you can see, it's not because the lawmakers are trying to keep us from having fun. It's because of the terrible damage it does to people's lives. This is a good example of a law that was made to protect people. It's too bad so many choose to ignore it.

"A person who willfully breaks the law pays a penalty, whether he gets caught or not. He pays the penalty in damage to his conscience, as he attempts to silence and destroy that little voice inside that warns him he's doing wrong. He pays the penalty as the wrong he's done begins to destroy him. And of course, he pays the penalty when he is finally caught and punished. It isn't funny. It really isn't worth ruining your reputation and letting your life go down the drain for a thrill or a dare."

As Pat finished speaking, the auditorium broke out in polite applause.

"Thank you," Pat said. "We've got about five minutes left. Does anyone have a question?"

"What happens if somebody gets caught making meth?" asked a boy behind me.

"He's in an awful lot of trouble. Depending on the amount involved, he could be facing as much as twenty-five years in prison, maybe more, and heavy fines on top of that."

What? My breath caught in a gasp. This had to be some kind of nightmare.

Heather must have seen the distress on my face, for she leaned over and whispered, "What's wrong?"

"Mind your own business," I hissed back. Heather stared at me in confusion, then turned away. I held my breath and dug my fingernails into my palms even harder, desperately trying to distract myself.

When Pat had finished answering questions, the principal made a few remarks and dismissed us. The room buzzed with laughter and talking as everyone rose at once.

In the aisle, Janet stepped to my side. "Tess, what's the matter? Don't you feel well?"

"I'm fine."

"Then come on, I'll introduce you to Pat. You'll like her."

It was then I realized that Pat hadn't left yet. She was standing in the hallway outside the auditorium, shaking hands and talking with the students as they came out.

I pulled away from Janet. "Listen, I just remembered something I gotta do. I'll catch up with you in a couple minutes." I started working my way through the crowd toward a side door.

"But Tess…" Bewildered, Janet hurried after me. "Tessa, wait!" Finally catching up with me at the door, she grabbed my arm and turned me halfway around. "Tess, what in the world is going on with you? You're so different; it's like I don't even know you."

I couldn't look at her. I just shook my head and pushed open the door.

"Tessa, please. Say something. Don't just walk away from me!"

The distress in her voice broke my heart. I wanted to stop and apologize, but I couldn't. Not with shame written all over my face and tears welling in my eyes. The tears came faster than I could wipe them away. By now Janet probably suspected the worst. Even if I did try to smooth things over, it wouldn't do any good.

It wasn't until I turned the corner that I dared look back. Janet was nowhere to be seen, but someone else appeared to be trailing me. A girl whose name I didn't know. I walked faster.

13

Reaching the nearest set of restrooms, I pushed the door marked "Ladies" and stepped inside. The stranger followed.

"Tess, isn't it?" she asked, with a slight accent. "I'm Lorraine."

Lorraine was new at school as of a few weeks ago. I'd never officially met her, but I'd seen her in the halls, her stringy, dyed-black hair almost hiding her face. She wore black nail polish, skin-tight black jeans, and way too much make-up.

"So you couldn't stand it either," she said. "Don't you just hate it when they try to scare you?"

I turned to look at her. "What're you talking about?"

"You know. That cop. Pat. You'd think she's on some sort of mission. What a pain."

I felt reassured. Here was a person who would understand where I was coming from. "You can say that again," I agreed. "She actually arrested me once."

Lorraine's face crinkled with interest. "Yeah? What'd you do?"

"Not much. I picked up a couple things at a store, and a clerk saw me."

"Cool. Say, I gotta run, but here." She handed me a tiny package wrapped in white paper.

"What is it?"

"Shhh. Just try it." She walked out, leaving me with the package in my hand. Curious, I turned it over, tugged at the piece of clear tape on the bottom, and slowly unwrapped two handmade cigarettes. Except for being a little shorter, they looked very much like the ones Walter made from the harvest of his secret garden.

I glanced over my shoulder as I crumpled the paper around them again. I would be in big trouble if I got caught with this – not only with the school authorities, but more importantly, with Mom. She'd probably turn me over to Walter like she did last spring when she found one of his joints in my jeans pocket while doing laundry.

I tried to push aside my uneasiness as I hurried to class. Nobody had seen. There was no way I could be found out. But my mind swirled with questions. Was marijuana harmful? Could people tell if I used it? What would my friends think if they saw me with Lorraine?

I already knew the answer to that one. Lois would turn it into a gossip item. Sandy would shrug it off and go blithely on her way. The only ones who would've really cared were Janet and Heather. And I had just made it abundantly clear that I wanted nothing to do with either of them. Rather a stupid move, but there was no undoing it now.

Lois caught up with me after school that day. "What's with you this afternoon? Cops freak you out or something?"

I tried to laugh. "What do you mean?"

"You act like you think somebody's after you."

My heart raced. Was I acting that strangely?

"It's nothing," I said. "I-I've got stomach cramps. You know."

Lois stared at me incredulously. "Stomach cramps? You're that nervous? But I guess it figures. I'd hate to be you and have to worry about getting caught smoking."

"Aww, shut up. Who said I smoke."

"I do. You positively stink. Especially after lunch."

I could feel my face getting hot at the raw compliment. "What do you expect me to smell like, when both my parents smoke? Fresh air and roses?"

"If it's that bad, you better move out before it kills you." For a moment, Lois looked serious. But seconds later she was her old teasing self again.

"I bet I've got it. Pat's the one who caught you when you ran away."

I forced another laugh. "That just shows how little you know about anything, snoopy-nose. Running away's not a crime."

Her eyes went round with astonishment. "No? Then how come they call the police?"

"Don't ask me. People call the police for everything nowadays – bats in the living room, leaking pipes, cars that don't start." I swung my knapsack onto my shoulder and said, "Mom's waiting for me. See you."

"Bats in the living room . . . Tessa! That's disgusting!" Lois's piercing voice echoed after me as I walked out the doors. I knew I'd have to face her prying questions for days, but at least I had won this first time. I was pleased with myself.

***

After lunch the following day, Lorraine approached me again. "Well?" she asked, in a half whisper.

"Well, what?"

"Did you try it?"

I shook my head.

"Good grief, girl, what're you waiting for?"

I felt my face flush. "I'm just not sure about it."

Amazement shone on Lorraine's face. But before she could reply, two more girls joined her. "Hey, what're you doing?" said one of them, draping an arm across her shoulders.

Lorraine half turned. "Why Britt, haven't you met Tessa yet? Tess, this is Brittney."

Brittney smiled and said, "Hey." She was a big, good-looking girl, with thick auburn hair and fine features. I later discovered her mother was the pianist at the Lutheran church across the street.

"And this is Crystal." Crystal was standing behind Brittney and wouldn't look at me at all. She was thin, with dark, brooding eyes and a deep scar on her cheek.

"We're a pretty diverse bunch," Lorraine said, with a laugh. "So, what grade you in?"

"Does it matter?" I shifted my weight and glanced across the room where Janet and Heather stood talking with a few friends.

"You new here?"

"I have friends, if that's what you mean."

"You mean those two?" Lorraine jabbed a thumb toward Janet and Heather. "I've met them. They don't seem like your type."

I took a step backward. "Oh yeah? And just how would you know who's my type?"

Lorraine threw her head back and laughed, revealing severely crooked front teeth. "I like your style, Tess. Join us outside McDonald's tomorrow noon, okay?"

I took a few more steps backward. "I can't. I don't live in town."

"Your old man won't drive you, huh? Tough. Well, we'll have to think of something else then."

"Yeah, I guess so." I edged away, wishing the bell would ring. Lorraine's forwardness made me uncomfortable.

14

W alter was released from jail the week before Thanksgiving. In his usual fashion, he had promised Mom he'd work in the furniture shop and finish up his orders as soon as he got out. And Mom, desperate for any kind of good news, believed him. That is, until she pulled into the driveway after picking me up at school that afternoon.

"Oh, come on." She shook her head at the beat-up station wagon and two pickup trucks parked at various angles in front of the shop. "He's having a party already?"

"Doesn't he always, when he gets out of jail?" I said.

Mom rolled her eyes. "I just wish he'd celebrate by working once in a while. He's eight weeks behind on his orders. More like ten or twelve on a few of them."

Throughout the evening, more cars trickled down the driveway. By dark, I counted seven. Mom observed the situation, once or twice hinting to me that she ought to crash the party.

"Why don't you?" I asked.

"It wouldn't do any good. About that time, the cops wouldn't find anything, and we'd have to deal with a very mad Walter." She shook her head. "Dish up the soup, would you, and we'll eat. There's no sense waiting for him. He'll be out there all night."

I knew she was right about that. Even so, I found it impossible to relax and enjoy my supper. The mere presence of Walter on the property was enough to keep me on edge.

That night, as I lay in bed with my door bolted shut, listening to the pulsing beat of rock music coming from the shop, I started to think about running away again. Walter's month-long absence hadn't changed him a bit. It didn't take a genius to figure out what would happen next. He'd pull me out of school, shove Mom aside, and haul me off to work for him again. And if I dared to resist or complain, he'd make sure I paid for it.

I heard water trickling in the pipes as Mom got ready for bed. Outside, a car engine revved, then died. It must be close to midnight. Pulling a blanket around my shoulders, I rose and went to the window. The night sky was moonless and black except for a faint orange glow off toward Northford. Somewhere in the distance a dog barked. Tomorrow I had school again. I should go back to bed and get some sleep.

Yet I continued staring out the window, turning the situation over in my mind. I knew the time had come to make a move. Running away might not be the best option, but it was the only one I could think of.

The plan I invented was pretty simple. I would get up before dawn and drive Mom's car into town. There I'd buy a ticket on a bus headed for some warmer part of the country, provided they were willing to sell me one. I had heard bus companies were cautious about selling tickets to minors. I'd have to lie about my age and hope they believed me. Still, it would look pretty suspicious – me walking into the bus station alone at five in the morning and trying to buy a ticket. Were they even open at five in the morning?

I went to bed, but I tossed and turned all night, torn between excitement and fear. I already had the money; all I needed were a few clothes and things. At ten minutes to four, I crawled out of bed and crept down the hall to the kitchen.

Flashlight in hand, I pawed through the assortment of plastic shopping bags in the bottom of the pantry. I wanted a big thick one with handles, not some flimsy thing from Walmart. When I had found one I thought would work, I returned to my room to pack.

Socks. Toothbrush. Money. Extra sweatshirt. Safety pins. One by one I checked the items off my list, moving about by the faint glow of a night light I had borrowed from the bathroom. Over in the corner, I could hear Genevieve nosing through her food bowl. She had rapidly outgrown the shoebox under the lamp, and I had moved her into a large plastic garbage can. She was now half grown, very friendly, and curious about everything. I would miss her terribly.

The final item remaining on the list was food. I made one more trip to the kitchen, scouring the cupboards for things that would be easy to pack. Spam fit the bill, as did a box of cheese crackers, two candy bars, and a couple slices of banana bread. By then my bag was bulging.

It was a quarter to five when I whispered goodbye to Genevieve, picked up my bag, and walked down the hall for the last time. I was more nervous than I'd ever been in my life, but I kept telling myself it was now or never. I set the bag down on the table and felt around in the shallow desk drawer where Mom kept the car key.

Nothing.

I pulled the drawer out farther, feeling around the stack of receipts, loose pens, scissors, calculator. The key was not there. I pushed the drawer shut and stood there in numb disbelief. This could not be happening. Everything was ready. It was time to go. How could such a small thing stop me? It was just too stupid.

I dug in my bag until I found my flashlight, then proceeded to do a thorough search of the drawer, the kitchen table, the counters, Mom's coat pockets, the bookshelf. I even crept out to look in the car. The key was nowhere to be found.

I returned to my bedroom too discouraged to think. School would start in less than three hours. Even if Mom would accept a claim that I was sick, I didn't want to stay home with Walter around. I dropped my bag next to my bed and crawled under the covers without even taking my shoes off. Why did nothing ever turn out right? Blood pounded in my head, each pulse jabbing into my temples like a nail. *There's no way out,* it seemed to say. *Quit trying. You're doomed.*

I pulled the blankets up over my head and inhaled the warm, stale air. *Just maybe, you'll suffocate down here,* I thought, recalling one of my childhood fears. Back then, I couldn't sleep with so much as a sheet over my nose. Mom's repeated assurances that air could go through fabric had little effect on me.

The warmth eventually made me drowsy. *Either I really will suffocate down here, or else I'll sleep for a few hours,* I remember thinking as I drifted off.

Despite my anxiety, we saw very little of Walter over the next few days. Once or twice he raided the cupboards for candy bars and soda pop, and one morning I awoke to a heated argument over an unpaid credit card bill. Otherwise, things were calm. But I knew better than to relax. I spent my evenings in my bedroom with the bolts pulled.

Thanksgiving was the one bright spot during this time. School let out a day early to allow families time to travel. We, of course, had no such plans; but I did spend a portion of the extra day helping Mom make an apple pie. It was more enjoyable than studying the geography of South America or learning about the classification of insects.

"Is this enough apples now?" I asked, adding yet another freshly pared apple to the short row on the kitchen table.

Mom turned from the counter where she was mixing the crust. "It might be. Cut out the cores and slice them real thin. We need six full cups."

"You know, I was thinking," I said. "Everybody else has turkey and dressing and mashed potatoes and–"

A mild crash from the other end of the kitchen interrupted me. "We're not everybody else, Tess."

"Of course not. But it would be kind of nice to have that stuff, don't you think?"

Mom unfolded the bottom crust into the pie plate and began rolling out the top in short, even strokes. "Maybe sometime," she said.

Her indifference frustrated me. I shoved my chair back so hard it fell over. "I'm sick of this!" I burst out. "What's the matter that we can't ever do anything?"

"Stop it. Be glad you're getting a pie."

I hacked at an apple, venting my anger on it. What could possibly be wrong with making a normal Thanksgiving dinner? But I should've known. Mom didn't want to bother, for some stupid reason.

"Uh-oh." Her exclamation interrupted my sullen mood. "Vicks just drove in."

"Oh great," I muttered. "Tell 'em we're not home."

"Right. Like that will solve anything." Mom brushed the loose flour from her hands and hurried to the front door.

Dan Vick was an older man, well-built and balding on top. One of Walter's original furniture customers, he had a reputation for being particular about quality and price. He possessed a booming voice and lately, an irritable temper.

"I'm here to pick up that bookshelf," he greeted Mom.

"I'm sorry, sir, but Walter's still working on it."

"He told me it would be done today!" His voice became hard. "Where is he?"

"He's gone right now."

"Gone again, huh? Well, this is some kind of racket," he stormed. "First he tells me it'll be done in a few days. Then he changes his mind; says it'll be a couple weeks. Last Friday he promised it would be done today. I've had it. I want my money back, or I'm calling the sheriff."

"I'm sure it'll be done real soon," Mom reassured him, beginning to close the door. "He's had some problems with it."

"Yeah, I bet. We'll see what the sheriff thinks about that."

"I can't imagine what that Walter thinks he's doing," Mom sputtered, as she locked the door and returned to the kitchen. "You can't run a business like that! Doesn't he have any brains at all?"

I looked up from mixing the pie filling. "I don't think he's even started the bookcase."

"I'm sure he hasn't. And the way he's going, he never will." She took the bowl from me and scraped the filling into the pie shell. "I'm not talking to any more of his customers. Period. I'm not answering the door, I'm not answering the phone, and I'm not taking any more messages! Either he's gonna be here, or he's gonna lose 'em. It's his problem."

Justified as it was, her outburst grated on my nerves. I was so weary of thinking about, hearing about, and worrying about the mess we were in that I wanted to scream.

Picking up a stray piece of apple, I slipped off to my room. Playing with Genevieve had become my favorite escape from the mounting tension in the air. I dropped the apple into her food dish, then reached down and tapped gently on her nest box.

Nothing happened. I tapped harder. Suddenly Genevieve scurried from the nest and ran up my arm. Chuckling, I shook her off. It was fun to let her explore the bedroom, but the other night she had been impossible to catch again. It was safer to leave her in the garbage can and watch her eat.

A short time later, Mom stuck her head in my room. "Oh, there you are." Then her nose wrinkled. "Phew! Don't you think that mouse is old enough now to fend for itself?"

"What do you mean? She's my pet."

"A very smelly one, I'd say. How about if we take a drive and find her a new home. We'll go out to that abandoned farm across the highway. There are plenty of old buildings there she can live in."

"I said, she's my pet. I'm keeping her." I folded my arms and stared at Mom.

"But Tessa, haven't you thought about what the mouse wants?" Mom countered. "She's not gonna be happy living her life in a garbage can. She wants to run and mate and have babies."

"I wasn't gonna keep her in a garbage can," I retorted. "I'm gonna build her a cage."

"She doesn't want to spend her life in a cage either. She's a wild mouse."

"But I need her, Mom," I pleaded. "She makes me happy. I'll take real good care of her, I promise. I'll build the cage tomorrow."

But Mom was shaking her head. "We're not gonna have a mouse in the house. They stink no matter how well you take care of them."

Tears crowded my eyes. Genevieve wasn't just a mouse. She was a playful creature whose silly antics brightened my days. She made me laugh when everything else was going wrong. How could I ever be happy without her?

My throat was so tight I could hardly speak. "If I let her go, can I have another pet?"

"Look, Tess, we can hardly afford to take care of ourselves right now. I'm afraid pets are out of the question."

"But Mom, Genny eats almost nothing. I'll pay for it. I'll keep my door closed so you can't smell her. I'll scrub her cage as often as I have to. You can't make me get rid of her!"

"I'm not gonna fight with you, Tessa. I've got my hands full with Walter. But that mouse has to go. I'll drive you out to the farm tomorrow."

I felt like my heart was being ripped in two. I sank down on my bed, covering my face to muffle the sobs. How could Mom be so cruel? Couldn't she see that I needed Genevieve?

After a time, my tears subsided. I heard Genevieve rooting around in the debris in the bottom of the can. Then she caught sight of me and stood up on her hind legs, jumping and begging to be lifted out. Fresh tears spilled down my cheek as I reached into the can. If only I could keep her secretly! But none of the scenarios I pictured had a good ending.

Maybe it's for the best, I consoled myself. *At least she'll be safe at the farm. Otherwise, who knows what will happen to her when I run away.*

I watched Genevieve streak across my bed and leap to the floor. I quickly shut the door and checked to make sure the furnace vent was plugged with a piece of cardboard.

The one thing that continued to delay my plans to leave home was my inability to find the car key. I had checked Mom's purse. I had combed her drawers. I had even searched her pants pockets while she lounged on the couch in her bathrobe, but without success. Where could she be keeping it – on a string around her neck? Knowing her, she might be. And if so, I would never get it.

16

i had a hard time falling asleep that night. Genevieve was making a lot of noise, which didn't help. I kept thinking about her and how much I was going to miss her. Though I felt ridiculous crying over a mouse, I couldn't stop the ache inside. Hours crawled by. At last, exhausted from sleeplessness and crying, I rose and downed one of Mom's sleeping pills. Back in bed, I soon sank into a dreamless slumber.

I awoke with a jerk, my heart pounding. I could hear muffled voices and the thud of something heavy hitting our front door. Terrified, I stumbled out of bed to check the bolts on my bedroom door, then with shaking hands groped through the darkness for my clock. Four thirty. I stood trembling, clutching the clock, too terrified even to call out to Mom. A thief would never make this much noise. It had to be someone with more sinister intents.

The thuds were soon followed by the crack of splintering wood. Dropping to my knees, I began frantically pulling the stuff out from underneath my bed. It was a pretty obvious hiding place, but I had nothing better.

There was a final splintering sound, then a window-jarring bang as the heavy front door slammed against the wall. I dove under the bed, making sure all of me was completely out of sight. I lay panting, listening to the heavy tread of footsteps in the next room. A man coughed harshly. Then Mom's bedroom door creaked open.

"Walter Miner!" she exploded. "What do you think you're doing!"

I crawled out from under the bed, still shaking, drenched with sweat and disbelief. It was Walter? How crazy could he get?

Walter's usually deep voice was husky and thick, as if he had laryngitis. "Don't think you can lock me out of my own house. I've got ways of getting in."

"What are you talking about? Where are your keys?"

"Never mind my keys. I'm looking for something." I could hear his footsteps going toward the kitchen.

"Where have you been, anyway?" Mom demanded. "You promised me you'd work on the furniture!"

"Leave me alone. I'm busy." Walter's voice was muffled by the rattling of pans. It sounded as if he was digging through the stove drawer.

"You're busy," she spat. "I bet. Did you ever start Vicks' bookcase?"

There was a screech and a thump as he pulled the drawer all the way out.

"Look," she said. "The phone bill is due. The electric bill is due. So is the rent, the car insurance, and almost everything else... Are you listening to me?"

"You better get going on it," he said, slamming the drawer shut.

"Me! Where do you expect me to get the money?"

Walter murmured something unintelligible. I heard shuffling noises, followed by a slammed cupboard door. "What the hell did you do with my beer?" Walter exclaimed. Although louder now, his voice retained its tortured, raspy quality.

"Forget your stupid beer. If you don't pay the rent pretty soon, we're gonna be homeless, you hear?"

"Quit bugging me!" Walter shot back. "I hate coming home, and I hate you! All you wanna do is fight."

"You don't care, do you." Mom's voice shook with anger. "You don't care about a single damn thing except your drugs. How about if I tell all your customers what's really going on. You want me to do that? Do you?"

I didn't want to listen to this. It was the same old fight they'd had the other morning. I switched on a light and changed out of my sweat-soaked pajamas. I was so exhausted from the stress that I felt sick. I climbed back into bed, turning the radio on close to my ear to cover my parents' voices. I lay awake for a long time, finally drifting into an uneasy sleep around dawn.

***

I slept until almost noon. When I ventured out for breakfast, the first thing I noticed was the armchair propped against the front door. Except for a few dents, the door itself seemed intact; but the frame around the latch was all splintered away. It looked like Walter had used a crowbar on it.

I found Mom in the kitchen, dusting and reorganizing the pantry. "What happened?" I asked.

"Oh, not much. I threw his beer out and he's mad. I'll fix the door later. Say, how'd you like to go out to eat? Turkey and dressing and everything?"

Her offer surprised me. With all the trouble, I had forgotten it was Thanksgiving. "Sure. That'd be great," I said.

"Good. We'll leave as soon as you're ready. Oh, and don't forget the mouse. We'll stop by the farm on the way."

Back in my bedroom, I pulled on a nicer sweater, brushed out the tangles in my hair, and lured Genevieve into her nest box with a piece of walnut. Taping the lid down securely to prevent mishaps, I hurried out to the car where Mom sat waiting.

Light rain spattered the windshield as Mom turned the car around and started down the driveway. But almost immediately, she slammed on the brakes. I looked up. My breath caught in a gasp. Coming up the driveway right at us was Walter's truck. The left headlight was smashed out and the fender badly dented. He swerved only inches in front of us and parked crosswise in the driveway.

"Where do you two think you're going?" he demanded, leaning out the window.

"None of your business!" Mom yelled back.

Rage leaped into Walter's eyes. He flung the door wide to jump out. It scraped the hood of the Grand Am and caught fast. Mom jammed the car into reverse. With a squeal of metal, the vehicles separated, leaving a deep scratch on the hood of the otherwise sharp-looking car.

Walter was livid. He ran up and pounded on my window. Mom hit the gas, and we tore out through the front yard, crashing right through the patch of wild raspberries that bordered the road. Once on the blacktop, she floored the pedal.

I was shaking, and it wasn't from the crazy ride. "Think he'll follow us?" I asked.

Mom's face was pale. "Who knows. I'm not taking any chances."

That she wasn't. From where I sat I could no longer see the needle on the speedometer, which told me she was going at least seventy-five. I felt dizzy. I'd never gone this fast on the back roads, even with Walter.

Several miles down the road, she eased up. "Look at that," she announced, casting one final glance in the rearview mirror.

"What?"

"We did it. Thanksgiving dinner coming up, and no Walter in sight." She slowed the car to negotiate a left turn.

I tried to laugh, but fear choked the sound. I didn't want to see the fight this would cause. My hand touched the box on my lap. I could feel a quivering inside it, and it made me want to cry. Oh, why wouldn't Mom let me keep the mouse?

Mom pulled into the gravel driveway of the old farm and parked in front of the steel gate. "No Trespassing," she read. "Well, who will know. Go on, Tess."

The rain was coming down harder now, pelting the car roof. I pulled my jacket closer around me and stepped out into the cold. A gooseberry bush clawed at my sleeve as I scooted around the gate. A squirrel nosing through the thick carpet of leaves dashed for a tree, chattering noisily. I kept walking. Ahead of me, half hidden by a giant box elder tree, stood a pole shed full of junk cars. Maybe Genevieve could live in there.

I ducked under a low-hanging branch and stepped inside. The shed smelled of musty hay and generations of mice. I skirted an old tub heaped with tires, stumbled over a rusty bucket full of chains, and squeezed around a station wagon with a smashed windshield as I made my way toward a row of dusty hay bales along the wall.

Setting the box on a bale, I raised the top. Genevieve sat still for a brief moment, her ears flat and her eyes bright with mischief. Then she scurried over the side and disappeared behind the bales.

My eyes filled with tears. "Bye, Genny," I said softly. "You be careful now. Live a nice long life and have lots of babies." Turning, I slipped out and ran all the way back to the car.

17

Dinner that day turned out to be quite different from what I had expected. Mom had found a church in Northford that was advertising a free meal to whoever wanted to come. By the time we arrived, the parking lot was jammed. We had to park on the street and walk. Just inside the main entrance, a large sign directed us to the basement, where we joined a double line of at least a hundred people.

The line crawled along, giving me time to observe the people around me. There was the older man in a tattered jacket, carrying a dirty canvas gym bag. The lady with a tight-fitting bandanna on her head, herding three young children ahead of her. The girl my age wearing baggy sweatpants and an oversized pink coat. The short man behind us who couldn't stand still and laughed at the slightest amusement.

I felt seriously uncomfortable. I knew Mom had been fussing a lot about money, but we couldn't be this hard up.

Beside me, Mom kept fidgeting and shifting her purse. I leaned close and whispered, "What are we doing here?"

She just raised her eyebrows. "You wanted dinner, didn't you?"

"Well yeah, but . . . *here*?"

"You know a better place?"

She was skirting my questions again, the way she usually did. It was frustrating. "I thought you didn't like churches," I faltered.

Mom's face reddened. She shrugged and faced ahead toward the kitchen, where several ladies were busy dishing up plates of food.

The truth hit me hard. All that arguing about unpaid bills wasn't just Mom's attempt to coerce Walter into working. It was real. We could have stayed home and had another meal of condensed soup and tuna fish sandwiches. But we were here because Mom wanted to give me the Thanksgiving dinner I'd asked for.

A lump filled my throat. Mom did care about me. She just didn't show it in the ways I usually wanted.

Like everyone else, Mom and I received foam plates heaped with roast turkey, dressing, mashed potatoes, and squash. There was even a spoonful of cranberry sauce. I paused to pick up a glass of punch before taking a seat at one of the long tables in the next room.

As I dug into my plate of food, I began to relax. Nobody was paying us any attention. Lively music poured from the speakers at the far end of the room, blending with the din of conversation. Across my mind flashed the thought that Walter would never find us here. I was safe.

A crushing weight lifted from my spirit. *I'm safe.* I repeated the strange words to myself. *I'm really and truly safe. Walter cannot get me.*

Happiness bubbled up inside me. I found myself smiling. *Is this how everybody else feels all the time?*

The wonderful feeling stayed with me until we got in the car and started home. I didn't dare say so to Mom, but somehow I knew the peace I'd felt had come from God.

18

Five inches of fluffy snow fell in Northford the night of December first, ushering in winter and the beginning of the holiday season. I forced myself to laugh and joke with my friends at school, but a sense of foreboding plagued me. Every time someone mentioned Christmas, I got a cold feeling inside, as if it wasn't going to happen this year.

"Guess what Mom's getting me for Christmas," Sandy boasted over lunch one day. "A digital camera – one of those fancy ones – and all the lenses."

"Don't you already have a camera?" I asked.

"Yeah, but it's junk. The pictures it takes are all grainy. If I'm gonna be a professional photographer, I need the right equipment."

Lois sighed dreamily. "You're lucky. I want so many things I don't know where to start. What I would really like is a snowmobile, but Dad's been tough to convince. He keeps saying I'm not old enough." She rolled her eyes. "How about you, Tess? What do you want?"

"She needs a smart phone," Sandy pronounced. "Poor Tess, stuck somewhere back in the Stone Age. Wake up."

I laughed, though the comment stung. "I can't help it. My dad thinks I'm not old enough."

"Are you serious? Even my three-year-old brother can work those things. Last night he got on his monster site with Mom's phone and downloaded something. She's still trying to figure out how to get rid of it."

"Good grief, don't tell that to my dad or I'll never get one," I said. "Do you know what he gave me for my birthday last spring?"

"What?" Lois leaned forward eagerly.

"A Barbie doll."

"Yuck. What'd you do with it?"

"What do you think? I didn't even take it out of the box; just threw the whole works in the garbage."

Lois's face fell. "Aww. That's so lame. You should have saved it to play tricks on him. You know, wait til Christmas when all your relatives are there, then wrap it up and give it to him as a present. Wouldn't *that* be funny!"

I couldn't see much humor in Lois's suggestion. Playing a trick that made Walter look stupid in front of others would be akin to teasing a mama grizzly bear. But both my friends were laughing, so I joined in.

Sandy put her hand on my arm. "Hey, listen. A bunch of us are going to Alyssa's place tomorrow night for a slumber party. Why don't you come too? We're gonna watch movies and play games and–"

"Laugh so hard we throw up, probably," Lois finished.

I shook my head. "I'd really like to," I said. "But…"

"But you gotta ask Mommy," Lois teased.

"I didn't say that. What I meant was I'm busy tomorrow night."

"Aww, come on," Sandy groaned. "Doing what? Sharpening your stone tools?"

My face burned. Having to turn down invitations was painful enough without being teased on top of it.

"We've got people invited over," I lied. "I have to help with dinner."

"So tell your mommy you got something else going on. Come on, Tess," Sandy coaxed. "It's gonna be loads of fun. Doesn't your mom ever let you do anything?"

"I tell you what," Lois said. "Don't say anything to her. Tomorrow I'll lend you my cell phone, since you don't have one, and you can call her up and tell her what you're gonna do. She'll have to say yes."

I was silent. I could picture how angry Mom would be if I tried such a thing. Yet other girls did it. Their parents didn't seem to mind.

"I guess it's kind of short notice for you," Sandy apologized. "Alyssa sent all of us a text last night."

"See?" said Lois. "Tell your mom she has to get you a phone for Christmas, or you'll never speak to her again. I should have saved my old one for you; it would be better than nothing."

I forced a smile as I shoved my chair back and picked up my empty tray. Inside I felt like punching someone. My friends had parents who gave them pretty much whatever they wanted – within reason, anyway. Mom never gave me anything. Oh, sure, she supplied me with basic necessities, and she saw to it that I had presents at Christmastime – stuff like sweaters and candy and cheap jewelry. But when it came to the important things, smart phones and fashionable clothes and blank checks, I was sunk before I even asked.

"Wait, Tess." Lois caught my elbow. "Before you disappear for the afternoon, you've got to answer my poll question."

"What question?"

"You know. What are you hoping to get for Christmas?"

I shook my head. "For Pete's sake, Lois, that's still weeks away. Give it a rest."

"But I need your answer so I can finish my class project."

"Well, then just come up with something."

Lois looked hurt. "Tess, please. Everybody else is giving me feedback. What's eating you anyway? I thought we were friends!" She turned her back and began questioning the next student passing by, who happened to be Janet. I lingered a moment, curious what her answer would be.

"My parents always surprise us," Janet said. "I haven't the faintest clue what they'll get me."

"If you had to pick something, what would it be?" Lois pressed her.

"Oh, I don't know. Maybe a box of chocolate truffles."

"No, no. I mean something bigger. How about a snowmobile? Or a drum set? Or–"

"Or time spent with my family and friends?" Janet finished for her. "That's what I really look forward to about Christmastime. Mom and I bake cookies and do a ton of decorating, and besides that I'm helping organize the Christmas Eve service at church this year. It's gonna be fantastic."

Lois wrinkled her nose. "Whatever. We go to a Christmas Eve service. They sing all these dumb songs, and then the pastor gets up and preaches a long sermon. It bores me to tears, but Mom always insists I have to go because it's Christmas."

"You should come to ours," Janet said. "You'd like it."

"I can't." Lois waved her hands helplessly. "We'll be visiting my grandparents, and we always go with them."

I snickered as I walked away. At the rate Lois was going, it would take her many days to poll everyone. Maybe by that time I could come up with something.

Near the counter, I met Lorraine and Brittney. "You coming to Alyssa's party tomorrow night?" I asked.

"Nah. Slumber parties are kids' stuff," Lorraine scoffed. "I wouldn't be caught dead at one of them."

Brittney laughed and agreed.

"But speaking of parties…" Lorraine leaned close and whispered in my ear. "Is it true that your old man grows weed?"

I drew back from her in shock. "Where'd you get that idea?"

She just laughed at me. "Hey, you do that pretty good. You could be rich, you know."

I didn't try to answer. Inside I felt a vague fear. What else did Lorraine know? And how did she know it?

The question haunted me the rest of the day. Possibly Lorraine was just trying to feel me out. Of course, there were a few people around Northford who knew what Walter was into, but they also knew better than to tell anyone. Lorraine had to be just guessing. And since I'd reacted with proper astonishment, I was sure I'd heard the last of it.

Heather caught up with me after school as I was hurrying toward the doors. "Hey Tess, you got a minute?"

I would have ignored her, except that she was now standing directly in front of me. I exhaled to show my annoyance. "Not really."

"I'll be quick, okay? It's just that I've been meaning to ask you something, and you're never alone. Tomorrow night Janet and I are going with some other young people from church to see a movie. We'll order pizza afterwards. You interested by any chance?"

I shook my head. "Nah. My mom doesn't like to take me places."

"Then listen. If you want to go, ask her if we can pick you up on the way past. It wouldn't be any bother at all. You know where I live, right?"

"Uh, no." I shifted my knapsack from one hand to the other.

"My grandparents own that yellow house up the road from you. We're neighbors."

I dropped the knapsack on my feet and said, "I didn't know that."

Heather smiled. "Just think about it and let me know, okay?"

I nodded and pushed the door open. I already knew I didn't want to go. Not at the expense of being judged by a bunch of self-righteous church kids. The slumber party would be a lot more fun. If only my friends would quit teasing me about that technology stuff.

On the way home, I posed my request. "Mom, I really need a cell phone."

Mom braked hard to avoid rear-ending another car stopping for a yellow light. "You need a cell phone," she repeated. "Why?"

I squirmed. "I just do. Everybody has them. I'm sick of being left out all the time because I don't. I mean, it's like I don't even exist."

"Tess, I can't afford to buy you something like that." Mom's voice was flat.

"You mean you don't want to," I challenged. "You never did let me have any fun."

"Tess, that's enough. I'm not buying you a cell phone, and that's final."

Angry tears stung my eyes. "You know something? You're mean. You're every bit as mean as Walter!"

All that evening, as I ate supper, dried the dishes, and worked on my homework, I fumed. *I'm not a little kid, and I'm not gonna let Mom push me around like one. If she won't get me what I need, I'll do it myself.*

I waited until after I'd showered and put on my pajamas. By then Mom was dozing on the couch. Taking my flashlight, I padded into her bedroom and pulled five twenty-dollar bills from her purse. Never before had I taken so much, but I felt confident she wouldn't miss it. If she did, chances were she'd blame Walter.

Trembling with excitement, I packed the money in my knapsack along with a few underclothes and my frilliest pajamas. I could hardly wait for tomorrow.

19

It was a long time before I settled down enough to fall asleep. When I did, I dreamed I couldn't watch the movies at the slumber party because they were designed to play on the viewers' cell phone screens. But I awoke with renewed enthusiasm. Even if things didn't go perfectly, I was still going to have more fun than I'd ever had in my life. Nothing could stop me now.

I felt a pang of guilt as I sat down to my breakfast of scrambled eggs and toast. What if Mom would miss the hundred dollars? I should put it back. But then I noticed her purse already hanging on the doorknob, ready for her to grab when we left. Returning the money now would be impossible.

I haven't done anything wrong, I reasoned, as I tied my shoes and pulled on my coat. *Mom should have gotten me a cell phone. So I'm just getting one myself.*

"Ready to go?" Mom asked me.

"Yeah, I guess so." I couldn't meet her gaze.

I struggled to act normal on the way to school, fighting off the worry that kept invading my mind. I didn't want to attract suspicion by any unusual behavior. But Mom seemed none the wiser as she dropped me off at the front entrance. I hurried inside without a backwards glance.

"Hey, Tess," Sandy greeted me. "You coming tonight?"

I grinned and nodded. "Mom doesn't know yet."

"Way to go," Lois cheered. "You gotta live your own life, Tess. Why be hung up on your parents? Oh, I just know we're gonna have so much fun with you! Wait til I tell Alyssa."

Sandy linked her arm through mine and together we walked down the hall. I couldn't keep from smiling, even laughing, out of pure happiness. *This is the way life's supposed to be. Why'd I wait so long to do this?*

I held my head high as we walked into class and sat down. Across the room, Janet caught my eye and smiled. I looked away. Just seeing Janet made me feel guilty these days.

At lunch, Lois pulled me over to sit with Alyssa and her friends. Alyssa was a loud, fun-loving girl who laughed almost as much as she talked. She had a good sense of humor and even got me laughing a few times. I could see why the girls flocked to her parties.

As the lunch period drew to a close, Lois took me aside. "Hey, you gotta call your mom yet, don't you?"

I nodded.

"Here." She handed me her cell phone. "Just punch the number and listen."

My finger shook as I touched the little numbers on the screen.

"Hello?" That was my mom's standard telephone greeting. Flat, with an edge of rudeness to it.

I swallowed hard. I had to say something. "Uh, Mom, this is Tessa. Look, I'm gonna–"

I got no further. Mom's anger erupted like a nest of yellow jackets. "You thief! What have you done with my money this time? Speak up or I'll call the police!"

I was speechless. Not knowing how to hang up on a cell phone, I listened helplessly.

"Don't tell me," she continued. "You bought a cell phone. Well, you'll pay for it. You're gonna be one miserable kid when I get my hands on you." Then the line went dead.

Thoroughly shaken, I stared down at the phone in my hand.

"What's the matter?" Lois asked, taking the phone. "Did she say no?"

I shook my head. "I-I can't go." Tears filled my eyes. I stumbled out into the hall, shoving past Heather and a couple of other students standing near the doorway.

"Why Tess, what's happened?" Heather asked.

Ignoring her, I started down the empty hall in the direction of my locker. Why wouldn't that girl leave me alone?

Heather caught up and began walking beside me.

"What's the deal?" I demanded. "It's against the rules to be out here during lunch period, you know."

"Yeah, I know that."

For some reason that made me angry. "Then what? You obsessed with trying to help people or something?"

"No." She hesitated. "I know you think I won't understand, but maybe you're wrong. Will you tell me what's the matter?"

I walked faster. "I'm fine. I don't need you." I yanked my locker open and began shuffling through my books, keeping my back to her so she couldn't see the tears welling in my eyes.

"Tess, listen. I care about you. I pray for you every day."

"You're crazy." My voice was a choked scream. "Just go. Leave me alone!"

"I'll go if you want," Heather said. "But I'm still going to be your friend."

I tugged a tissue from my purse and dabbed my eyes, then straightened and glanced around. Heather had slipped away. I was alone. I leaned against the open locker and silently cried.

***

I had to force myself to walk out to the car after school that day. I slid into the back seat without a word and waited for Mom to scold me.

She didn't. As she put the car in gear and started across town, the silence became oppressive. I wanted to say I was sorry, but the words wouldn't come.

Mom turned at Willow Street and pulled into the parking lot of Allen's Super Foods. Then she faced me. "Where's the money?"

"In my knapsack."

"Get it."

I pulled out the wad of rumpled bills and handed it to her.

"No, you keep it," she said. "Put it in your pocket and come with me."

As I followed her into the store, a feeling of dread tightened in my stomach. What was she up to? I never went to Allen's with her anymore because all the clerks recognized me as a shoplifter.

Mom stopped just inside the doors. "There's a cart load of groceries up there behind the customer service desk. I picked them up this morning; but thanks to you, I didn't have the money to pay for them. Now, do you want a cell phone, or would you rather eat?"

I stared at her. "Eat, of course. But..."

"Then you go pay for them."

I glanced over at the service counter. There sat Bruce, watching the whole scene with a look of satisfaction. I cringed. "Mom, please. Don't make me."

My mother was unmoved. "You gotta learn somehow. This isn't the first time you've robbed me. Now get up there. Or would you rather face Walter?"

She had me cornered, and she knew it.

"I hate you." I glared at her, then marched up to the counter and slapped the money down.

"Ah, Tessa." Bruce gave me a long look. "So we meet again, eh? What can I do for you?"

I could have killed him for that ugly smirk on his face. "I'm paying for them groceries. You know that."

"Which ones?"

"My mom's, of course."

"That's $76.13." He shoved the change toward me. "Now beat it, punk."

Mom came over at that point and took the cart. I turned and all but ran for the door. I felt angry and miserable and ashamed of myself all at once. I hunched in the back seat of the car, wishing I could disappear.

Mom loaded the trunk and then climbed into the driver's seat. "Never, ever do that again," she said. "Do you understand?"

I didn't raise my head.

"I did this because you need to understand how serious stealing is. Someday you'll thank me for it."

Yeah, right. I felt more like punching her.

"You should know that Walter once spent a year in jail for burglary."

Somehow the revelation didn't surprise me.

"It was a long time ago, back when your sisters were little. You worry me, Tess. You have a lot of Walter in you. If you don't watch yourself, you'll end up just like him."

Much as I resented the lecture, her warning stuck in my mind like a burr. What did she mean, that I had a lot of Walter in me? How could I, when I hated him so much?

At home I locked myself in my room, partly because Walter was around, but mostly to avoid having to interact with Mom. I felt miserable. If only I hadn't stolen the hundred dollars, I might be at Alyssa's party enjoying myself. Instead, here I was, stuck at home again. Why had I been so stupid?

***

The following day was a Saturday. I spent the morning sorting through the junk in my closet, the radio blaring to drown out my parents' off-and-on arguing. Around noon, Mom dropped by to say she had to run a bank deposit into town. Normally I would have stayed home, especially since I wasn't on speaking terms with her. But because Walter was around, I decided to go with her.

The transaction at the bank took only a few moments. Mom swung by the convenience store across the street and bought some bread and a couple packs of cigarettes. Then she turned right on Bridge Street and began driving up through town. "Let's stop by the bakery and get something special for dessert tonight," she suggested. "Sound good?"

I shrugged. "Whatever. Last I heard, you didn't have money for stuff like that."

"You're right, I don't. I might not do this again, but I'm doing it today." She pulled over in front of the bakery. "So, what do you want?"

"Nothing. You're just trying to buy me off over yesterday. Aren't you!" I tossed her an angry glare.

"Now wait a minute. I know I was hard on you yesterday, but you needed it."

I turned my gaze to the stream of cars rushing past my door.

"You know, I don't appreciate the reputation I'm starting to get as your mother. And it was very embarrassing yesterday when I went to pay for my groceries and discovered I only had thirteen dollars. Maybe what I did wasn't fair. But all the shame and embarrassment coming to me isn't fair, either."

I continued to stare out the window. Mom had it all wrong, but what was the point of arguing with her? Even Walter could not win arguments with her.

The car door slammed as Mom left to go into the bakery. I glanced over, and my eye fell on the key still stuck in the ignition. *The missing key!* A shiver of excitement ran through me. Why not hijack the car right now? It would serve her right.

My heart beat so fast I thought it would break out of my chest. I slipped over into the driver's seat and reached a shaking hand for the ignition.

At that moment, Mom's words from yesterday echoed through my mind. "If you don't watch it, you'll end up just like Walter."

I hesitated. *Do I want to prove her right? Isn't stealing the car just because I can, something a criminal would do? Maybe I'm a lot like Walter already.* The thought bothered me. After a moment of indecision, I moved back to my own side of the car.

When Mom returned, she set the white paper bag on my lap. "I got your favorite. There was only one left."

I said nothing, but on the way home, I opened the bag and peeked inside. Sure enough, Mom had gotten me a cherry bismarck.

I shook my head. She was still wrong about yesterday. But at least she wasn't mad at me.

20

Mom and I spent the latter part of Sunday afternoon much like the other inhabitants of Northford – watching the football game over a bowl of popcorn. I probably should have spent the time doing homework, but Mom didn't mention it.

The game was a tense one. Although the Packers were a comfortable fourteen points ahead at halftime, the Cowboys steadily closed the gap after that. With fifty seconds left on the clock and our team down by three points, I thought surely the game was lost. But then we intercepted a pass and ran it back for a surprise touchdown, ending the game.

"Wow, that was close." I stood up to stretch. "Maybe we'll make it to the playoffs yet. Can we have a pizza to celebrate?"

"A pizza?" Mom looked doubtful. "I'm afraid not. There aren't any more pizzas in the freezer."

"Couldn't we make one?"

Mom glanced from her watch to the cuckoo clock by the door. "It's past seven. You want to start a pizza now?"

"Why not?"

She laughed. "Well, I suppose. C'mon, you can help."

I shredded two kinds of cheese, cut a green pepper and a package of cold meat into narrow strips, and drained a can of olives while Mom prepared the crust dough and sauce. After letting the crust rise a few minutes, we piled on the toppings and slid our creation into a hot oven.

"You better take a shower while this bakes," Mom said. "It's getting late, and you do have school in the morning."

A tantalizing aroma greeted me when I emerged from the bathroom some time later. Mom had the table set and was cutting the pizza with a chef's knife.

"It looks good," I said. I couldn't remember the last time we'd had homemade pizza. Long strings of cheese trailed across the yellow vinyl tablecloth as Mom scooped a wedge onto each of our plates.

"You'll need a fork," she advised. "The crust is a bit soft."

I took a bite and chewed thoughtfully. Our pizza tasted nothing like the frozen disks we bought at Allen's, but it wasn't bad at all. I took another bite.

We ate half the pizza before declaring ourselves full. "We'll keep the rest for tomorrow," Mom said. "You got any room left for ice cream?"

"Aren't we out?"

"I think there's a tiny bit left. We'll split it." She started toward the refrigerator, then stopped dead as if she'd hit a concrete wall. "What in…"

Cold fear touched my heart. For I too saw it – the evil red and blue lights glinting off the kitchen windows.

Mom reached over and flipped off the chandelier, leaving only the dim light above the stove. Together we hurried to the window. Parked in the driveway behind Walter's truck were two police cars. Walter was leaning casually against the driver's door of the truck, talking to the officers. The pulsating lights lent an eerie yet fascinating aspect to the scene.

"This doesn't look good," Mom muttered. But after a few minutes, the officers simply got into their cars and left.

"Uh-oh. Here he comes." Mom hurried to clear the table. "Just act like nothing's happened. Start the dishes."

The back door slammed with enough force to rattle the glasses on the table. "You dirty traitor!" Walter screamed. "You're gonna pay for this one!" Clods of grimy snow flew from his boots as he kicked a chair out of the way and advanced on Mom with doubled fists.

Mom's face went white. She grabbed the iron fry pan off the stove and swung at him with all her might. Walter jumped sideways and slammed her up against the stove. The fry pan crashed to the floor. Walter grabbed her hair and began slugging her in the face.

It all happened so fast. I stood frozen in horror, the dishcloth in my hand slowly dripping water onto the rug. Mom was screaming. Blood streamed from her nose down onto her pink sweater. Walter shook her and threw her to the floor. He bent, reaching for the iron fry pan. I had to do something.

I threw myself onto him, wrapping my arms around his chest, and kicked him in the shins as hard as I could. He wheeled and struck me in the thigh with the fry pan, a glancing blow, but hard enough to hurt. I broke free and dashed for my room. Walter chased me, his heavy boots clumping on the floor. I slammed the door and frantically pulled the bolts. Would they hold or not?

A thunderous crash shook the door. "Open up!" Another crash followed, and then another. I backed up against the far wall, trembling like an aspen leaf. What had I done? If those bolts gave way, I'd be dead. Vividly I recalled how he'd broken in our front door the other night with nothing but a crowbar. I had to get out of here.

I shoved open my window and hit the rusty screen hard with my fist. The frame bent outwards an inch or two, but the screen held. Wildly I glanced about for something sharp enough to cut it.

Another crash shook the door. This time I heard little splintering sounds. I grabbed the kitchen scissors off my bed and half cut, half tore a giant X across the screen. I hoisted myself onto the sill and slid through the opening feet first.

I dropped into shin-deep snow. The wind rushed upon me, stinging my face and snatching my breath away, but I scarcely noticed as I ran across the front yard toward the road. My mind raced. Should I hide in the brush? Hitchhike? Try to walk all the way to town? As cold as it was, I knew I wouldn't survive long. Already my throat hurt from gulping the freezing air.

I know, I thought. *Heather's place. I'll go there.* I shot a quick glance over my shoulder. Walter wasn't on my tail, not yet. I pulled my turtleneck up over my mouth in a crude effort to protect my face and throat from the biting air, and kept running.

21

I slowed to a walk when the pain in my side became unbearable. Running had kept me warm, but now the icy wind took its toll. The open farm fields on either side of the road offered no protection. My nose was running like a faucet. I pressed onward at a steady hike, my fists jammed deep into my jeans pockets. It couldn't be much farther to Heather's. If I kept going, I'd make it. But I knew I was much colder than I felt. How did I keep ending up in situations like this?

My mind shifted to what Heather would say when she opened the door and saw me. Her eyes would widen in questioning surprise. *You said you didn't need me. Remember? You pushed me away when I tried to help you. It's not like we're really friends anymore. Why don't you ask that Lorraine to help? You two have been pretty thick lately.*

But she'd flash that bright smile and invite me in. Maybe she'd even make me some hot chocolate. She'd say how nice it was of me to come over, and I would laugh and say I'd always wanted to. Then the two of us would sprawl on the floor in front of the TV and watch all the late shows until we couldn't keep our eyes open anymore.

But when the yellow house came into view, it wasn't the welcome sight I had imagined. The place was dark. What if they were all in bed? Worse yet, suppose no one was home. What time was it, anyway? I felt for my watch, but my wrist was empty. Somehow I had left my watch at home.

I hesitated at the end of the driveway. The thought of going up and ringing the doorbell filled me with nervous dread. Maybe it was the wrong house. Maybe someone would see me wandering around out here and call the police. Maybe Heather's grandparents would be mad if I woke them up.

Still, what did it matter? My hands were screaming with cold, and my face was so numb I was sure it was frostbitten. I would freeze to death out here. I plodded up the driveway and touched the lighted button at the door with one numb finger. *Push. Don't think, just do it.* I held the button down for a long moment, then clung to the wooden railing and waited. A dog barked inside. Then a bright light shone in my eyes.

"Can I help you?" said a man's voice.

I squinted against the light. "Uh . . . does Heather live here?"

"Yes. Do you know her?"

"Yeah. I'm . . . a friend of hers."

I heard some murmuring inside the house, then a click as the screen door was unlocked.

"Goodness, child, where's your coat?" The man held the door wide. "Come in and get warm."

A rush of warmth enveloped me as I stepped inside. But when I saw Heather's grandparents standing there in their bathrobes, I felt ashamed. A tan and white collie stood beside them, eyeing me.

"I take it you're Tessa," said the man, after an awkward pause.

I nodded, my eyes on the floor.

"I'm Tom Erickson. Pleased to meet you."

"Heather's not here tonight," said the lady, "but she's mentioned you a few times, I believe."

"Don't you live just down the road there?" Tom asked.

"Yeah." My teeth were chattering.

"So what are you doing over here this time of night?"

"I, uh..." What could I say?

"Come on, speak up. Do your parents know you're out? How did you get here?"

"I-I walked."

"In this weather, without a coat? For heaven's sake, child, it's ten below out there!" Tom shook his head. "I'm sorry. You must be frozen. Why don't you kick off your shoes and sit down."

"Thanks." I didn't bother with the laces; I simply bent down and pried the frozen tennis shoes off my stiff feet. Snow had worked down inside the shoes, and my socks were caked with it. After a moment's hesitation, I pulled them off too.

"Take a seat," Tom encouraged me, motioning toward the couch. "Don't worry about a little snow."

"Would you like some hot tea?" the lady asked, as she laid a pink flowered quilt across my lap. "I'm Patty, by the way."

I nodded and pulled the quilt up around my shoulders. Patty looked so warm in her pink fuzzy bathrobe and purple slippers. My hands had stopped hurting, but they still felt like ice.

Patty brought my cup of tea on a small saucer. "I hope it's not too hot," she said.

I took the cup and held it between my hands. The heat stung, but even that felt good. Steam rose up in my face and I closed my eyes, breathing in the gentle fragrance, letting my head droop. Tea was comforting in a lot of ways, some of which had nothing to do with actually drinking it.

***

Once I was comfortably situated with my tea, Patty settled on the other end of the couch and reached for her knitting. Tom took the mauve armchair across from me, and the questions began again.

"So, what's going on?" he asked.

I just shook my head. I couldn't tell them what had happened, and I was not in the frame of mind to invent another story. But Tom persisted.

"Have you run away?"

"I-I guess." I was still shivering.

"How come?"

"My mom and dad were fighting."

"I see. It must've been pretty bad."

"Sorta." I set down my cup and pulled the quilt closer around myself. Was Walter still looking for me? Mentally I retraced my steps, trying to picture any trail I might have left. The cut screen was obvious, as were my tracks across the front yard. I wasn't worried about them. But wait, wouldn't I have left footprints along the road as well? What if the wind hadn't covered them yet?

I felt sick. Why hadn't I thought to walk in the middle of the road? If Walter looked hard enough, he'd find me. I cast a fearful glance toward the door, which was still ajar. "Would you mind . . . locking the door?"

Tom's face registered surprise, but he rose and secured the door. "Is somebody after you?"

"My-my dad." My voice shook. I felt like I was going to cry.

"I see. So this here fight . . . you mean your parents were arguing? Or is it physical?"

I couldn't answer. Across my mind flashed the terrifying image of Mom sprawling to the floor as Walter reached for the heavy iron fry pan. I had to stop him!

"Tessa?" It was Patty's voice this time. "Is something wrong? Do we need to call the authorities?"

I managed to shake my head. Mom was fine. She had to be! With the time I'd bought her, she could have called the police, maybe even jumped in the car and driven off. She was probably on her way into town at this very minute.

Silence followed, broken only by the click of Patty's knitting needles. Under the end table beside me, the collie yipped softly in its dreams.

"Someone needs to know where you are," Patty said at last. "Is there someone we can call? A relative or maybe a family friend?"

Another hard question. I picked at a tuft of yarn on the quilt. All I knew about our relatives was that they lived somewhere down south. At least, Mom's did. I'd never heard a thing about Walter's family.

Over in the armchair, Tom stifled a yawn. "Patty's right. There must be someone you can think of."

"I'm trying! But we're not exactly from around here. Walter's got friends, but they're all a bunch of jerks."

"Well, in that case maybe I should call the sheriff's department and let them know where you are. Or is it safe for you to go back home?"

My head spun at the mention of the police. "Can't you wait until morning?"

"What would you do then?"

I couldn't answer that.

"I suppose you could try to call my mom," I said. "But if you get Walter, don't talk to him. Hang up or something."

"All right." Tom reached for the cordless phone on the end table. "What's the number?"

I told him and he punched it in, then held the phone to his ear. Moments later, he lowered it with a puzzled expression. "It says that number's been disconnected."

"Disconnected?" Visions of Walter cutting the phone cord flooded my mind. But no, that was too absurd. "Maybe you have a number wrong," I said.

Tom held up the phone for me to check. But everything looked right. I held my breath as he dialed once again. He listened, then shook his head. "I can't get through."

Fear broke over me like a tidal wave. What if Mom hadn't gotten away? With that thought came the most vivid and horrible picture. I could see Mom slumped on the kitchen floor, a dark pool of blood around her head. Her long brown hair, now dark and matted, half covered her face. She wasn't moving.

It was all so horribly real. I didn't want to believe it, but the dreadful picture wouldn't go away. Through my sobs, I heard Tom get up and leave the room. Was he going to call the police? It didn't even matter. Nothing mattered.

A short time later, I felt a hand on my shoulder. I looked up. There was Tom, dressed in a red flannel shirt and jeans. "I'm going to drive over to your place and try to talk to your mom before it gets any later. You don't want to come along, do you?"

I shook my head and buried my face in my hands again.

Tom wasn't gone long, maybe ten minutes, but it felt like an eternity. His face was serious as he walked in and took his seat. "I talked to your mom. She's going to come and get you in a little while."

"She's okay?" The weight of anxiety fell away, and I could breathe again. Then I thought of something else. "She's not mad at me, is she?"

Tom smiled and shook his head. "I don't think so."

The three of us settled in to wait. Beside me, Patty's knitting needles clicked steadily as she worked one long row after another of maroon and white variegated yarn. The irregular patches of color unfolding on the swatch fascinated me.

"What're you making?" I asked.

"This is going to be a sweater for my granddaughter. I was hoping to get it done in time for Christmas, but the way it's going, it'll probably be a late birthday present instead."

"It's pretty."

"Yeah, I think so too. Variegated yarn's fun to work with."

More time passed. I finished my second cup of tea and declined a third. Across from me Tom was snoring. Patty's knitting needles slowed, then stopped altogether as she laid aside her work. She turned out all the lights except the dim lamp in the corner and then sat down again, wrapping herself in an afghan. I fought to keep my eyes open, but somewhere between twelve thirty and one, I gave up.

22

I awoke in the gray dawn to the aroma of pancakes. The living room was deserted, the only sign of the all-night vigil being a red plaid blanket crumpled on the seat of the armchair. Around the corner in the kitchen, I heard Patty humming a tune as she stirred something in a bowl. I stretched my cramped legs, then settled back on the couch. Although it was Monday morning, going to school was the last thing on my mind. Why hadn't Mom come for me?

Somewhere off the kitchen, a back door opened, and I heard Tom stomping snow from his boots. "It'd be a fine day if it wasn't so cold," he said. Moments later the collie came bounding into the living room. It planted big snow-covered paws on my lap and reached up to lick my cheek.

"Sadie! You know better than that!" Patty scolded from the doorway. "Get down, you naughty girl." She shook a spatula at the dog. Sadie hung her head and slunk over to the doorway, but when she saw me watching, she grinned and waved her fringed tail. I almost laughed.

"Hope she didn't wake you up," Patty said.

"No, I was just sitting here."

"Would you like to eat with us? Breakfast is about ready."

"Okay," I said. The wonderful smells in the air were making me hungry.

As I walked into the kitchen, Tom looked up from drizzling syrup over his stack of pancakes and bid me a cheery good morning.

TESSA

Patty forked a fried egg and two pancakes onto my plate. I slid into a chair, then self-consciously bowed my head while Tom said a short prayer.

"How late are you working today?" Patty asked him afterwards.

"Let me think . . . we've probably got four or five hours left on Millers' job, and then I have to look at some leaking pipes. We've sent the guys out there at least three times, and the lady keeps calling and saying it's still not fixed. I'll try to be home by six."

"What do you do?" I asked.

"I'm a master plumber at P&B Plumbing – you know, the place with the big sign as you're going into town."

"Where does your dad work?" Patty asked me.

"He's got a shop where he builds and refinishes furniture."

"Really. Does he get a lot of work?"

"Enough, I guess."

"So your mom never came," Tom said, stating the obvious. "Is there anything else we can do for you?"

"I don't know. Guess I'll keep waiting for her."

I swallowed the last few bites of pancake and excused myself. Returning to the living room, I stood before the double windows and gazed out upon the wintry landscape. Despite the dazzling sunshine, the temperature remained in the single digits below zero. I watched the wind swirl loose snow over a peaked drift near the corner of the house. Anxiety clouded my thoughts. *What if my mom never does come? Is she really okay? Or did something awful happen after Tom left?*

"I hate to leave with things so uncertain." Tom's deep voice drifted in from the kitchen. "But I really need to be there to finish that job."

"I know. I'll call you if anything changes," Patty said.

I heard a rustle as Tom pulled on his jacket. He opened the door. "I'll be back as soon as I can."

"Have a good day. Drive carefully," Patty called after him.

I watched the red SUV back out of the driveway and disappear down the road in a haze of blowing snow. Patty came in and joined me at the windows.

"You watching for your mom?"

I shrugged and kept staring out at the snow.

"Listen, I don't know what's going on in your family, and you don't have to tell me; but whatever it is, God can straighten it out. He sent you here last night so we could help you. He loves you, Tessa. So do we."

I didn't want to hear this. If God loved me even a little, things wouldn't be in such a horrible mess. Any idiot could see that.

"Would you like me to pray for you?"

I sighed, not caring whether it was rude. Prayer was the last thing I needed right now. Patty reminded me so much of Heather – always poking her nose into my affairs, always wanting to help.

"That's okay. I have to clean up from breakfast, but if you need anything, just let me know."

I was relieved when she left. But as I continued to gaze upon the frozen world before me, such an ache filled my chest that I couldn't stand it. Maybe I should have let her pray for me.

***

Mom's black car pulled in about noon. I dropped the magazine I'd been reading and watched as she limped toward the house. I winced when I saw her face. Both eyes were blackened, and there was a nasty bruise in front of her ear and another on the side of her mouth. Her long brown hair whipped in the wind.

"Mom's here," I called, and hastened to open the door.

Mom leaned hard on the door frame as she stepped inside. "Hey, Tessa." She tried to smile, which only made her look worse.

"Oh man, he got you real bad." My throat tightened in sympathy.

"So tell me, how do you like it here?" Mom asked. She spoke slowly, grimacing as if it hurt to move her mouth.

I shrugged. Patty hurried in from the kitchen. "My goodness, Julie, what happened?"

Mom ignored the question. "I need to ask a favor of you." She took off her gloves and unzipped her coat. Underneath, she was wearing an old gray sweatshirt and blue jeans. "I know you're good people. Would you let Tessa stay here for just a few days?"

I could see the surprise in Patty's face. "Well, we'd have to consider it. Why?"

Mom kind of laughed. "Why? So she don't look like I do tomorrow, that's why." Then her manner changed. "Please. I need a few days to decide what to do. I know it's asking a lot, but I just don't know what else to do. We don't really know anybody around here."

"Well, this is rather unexpected," said Patty. "But if you're serious, I'll call Tom at work and see what he thinks about it."

"Call him. I can wait." Mom limped over and lowered herself into the armchair.

I remained standing near the door, annoyed that Mom had not asked my consent before proceeding. But why raise a fuss when Patty might turn her down anyway? She seemed cautious about the idea, and judging by the snatches of conversation drifting in from the next room, Tom wasn't thrilled by it either.

At least ten minutes passed before Patty returned. She perched on the arm of the couch. "All right. I talked with Tom, and we're okay with her staying a couple of days, if you give us a signed note with your permission."

Mom frowned. "A signed note? Come on, can't you guys just trust me?"

"It's not that we don't trust you," Patty said. "What if Walter shows up over here tomorrow claiming we kidnapped her or something?"

Mom shook her head. "Whatever. Give me some paper, and I'll write a note."

"Aren't you gonna ask what I think about this?" I cut in. "Or doesn't it matter?"

"I asked you. You didn't answer. There something you don't like about it?"

"You wouldn't care even if there was."

"Tess, it's just a couple days."

"Right." I rolled my eyes and stalked out of the room. Staying with Tom and Patty sounded like a good idea, but why did she always have to go over my head like I was a toddler?

I wandered through the kitchen into the small but cozy dining room. A wooden table and four chairs stood in the center of the room against a backdrop of lacy yellow curtains. In the corner was a desk with an old-fashioned telephone and a laptop computer. Off to my right, a doorway opened into a small bathroom. It was here that I positioned myself to eavesdrop on the rest of the conversation.

"I'll come in the morning and take her to school," Mom was saying. "I brought her some clothes and things."

"How long were you thinking she'd be here?" Patty asked.

"Oh, if you get tired of her, just let me know."

"That's not the point. She's your daughter and you ought to take care of her, not us. This is a special and very temporary arrangement."

"Of course."

There was a pause, then Patty spoke again. "I don't know if you're interested, but our church runs a temporary shelter in Northford for women who are caught in abusive situations. I'll give you their number. Even if you and Tessa didn't want to stay there, you could talk to somebody, maybe get some help."

Mom's reply was curt. "I'm working on it. Don't worry about it."

"Okay. If you say so. But if I were you, I'd get away from that guy before it's too late. He sounds like a real character."

"Oh yeah?" There was suspicion in Mom's voice now. "What all is Tess telling you?"

"She doesn't have to say anything. It's pretty obvious."

"What's obvious?"

"That you're in a pretty difficult situation."

Mom was silent for a few moments, then she said, "I'm assuming you guys know how to keep things quiet."

"You mean…"

"Just answer me. You gonna keep things quiet or not?"

I pressed my hands against my chest. Why Mom was grilling Patty I wasn't sure, but one thing I did know. Patty's response would determine whether or not I was allowed to stay.

Patty stammered as she tried to answer. "Well, uh . . . honestly, Julie, you puzzle me. I can't imagine why you wouldn't want to get help, but I'm not going to do it for you. I don't get involved in other people's affairs without a really good reason."

"What would you call a good reason?"

"Just what are you driving at, Julie? If you want me to promise I won't say anything ever, even if I think you're in danger, you
can stop right now. I have to do what I believe is right. If that isn't
good enough for you, you'd better take your daughter with you
when you leave."

Mom sighed. "Look, I'll give it to you straight. Tess talks too
much. Most of what she says isn't true, the rest is exaggerated, and
none of it is your business. Get it?"

Anger surged through me. That charge wasn't true, and Mom
knew it.

Patty's reply was firm. "Like I said, I'm not making any blanket
promises."

"Sure. I'm just telling you. You go messing with other people's
business, you're gonna be sorry. *Dead* sorry."

My heart stopped. I shrank back into the bathroom. What was
Mom doing? After last night, any fool could see we'd be better off
if Walter got caught and thrown in prison.

Suspicion leaped into my mind. Could Mom be involved in
Walter's dealings? Sickening as the thought was, it made sense – a
lot of sense. Who else could have drawn those intricate diagrams
taped on the refrigerator at the farmhouse? It certainly wasn't Walter,
whose skill with a pen barely rivaled a second-grader's. And what
about those weird phone calls she'd been making lately?

I felt like I'd been kicked in the stomach. How could Mom do
this to me? If she got arrested along with Walter, I'd be completely
alone. I'd be at the mercy of whatever the state decided to do with
me. Would I end up in foster homes? Or would I be charged for my
own involvement and sent to jail or juvenile detention?

Out in the living room, everything had gone quiet. Mom must
have left. But I was paralyzed – too depressed to move, much less
go out and face Patty. What must she be thinking?

I sank to the bathroom floor and there, arms wrapped around
my knees, I sat until my mind was numb and my back ached.

I didn't hear Patty come in. She got down on the floor next to
me and took my hand in hers, gently unclenching my fist. "I know
how you must be feeling," she said. "But it's okay. You were smart

to come here last night, and Tom and I want you to know you're more than welcome. Anytime."

I couldn't see how that would help anything, but I nodded.

"One more thing," she continued. "Tom and I are your friends, and we'll do whatever we can for you, but the one who can really help you is Jesus."

I chewed my lower lip. Jesus, wasn't he up in heaven somewhere? A lot of good he could do me. Supposing he even existed.

"Tom and I have been praying for you, even before you came," Patty went on. "Jesus knows all about your situation and how to deal with it. He knows about the fear and the trouble you have with your dad. He cares, Tessa. And I believe he's working right now to help you, even though it doesn't look like it."

I wished I could believe her. Anything would be better than this debilitating fear. But how could I be sure what she said was true?

Patty smiled and patted my shoulder. "Come out to the kitchen, and I'll make you a sandwich. Do you like toasted cheese?"

I nodded. I didn't know why, but listening to her had made me feel better.

23

How would you like to come along into town?" Patty asked me midway through the afternoon. "I have to get a few things at the store, and if we leave right away, we can swing by the high school and pick up Heather."

I gulped. I had forgotten about Heather. She probably didn't even know I was here.

"She'll be delighted that you're staying over," Patty assured me. "You want to come?"

"I suppose." I'd had enough of sitting at the table trying to do homework while my mind spun with anxious speculations about Mom.

I pawed through the two black trash bags of belongings Mom had left me until I found my jacket. Then I followed Patty out to the tiny one-car garage. She pulled the wooden door up by hand, revealing a mid-sized red car with a few rust spots. Except for the color, it was a carbon copy of the old white Impala that Walter had parked behind the abandoned farmhouse.

"We've got a car just like this," I said, as I opened the door and slid into the back seat.

"Really? I've never seen it over there."

"It's in the repair shop right now."

Patty backed the car out, pausing at the road. Her gaze lingered on me. "Tessa, you need to wear a seat belt."

"Aww, come on. Do I have to?" I pulled the belt across my lap and clicked it shut.

"Yes, as long as I'm the driver, you do."

"Mom doesn't make me wear one," I argued.

"Well, it's never too late to develop a good habit," was Patty's reply.

I let the subject drop. I was more concerned how Heather would react when she found out I was staying at her house. Wouldn't she feel I was intruding? Taking away time and attention that was rightfully hers?

But the grin that spread across Heather's face when she saw me dispelled my fears. "What are you doing here?" she exclaimed, as she climbed in back with me. "You weren't in school either."

"It's a long story, but I guess I'm staying at your place for a couple days."

"Awesome."

"My mom said I could. Actually, she more like told me I had to. So I don't know; I guess it'll be fun."

"Of course. Sleepovers are always fun." Heather's eyes sparkled, as if she could envision the good time we would have.

I shrugged. "I wouldn't know. I never did it before."

"You've got to be kidding. Not even at your grandparents'?"

I shook my head. "Walter wouldn't let me."

"Who's Walter?"

"My father."

"How come you call him 'Walter' and not 'Dad'? Is he really your father?"

"Yeah, as far as I know. He doesn't act like it though."

Patty pulled into a parking space at Allen's grocery store. "Maybe you girls want to stay here and talk," she said. "I'll just be a few minutes."

I nodded. That was fine with me. The last thing I wanted to do was explain why I couldn't go into the store with them.

"So how's your mouse doing these days?" Heather asked.

I pulled my hair loose from its ponytail, then smoothed it out and gathered it up again. "She's okay, I guess." I desperately wanted to change the subject. "Hey Heather, you ever drive a car?"

"Not yet. I'm planning to take driver's ed in the spring."

"I guess it's not too terribly hard," I said.

"What, driver's ed?"

"Driving. You know, stay in your lane, don't hit anybody, make sure you stop at the red lights."

Heather laughed. "Yeah, but there's a lot of laws you need to know about. Like who goes first when you get to a four-way stop."

Patty returned with two sacks of groceries, and the conversation took other twists. I withdrew, keeping my thoughts to myself as the traffic and noise of the city gave way to wooded hills and snow-covered farm fields. At the crest of the hill where we turned left onto Vance Road, I noticed two sheriff cars sitting side by side in the driveway of the power substation.

"I wonder what they're doing," Heather commented.

I said nothing, but their presence a quarter mile from my home alarmed me. It was probably the same guys who'd followed Walter home last night. Maybe they were waiting for him.

Sadie greeted us at the back door with barks of delight. I scratched around her collar and she leaned into me, panting and wagging her tail furiously.

"She really likes you," Heather said, as she hung up first her coat, then mine in the closet.

I continued scratching Sadie's neck. Much as I loved dogs, we'd never had one of our own.

"You can take her out and play with her if you want," Patty said. "She'd like that."

I didn't answer. I probably shouldn't go outside; if Walter happened to drive by and see me, I'd be in big trouble.

"So, what would you like to do?" Patty asked me, after she'd put the groceries away. "I'm making meatballs for supper. You could help with that, or if you'd rather, you could join Heather in the dining room and do some more homework."

"I'll help out here."

I watched as Patty scooped a chunk of hamburger into a mixing bowl, then cracked two eggs over it.

"Your eggs are brown," I said.

"Yeah, we've got a little flock of chickens out back. Most of them lay brown eggs."

"They lay eggs – like every day?" My curiosity was piqued.

Patty smiled. "Like every other day. They kind of switch off. I've got sixteen hens, and they give me ten or eleven eggs every day. You want to see them?"

"Sure." It would be fun to see some farm animals up close.

"After we get the meatballs in the oven, I'll take you out there. I have to feed them anyway." She added a heaping cup of Parmesan cheese and several handfuls of crushed saltine crackers to the bowl, then pushed it toward me. "Here, why don't you mix this. I just use my hands, but if you want a spoon, they're in that drawer in front of you."

I stared down at the square mass of raw hamburger in the bowl. Somewhere I'd heard this stuff was contaminated with all sorts of unmentionable things. But if I used a spoon, Patty would think I was squeamish. It wouldn't kill me, I decided, and I could wash my hands when I was done.

"Good job," Patty said when I was through. "Now we roll the meatballs." She made one to show the correct size, and after that we worked with the bowl between us until we had forty-seven little balls lined up on the tray.

I retired to the sink to scrub my hands while Patty slid the tray into the oven. A sheet of yellow paper tacked on the side of the refrigerator caught my eye. This must be Mom's note. Grabbing a towel, I stepped closer and read.

Tessa has my permission to stay at Ericksons' house until I say. She will be free to leave at any time and must leave when I say. She may not stay longer for any reason.

At the bottom of the page, Mom had signed and dated it.

Uneasiness churned in my stomach. Mom never wrote but one short line in her notes to the school office. Clearly she was making a point here, but what was the point? That Tom and Patty could not imprison me at their house? It made no sense.

***

A wash of subdued orange and pink was all that remained of the modest sunset as Patty and I walked down the shoveled path to the chicken coop a few minutes later. Patty carried a two-gallon bucket of feed in one hand. Sadie bounded ahead of us, her breath making little clouds of fog in the frigid air.

Patty pulled open the main door and stepped inside. I followed. Immediately half a dozen chickens clustered around my feet and began to peck the snow off my shoes. Their beauty and diversity amazed me. Yellow, black, red, speckled and striped, no two were alike. I stooped to touch the yellow one. It shied away, but then circled around to peck at my shoes from behind.

Patty gathered eggs from the wooden nest boxes along the wall, then tossed corn from her bucket in handfuls onto the floor. The chickens scattered for it like children after parade candy.

I laughed at their eagerness. "Where'd you get them?"

"My brother gave them to us when we moved here last summer. I'd love to have some other animals, but without a barn, it's going to be a while." She led me back outside and latched the door. Sadie bounded up to us, a frozen tennis ball in her mouth.

"Well, where'd you find that?" Patty said. "Give it here."

Sadie swung her head up and down, the ball firmly clenched in her teeth. I reached for her and she pranced away.

Patty laughed. "You could chase that dog all day and she wouldn't give you the ball. Tom's the only one who can get it away from her."

Back at the house, Heather met us looking downcast. "Grandma, I can't get this equation to come out."

"All right, honey. Let me get something started in the kitchen, and I'll come look at it."

Patty pulled the meatballs from the oven, then opened a jar of spaghetti sauce and emptied it into a pan on the front burner. "Would you watch that for me and turn it down if it starts to splatter?" she asked me.

"Sure." I got out a spoon and stirred the sauce a few times, but it was still cold. So I turned it up, put the cover on, and wandered over to the windows to admire Patty's houseplant collection. She had everything from cactus to marigolds to freshly potted amaryllis bulbs in the deep-silled windows behind the sink. I especially liked the plant with big shiny leaves and red flowers that resembled tiny roses. Carefully I pinched off a few blooms that had faded to a papery brown.

Behind me, I heard a loud sizzle. *Oh no, the spaghetti sauce!* I whirled in time to see the cover lift. A wave of bubbling sauce poured over the side of the pan and down onto the burner. I sprang to turn it off. My sleeve caught the handle of the pan, flipping it on end. I cussed as a splash of boiling liquid hit my hand. Spaghetti sauce was everywhere – flowing across the stovetop, leaking down around the other burners, dribbling onto the floor. I wanted to cry. How would I ever get this cleaned up?

The voices in the dining room ceased, and I heard footsteps. Through the kitchen window, I saw Tom's SUV pull in. I couldn't face three angry people. Would Tom beat me like Walter did?

I didn't wait to find out. Grabbing a paper towel for my hands, I fled down the nearby stairs to the basement.

The basement was pitch dark, but I was too scared to turn on a light. I bumped my way around, searching for a place to hide. There, behind the furnace!

I squeezed into the narrow space. At my back was a cold cement wall. I clawed a cobweb from my face and tried to quiet my breathing. Overhead, I heard muffled voices and footsteps, then water running. My hand stung where it had been burned, but the pain was nothing compared to my fear. Tom was a big man, over six feet tall and built like a football player. I wouldn't stand a chance against him. Why had I been so careless? What was wrong with me?

Light footsteps pattered on the wooden stairs. "Tess, you down here?" Heather called. I made no reply, and after a moment she went back up and closed the door behind her.

Maybe they won't find me after all. Maybe they'll think I ran away. The thought both relieved and pained me. Tonight after they were all asleep, I would sneak upstairs, get my coat, and leave.

A long time later, I heard Patty coming down the stairs in her slippers. She turned on the light. "Tessa? Where are you?"

She didn't sound mad. I slipped out from behind the furnace. "I-I didn't mean to do it."

"Of course not. Why are you hiding down here?"

Now I felt foolish. "I thought you'd be mad."

Patty smiled and shook her head. "I'm not mad. Come on, it's time to eat."

She turned toward the steps. Despite my embarrassment, I felt remarkably light, even happy, as I climbed the stairs behind her.

***

After supper, Heather and I withdrew to her bedroom. She played her new Taylor Swift album, and we sat on the bed and talked. I envied her pretty bedroom. Rose flowered wallpaper ran halfway up the walls, and above that they had been painted a delicate pink. Her bedspread was a patchwork pattern of rose and light pink with a matching pillow sham. Lace curtains hung at the window.

"I like the way you've got your room decorated," I said. "Did you do it yourself?"

"Partly. I picked out the paint and the wallpaper, but Grandpa helped a lot with putting it up. We just got the last bit done last weekend."

"That's cool." I racked my brain for something else to say.

"Yeah. You should've seen the room before we worked on it. The walls were dark blue, like a blue crayon. It took three coats of paint to cover it all up."

"Well, I'd say you improved it."

"Thanks. Grandma says it's a good thing, because she didn't know where to start."

"Have you always lived with your grandparents?"

"No, just since last summer. Mom and Dad are on a mission trip to Haiti, so I'll be here until school ends in the spring."

"Haiti? What're they doing down there?"

"Well, you know there's some tremendous needs there. My mom's a nurse, and she used to work with the Red Cross. My dad has worked in construction most of his life, but he's been unemployed since last winter. If there's one thing Dad can't stand, it's having nothing to do. One day last spring he was talking to our pastor. Mike happened to mention they needed help building houses in Haiti. He told Dad if he was interested, he'd put him in touch with some people who worked down there.

"Mom has always been interested in mission work, but she didn't want to travel around the world by herself. When it turned out Dad could go too, I guess that sealed it. So now she's down there helping sick people, and he's overseeing teams that build houses and schools and stuff."

"That's cool."

"Yeah. They're planning to stay down there for most of the winter. I kind of miss them, but Mom sends me pictures and calls sometimes."

A knock on the door interrupted us. "Girls, you'll have to wrap it up and get ready for bed," Patty called.

"Okay," Heather said. "Say, is Tess supposed to sleep in here?"

Patty opened the door. "Did you girls have some kind of plan?"

"No…" Seated beside me on the twin bed, Heather glanced around the small room.

"Actually, I was thinking she'd use the hide-a-bed in the back room," Patty said. "I straightened it up just yesterday, and I think it'll make a splendid bedroom for a few nights." She smiled at me. "Come on, I'll show you."

Patty took me farther down the hall, past the master bedroom. She pushed open a door and flicked on the lights. "What do you think?"

The room was large and unfinished, with a bare plywood floor and three big windows facing out into the night. Stacks of storage boxes and a chest freezer took up the far end of the room. But directly in front of me, a couch, an overstuffed armchair, a bookshelf, and an antique floor lamp had been arranged to form a sitting area. A large scatter rug in the center added a touch of coziness.

"It's not fancy, but I thought you'd like it better than sleeping on the couch in the living room."

I nodded. "It'll work." I almost added that I had slept in worse places, but I didn't want Patty to think I was complaining.

"Let's bring your stuff out here," Patty said, "and then you can take a bath while I make up your bed."

Back in the living room, we each grabbed one of the black trash bags Mom had left me. They were heavier than I expected.

"This is a lot of clothes for just a few days," Patty commented.

I said nothing, but as I emptied the bags on top of the chest freezer and began to sort the contents, the apprehensions I'd felt earlier returned in full force. I had enough clothes for about ten days. With a weekly laundering, I could easily get by for the rest of the winter. What was Mom thinking?

Maybe she's not coming back. Maybe she knows the cops are gonna close in, and she's gonna take off while she can.

I shoved that thought away as fast as I could. Mom might be crooked, but she would never abandon me. Or would she? The longer I contemplated the matter, the more uncertain I became. Didn't I have two older sisters somewhere? For all I knew, Mom might have abandoned them just like this. She'd already proven herself a liar; why should I trust anything she said?

Despite the hot bath I took and the flannel nightgown I put on, I still felt cold inside when I climbed into bed that night. I didn't even answer when Patty came by to tell me goodnight. I couldn't. I was sobbing under my pillow.

That night was awful. Even sleep brought me no peace. I dreamed Walter broke in during the night and kidnapped me. He tied my hands and hauled me into the woods, where he had built a bonfire. He had a huge pistol stuck in his belt. He was going to get warm, he said, and then he'd "take care of" me. Mom was there too, but she seemed indifferent to what was happening and wouldn't even look at me.

I managed to escape with Walter in pursuit. The path was rough, blocked by fallen trees and chest-high brambles. Worse, some kind of paralysis was setting into my legs. Only with great effort could I keep moving.

Clambering over yet another fallen tree, I found myself at the brink of a deep gorge. I could hear Walter's footsteps crackling in the dead leaves behind me. I crouched down, hoping he wouldn't see me; but as I did, my foot slipped. I tumbled over the cliff.

I awoke to my own screams. I was lying on the floor near my bed, drenched in sweat and shaking uncontrollably. The light was on, and beside me Patty knelt on the floor in her nightgown.

"There now, it's just a dream," she soothed me. "It's okay now." She guided me back to the rumpled bed and tucked a blanket around my shoulders. But I couldn't stop shaking. The dream had been so real.

"You're not gonna leave, are you?" I pleaded. More than anything, I wanted her to stay.

"Just for a moment," she said. "I have to put on a bathrobe before I freeze."

When Patty returned, she sat down on the bed and took my icy hands in her warm ones. "You still look scared. What's up with the bad dreams?"

I started to cry. I didn't even try to stop it. Patty put an arm around me and pulled me close, rocking me gently. "Is it Walter?"

I nodded.

"Tell me about it. What's he like to live with?"

More tears spilled down my cheeks. "I can't. I'm . . . not supposed to talk to anybody."

"Yes, you can. Nobody will find out. Now do you want to tell me or not?"

I sniffed a couple of times, struggling to compose myself. "If he knew . . . I was here . . . I'd be in really big trouble."

"Why's that?"

"I've run away before." I swallowed hard and fixed my gaze on the blue quilted blanket on my lap. "He always found me and punished me, but . . . last time he couldn't find me. One day the police picked me up. I didn't tell them anything, but they figured out who I was anyway and . . . and called Walter."

"What happened then?"

"You don't wanna know."

Patty stroked my hair. "Don't worry about bothering me. You need to get this out of your system."

"Well . . . it's bad . . ."

I stopped. How could I admit what had happened to me that night? It was too horrible, too shameful. Just the thought of recalling it caused me physical pain. Maybe it hadn't really happened like I remembered. Maybe I had imagined some part of it.

Patty helped me out. "So the police picked you up and called Walter. What then? Did he come get you?"

My voice choked as I tried to answer, and then everything fell apart. I began sobbing and beating the bed with my fists. I hurt. I raged. I yelled. Somewhere in there, though, I got the story out.

Patty listened with tears in her eyes. "Does your mom know about this?"

"I can't tell her stuff like this. She don't believe me."

"I see. But tell me, why does Walter care if you run away? If he is like you say, I don't see why he'd miss you."

"He's afraid I'll say something, especially if I get picked up again."

"Say something? About what?" Patty's arm around my shoulders was warm, reassuring, but I knew better than to answer truthfully.

"I don't know. He's kind of neurotic."

Patty talked with me a few more minutes, then offered to pray for me. This time I agreed.

25

To my surprise, Mom arrived promptly at seven thirty the next morning to drive me to school. She acted so normal that I felt guilty for distrusting her. But when school let out, for the first time ever she was not waiting out front in her black car. I searched the parking lot and checked the side streets. No sign of her. In growing dismay, I turned back toward the building.

The other students were scattering into the parking lot in little groups. A few stragglers were still getting on the buses. Should I ask someone for a ride? What if Mom came later and found me gone?

A horn blared on the street behind me, and a familiar voice shouted my name. I turned. Nosed into the curb was Patty's red car. I hurried over.

"Where's Mom?" I asked, opening the passenger door.

"She's at the hospital. Walter's been in a car accident. She called and asked me to pick you up. Sorry I'm late."

"That's okay." I swung myself inside, dropping my knapsack on the floor with a thump. "So, how is he?"

"I don't know. The doctors were still checking him over when she called."

"All right." I wasn't concerned. Walter had been in three accidents in the last year, and each time, he'd managed to walk away unharmed. He was as indestructible as he was mean.

I settled back in the seat and closed my eyes. But tired as I was, I couldn't relax. Mom's excuse didn't make sense. Why would she rush to the hospital to be with Walter, after the way he'd beaten her up the other night? Was she even able to walk across that big parking lot? The more I thought about it, the more I doubted her story. Even if Walter was injured, I couldn't imagine Mom going to see him unless she had to. Maybe she had abandoned me, and the accident story was a cover-up.

The next few hours passed in a fog. I could hardly function, let alone do homework. If only Mom would call and explain what was going on!

The call didn't come until seven o'clock. Tom answered, then held out the phone to me. "It's your mom."

I swallowed and took the phone. "Hi, Mom."

"I just wanted to touch base with you," she said. "You heard about Walter's accident, didn't you?"

"Yeah, Patty said something. Was it bad?" From the music and laughter in the background, I knew Mom wasn't calling from the hospital. I guessed she was at a bar.

"Kind of. He's pretty banged up. He's got a smashed arm and a broken leg. They think he'll recover all right, but he won't be going anywhere for a while. His truck is a total wreck."

"Really. What happened?"

"He crossed the center line on County P just out of town and hit a dump truck." She sounded disgusted. "I can't believe he's in as good a shape as he is."

"So he's in the hospital?"

"Yeah, for now. Say, I was gonna ask you. Have you still got a key to that old Impala?"

"Somewhere. Why?"

"Somewhere doesn't help me much. Is it there with you?"

"How should I know? It was probably in one of the pairs of jeans lying around my room."

"I think I packed all your good jeans. Can you check and see if you have it?"

"I suppose." Amid curious looks from the others, I carried the handset with me down the hall to my makeshift bedroom. In the pile of clothes on the freezer, I found my newest pair of jeans. In the front pocket was a ring with three keys.

"I've got it," I reported.

"Good. Maybe you could give it to me tomorrow when I come. I wanna get that car out of there before the snow gets too deep."

"Okay. Where are you, anyway?"

Mom laughed at that. "Steve's, on Grand Avenue. Remember?"

"Oh, yeah." I remembered the place all too well. Last winter we'd spent almost every weekend at that downtown tavern. Mom and Walter were good friends with the owners. Lately, however, Walter had been avoiding the place in favor of some less reputable establishments down by the river.

"So, how are things going for you?" Mom asked me.

"Pretty good, I guess."

"I never thought I'd make an arrangement like this," she apologized.

"It's okay. I sort of like it."

"Well, tell Ericksons I appreciate it. When those doctors got done with Walter, one of them asked what happened to me. I told him I fell down the stairs, but I don't think he bought it. He's like, 'That's some fall. How about if we check out that leg.' It hurts so bad I let them do it. But it turns out it's just a really bad bruise."

"That's good."

"Yeah. So, I'm gonna let you go here. I'll see you tomorrow."

I hung up feeling much better. Mom couldn't be lying. If she were really hundreds of miles away, she wouldn't need the key to the Impala. And the music in the background sure did sound like Steve's. I must be paranoid, thinking I could foretell Mom's plans by the number of socks she packed.

I laughed aloud at the thought. She'd likely packed my stuff in a tearing rush and not counted anything.

Later that evening, after another hot bath, I wrapped up in a blanket and wandered out to the empty living room. Heather had gone to bed, but from the light under their door, I knew Tom and Patty were still up.

I settled on the couch and pulled a magazine from the rack. After last night's bad dreams, I wasn't eager to go to bed. Maybe if Patty saw me out here, she would stop and talk to me.

In a few minutes, Patty emerged from her bedroom, carrying an empty mug. Sadie followed at her heels.

"Why Tessa, aren't you in bed yet?"

"It's dark and lonely out there," I protested.

Patty went to the back door and let Sadie out, then returned to the living room. "Tell you what. You go get in bed, and I'll come in a few minutes and say goodnight. How's that?"

"All right." I tried to hide the little smile that sprang to my lips. Everyone would say I was too old for that kind of attention, but Patty was a grandma. Maybe grandmas did things like this.

When Patty came, she tucked me into bed the way Mom used to. Then she asked God to give me a good sleep and keep the nightmares away. "Goodnight, I love you," she finished. Turning out the light, she went softly away.

I lay still, unwilling to move lest I break the wonderful spell she had cast. Inside I felt peace and a deep contentment that I hadn't felt in years. I wanted to stay awake and savor it, but the warm bed made me drowsy. Soon I drifted into sleep.

26

The insistent ringing of the telephone jolted me awake. It couldn't be Mom again, could it? I rolled out of bed and stumbled down the hall, rubbing my eyes. Patty stood talking on the kitchen phone. She was barefoot and held a wet toothbrush in her free hand.

"We'll work something out," she was saying. "No, it's okay, really. We'll be there as soon as we can." She hung up.

"What was that?" I demanded. By now Tom had appeared in his pajamas to see what the stir was.

"That was Julie. It seems she left the hospital and was going through State Street intersection when she got broadsided by some-body running the red light. She isn't hurt, but her car's in pretty bad shape. She asked if we could drive her home."

"Sure, why not," Tom drawled. "We are the late-night emergency crew nowadays. I guess I'd better get dressed again."

I slipped off to my room without a word. Fear clawed at my throat. Why was everything going wrong? My hands shook as I pulled on jeans and a sweatshirt. Tom and Patty might disapprove, but I had to see Mom.

I met Patty at the back closet, buttoning her coat. I ducked behind her and grabbed mine off the hook. She turned in surprise. "Why Tessa, you don't have to come."

"I don't mind. I'm used to staying up until midnight," I said. "I can even drive if you like."

Patty raised her eyebrows. "You can drive? You don't have a license, do you?"

"Well, no."

Tom appeared then in his red flannel shirt and jeans. Together the three of us trudged out into the cold and piled into Tom's SUV. Tom drove.

Mom had called a tow truck and then hitched a ride to the 24-hour convenience store on Park Avenue, where she'd told Patty to pick her up. When we arrived, the parking lot was deserted. Tom pulled into the space nearest the door and tapped the horn.

Mom hobbled outside. "Thanks so much," she said, as she opened the rear door and got in. "I could've gotten the tow guy to give me a ride home, but I didn't like the looks of him." Then she turned her attention to me. "Tessa! What're you doing here?"

On impulse, I fished in my pocket and handed her the key to the Impala. "Here. Might as well give this to you before I forget."

Her face broke into a tired smile. "Tess, you're amazing. A real lifesaver."

My cheeks warmed with the unusual praise. "Yeah. I even offered to drive, but Patty doesn't trust me."

"You brat," she scolded playfully. "You're gonna ruin my good reputation yet. What else are you telling them?"

"Oh, I told Heather all about Genevieve, and how much fun she had the night she ran loose in my room."

"Oh brother. That explains why your room still smells."

I laughed, and the conversation ended. We rode along in silence for several minutes.

"Well, this does it," Mom said then. "Tomorrow I'll have to figure out how to get me another car. Of course, there's the old Impala," she added, as if she'd just thought of it. "It probably still runs. But I'd have to get out there somehow. Even if I could walk, which I can't, it would take me like . . . two hours?" She glanced at me for confirmation.

"Yeah, probably." Worry tugged at my mind. Why was Mom talking so freely around Tom and Patty?

Mom was silent for a while. Then she leaned forward. "Sorry to impose on your kindness, Mr. Erickson, but could you drop me off at my brother-in-law's place instead? We've got an old car we keep there."

My heart lurched. *She wouldn't!*

"Where is the place?" Tom asked.

"It's only a couple of extra miles."

"I suppose. How do I get there?"

My anxiety diminished as I realized Mom was taking Tom to the farmhouse the back way. By going in through the field and parking behind the outbuildings, she would disguise both the location and the deplorable condition of the place. Tom would assume it was just another farm. The plan was daring, but with a little luck, it would probably work.

A few miles past Vance Road, we turned left. Dirt replaced the blacktop as the road narrowed and began to wind along the base of a high ridge. The surrounding land was mostly wooded, with an occasional isolated farmstead. Every now and then the road widened out to form a Y.

"Your brother-in-law lives way out here?" Tom queried.

"No, but he's got a cabin of sorts." Mom's voice was too sharp. "There's the driveway, on your left."

Tom slammed on the brakes and made the tight turn. The narrow field lane might have indeed passed for a driveway if it weren't for the two inches of fresh snow obscuring the wheel tracks. Tom drove slowly, rolling over bumps and slipping into ruts. To our right lay a snow-covered cornfield; to our left, a brushy woods.

"Don't get stuck," Patty warned, as the vehicle began to climb a slight incline. I nodded in silent assent. Even Walter's three-quarter-ton pickup had gotten stuck out here a few times.

Rounding the corner at the end of the field, Tom nearly collided with a rusty combine smothered in a tangle of vines and brush.

"Oh, that thing," I said.

Mom turned toward me so sharply I could almost hear her reprimand. *I'm running this thing. Don't ruin it.* Then she leaned close to the side window to watch for the turnoff.

"Okay, hold it. Turn left right here."

The SUV jolted to a stop. "Right *where?* This is getting crazy, Julie."

"Right between those trees. There's a gate, see?"

I nearly choked. Anybody could see the barbed wire had been cut.

Tom sounded skeptical. "It's how much farther to this place?"

"Oh, maybe an eighth mile."

"I'm holding you to that." Tom turned the steering wheel and proceeded through the narrow opening onto the next property. He drove slowly, following a faint trail that wound between patches of sumac. At length the headlights shone upon a group of dilapidated buildings.

I was so nervous I had to clench my jaw to keep my teeth from chattering. This was it. If anything went wrong now, we'd be in huge trouble.

"There's the car," Mom said, indicating a snow-covered shape next to a low shed.

Tom pulled up alongside it. "So, you guys actually own this car, Julie?"

"Of course we do. I hope you didn't think I was stealing it." Mom gave a quick laugh.

A brief, awkward silence followed.

"Oh come on," she groaned. "Don't you trust me at all?" She tugged a piece of paper from her pocket, unfolded it, and thrust it at Tom. "Look."

Tom flipped on the dome light. I craned my neck until I could make out the heading on the envelope-sized paper. It was the registration for the Impala.

"Okay." Tom sounded satisfied. "Will the thing start? I didn't bring my jumper cables."

Mom tucked the paper back into her pocket and opened the door. "I don't know for sure. Maybe you could stay a minute until I get it going."

"I know how to start it," I said.

"Will you shut up?" Mom slammed the door and began to brush the snow off the white car with her mittens. I hunched in my seat and wished I were back at Tom and Patty's, asleep. This trip had turned into a lot more than I'd bargained for.

The old car cranked slowly, but at last it roared to life. Mom lifted her hand in a gesture I took to mean "thanks and goodbye," then pulled a scraper from the back seat and began to chip ice from the windows.

"I guess we can go," I said. "You just sort of turn around and go out the way we came."

"So where does your uncle live?" Tom asked, after we'd made it back onto the road.

"My uncle?" I tried to think where he'd gotten that idea.

"Wouldn't your mom's brother-in-law be your uncle?"

"Oh. Yeah, I guess so." I tried to remember what Mom had said about this imaginary relative on the way there. "I wanna say Chicago, but I'm not real sure. He moves around quite a bit."

"And he comes up here to go hunting or something?"

"Yeah. In the fall."

"What does he do the rest of the time?"

"Go left here," I directed, as we came to the first branch in the road. "I don't know what he does. Why?"

"Just curious," Tom said, and dropped the subject.

It was past two by the time we returned to the house. I quickly got ready for bed. Then I slipped out to the kitchen for a glass of water. On the way back to my room, I heard talking in Tom and Patty's bedroom. I paused outside their door.

"You see what I mean," Patty was saying. "That Julie is a con artist, or worse. This is the last time I'm doing anything for her."

"Yes, she's quite a character," Tom agreed. "But I think I'm too tired to figure it out tonight."

Then the lights went out, and I heard them get into bed. "Oh Lord," Patty prayed. "Please, let us sleep the rest of the night. No more car accidents, nightmares, and doorbells."

"Amen," murmured Tom.

I could not dismiss my worries as easily as Tom had. I lay wide awake for at least another hour. Why had Mom taken such a foolish chance? Wouldn't it have been better to walk the two hours – even with a bruised leg? Maybe the whole incident had been some kind of setup, some plan to get out to the farmhouse without being followed. Maybe she was going to load the car with meth, then split for the Twin Cities or someplace and sell it.

Round and round my mind went, each possibility crazier and more frightening, until at last, exhausted, I sank into a restless sleep.

27

The remainder of the week passed without event. I had to laugh at myself for imagining so many awful scenarios, although I wondered if Walter's accident had played a part in preventing them. Mom picked me up for school every morning and dropped me off again in the afternoon like clockwork. She deflected questions such as how long I'd be staying with Tom and Patty, but she did keep me abreast of Walter's condition. He was doing well and would be coming home on the weekend, she said.

I didn't dare ask, but I hoped Mom would continue to let me stay with Tom and Patty. I felt safe with them. Sure, they had rules, some of which were stricter than Mom's. I had to go to bed by ten thirty, and there was no watching TV or videos unless all my homework was done.

But Heather's companionship more than made up for the annoying rules. She played CDs for me while we did the dishes, kept me company as I struggled with my never-ending barrage of homework, and even gave me one of her hand-crocheted pillows for my bed.

"I always wanted a sister," she confided one evening, after trying to explain for the third time why adding two negative numbers would not give me a positive. "So this is actually kind of fun for me."

Patty welcomed me in her own way, whether it was buying a nightlight for my room or inviting me to help make muffins for supper. At bedtime, she would tuck me in and pray for me. Afterwards, she'd often stay a few minutes and talk to me about God. I didn't follow everything she said, but I did notice I wasn't having nightmares anymore. Could it be that God was looking out for me like she said? It seemed preposterous, but I had no other explanation for my calm nights.

Saturday morning I slept in until ten o'clock, the way I always did. As far as I knew, everyone slept in on the weekend. To my surprise, when I got up I found the breakfast table cleared and the dishes already washed. Heather sat at the table in a patch of sunshine, working on a pen sketch of Sadie.

"Hey, you're pretty good," I complimented her. "Did you leave me anything to eat?"

"There was a bowl of oatmeal for you. Grandma must have put it in the fridge."

"Oatmeal." I made a face. I'd been hoping for pancakes again.

Heather's pen made short, fast streaks as she filled in Sadie's thick ruff. "Yup. It's good for you."

I made a growling sound. "If I eat oatmeal one more day, I think I'm gonna be sick."

Heather chuckled. "Nah. You'll get used to it. You're just spoiled."

"I am not."

Heather shrugged. Picking up a different pen, she began to add in the finer details on the face.

Spoiled, my foot. Bet she wouldn't survive even one night at Walter's farmhouse. I pulled a box of raisin bran from the pantry and poured myself a bowl.

Heather glanced up from her dog portrait. "See, you are spoiled."

"Shut up." I pulled out a chair and sat down across from her.

"Fine. Next time I'm not making you anything. You don't show up for breakfast anyway."

"I never asked you to make me anything! And by the way, I can sleep as late as I want, and you don't have anything to say about it."

Heather stood up. "You know what? You're a brat. A spoiled, lazy brat. I hope your mom comes and gets you pretty soon."

"And you're little Miss Perfect, huh? You're nothing but a smart aleck and a showoff."

"Girls, girls," Patty chided from the living room.

Heather shoved her chair into place and grabbed her unfinished drawing.

"Not gonna argue it, huh?" I said.

Heather spun around, her face red. "I'm not gonna argue with you because it's a sin!" She stomped into the bathroom.

"I don't care!" I fired after her, as the door slammed. Man, was Heather in a bad mood this morning, picking a fight with me like that. Oh well, at least I could enjoy my breakfast in peace now.

But a peaceful breakfast was not to be that day. About the time my flakes lost their crunch, the phone rang. Patty answered in the living room. "Tessa, it's your mom."

I groaned as I reached for the kitchen phone. "Yeah?"

"Can you be packed and ready to leave in half an hour?"

My head spun. "Uh . . . I suppose."

"Good. I'll be over to pick you up. We have a lot of work to do before Walter comes home."

I hung up without saying goodbye.

"What did she want?" asked Heather, appearing from the bathroom as if nothing had happened.

"None of your business, nosy." I upended my bowl and gulped down the remaining milk and cereal. Then I hurried down the hall to my makeshift bedroom, slamming the door behind me. Angry thoughts tumbled through my mind.

Leave it to Mom to do this to me. Why couldn't she have said something yesterday, when any other decent person would've mentioned it? But no, she had to keep me hoping til the last second, then drop the bomb and whisk me away before I could protest.

I seized one of the black trash bags and began shoving clothes into it so violently that it tore. The stupid, cheap bag! I kicked it, punching another hole in the side.

"Tessa! What's going on?" Patty poked her head around the door.

"Nothing. Mom's coming to get me." I continued stuffing clothes into the bag as fast as I could.

Patty walked in and sat down on the unmade bed. "I thought that might be it. Need help packing?"

"No, I've about got it." I kept my back to her as I dumped the box that held my dirty clothes into the second black bag.

"We're going to miss you."

"Yeah, I bet."

"Why are you so upset?"

"I'm not upset. I'm in a hurry."

Patty walked over to where I stood at the chest freezer, pretending to examine a hole in one of my socks. She put her hand on my shoulder. "Tessa, do you know why we care about you?"

I shook my head and stared harder at the torn sock.

"Because God cares about you. You're so very precious to him. He made you. He loves you deeply, and he causes us to love you too."

I blinked rapidly, determined not to cry. My throat felt like it had a block of wood stuck in it.

"I wish you could stay here longer because I know you're hungry for love. It's harder to believe God loves you when the people around you don't love. But if you'll open your heart to God's love, he promises to come and satisfy that deep longing inside of you in a way no one else can."

The tears were coming faster than I could blink them away. Whatever she was talking about, something inside me desperately wanted it.

Patty hugged me. "That's all right. Don't fight it, just cry."

"Sorry," I said, when I could talk again. I glanced at Patty. Tears glinted in her eyes as well.

"How come you're crying?"

Patty shook her head. "I couldn't help it. If you ever want to talk or anything, just call me, okay?"

"Okay."

She gave me another hug, and this time I hugged her back. It felt good.

"Come on, I'll help you get this stuff to the door," she said.

Heather trailed me to the back closet. "Hey, Tess. I'm sorry for what I said to you. I didn't mean it. Can you forgive me?"

I kept my face turned away as I zipped up my coat.

"I-I have some things I can't stand to eat either," she faltered. "Like dill pickles. So I'm sorry for picking on you for yours."

I looked at her then. Her face was earnest and sad.

"So can we still be friends?"

"Okay." I managed a smile. Then, on impulse, I reached out and gave her a hug. "I'm gonna miss you."

"Me too," Heather said. "But I'm really glad you could come."

Outside, a horn honked. Did Mom expect me to be standing there ready to run out the door the instant she drove in?

Patty grabbed one of my bags, and together we walked out to the car. Mom limped around to open the trunk.

"Thanks a million," she said to Patty. "Sorry we've been such a bother to you guys."

"It's okay," Patty said. "Take care now."

Then Mom slammed the trunk, and Patty turned back to the house. We drove home in silence.

28

The kitchen was a mess, with muddy boot prints on the linoleum and last week's dirty dishes still scattered on the counter. A heap of laundry lay on the table. But it wasn't until I stepped around the corner into the living room that I understood Mom's urgent need for help.

Mud had been tracked onto the carpet and the couch, then left to dry. Food wrappers and crumbs littered the floor. A pair of filthy blue jeans was thrown across the arm of the chair. Beer cans were scattered everywhere. But strangest of all, a piece of paneling had been ripped from the wall behind the TV, exposing chipped plaster in hideous shades of green and olive.

"Pretty bad, huh?" Mom came to stand beside me. "Looks like Walter stayed a night or two. I just found it this morning."

"This morning? But he's . . . I thought you said…"

"I haven't been here," she said. "I've been staying in town with Steve and Wendy all week."

"Oh."

"I paid the phone bill and most of the back rent on Thursday. We should have phone service again soon."

So that was why the phone didn't work. Things would go more smoothly if only Mom would tell me things like that. I cast a glance down the hall toward my bedroom. The door hung partly open. "So . . . did he actually break into my room or what?"

"Yeah, unfortunately. I wasn't in no shape to stop him. I wish I could've called the cops right then."

"I thought of it, but I didn't have a phone."

"Of course. What I'd like to know, though, is why you didn't call them when you got to Erickson's."

I stared at her. "You . . . you wanted me to?"

"Well of course! What the hell did you think was going on back here?" Then her voice softened. "I'm sorry. It's been a hard week. Why don't you put your stuff in your room, and then you can help me clean up this mess."

I was surprised at the fear that gripped me as I started down the hall toward my bedroom. As I drew nearer and observed the multiple dents in the door and the wall, the fear intensified. Maybe Walter was still inside, hiding behind the door or in the closet with that iron fry pan.

Silly thought. I reached out and with one quick motion shoved the door wide. Floor boards creaked as I stepped into the room. Someone had closed the window, but the ruined screen was just as I had left it, the jagged corners protruding outward like rusty metal wings. A piece of red fuzz from my sweatshirt clung to the bent wires. I turned away. Maybe later I could cut the screen out. I did not want to remember that night!

After checking the closet to reassure myself that Walter couldn't possibly be there, I carried in my bags of clothes and dumped them at the foot of the bed. On my way out, I tried to close the door, but the frame was too splintered to hold the latch. I gave up and returned to the living room, where Mom set me to sponging mud off the carpet with a rag and a bucket.

Cleaning the mess up took several hours, and then we had to rearrange furniture to make the walkways wide enough for a wheelchair. Sometime around two, we finished and ate a quick lunch.

"I sure appreciate your help," Mom said, as she ladled hot tomato soup into two bowls. "All I have to do now is take care of him. That's gonna be interesting."

"Can't he do anything for himself?"

"Not much." Mom crumbled a handful of crackers into her soup. "The broken leg would limit him enough, but he had to smash his arm too. So he can't use crutches, and he's not going to be lifting himself into or out of his wheelchair or the car or anything else without help. He can feed himself, but beyond that he's practically an invalid. And a very angry one at that."

"He's mad about the accident?"

"Oh yeah. It's all my fault, he says."

"Huh?"

"Sure. I called the cops on him, supposedly, which got him upset, which led to us having a fight, which led to him getting really jazzed up on whatever all he takes, which led to him swerving over the center line in broad daylight and hitting a dump truck. You get the idea."

I groaned. "Maybe you should put him in one of those drug rehab places, like the doctor said."

"It wouldn't do any good. He denies everything, even when the doctor's standing right there with the test results."

"Oh wow." I finished off the crackers, then ran my finger along the bottom of the empty wrapper, collecting the loose salt and crumbs.

Mom rose and began to stack the dirty dishes. "Say, I was gonna ask you. Do you have any idea where he keeps that gun of his?"

"Which one?"

She stared at me. "What do you mean, which one?"

"He's got several of them."

Mom's frown deepened. "Great. How long has that been going on?"

"I don't know. Couple months, anyway."

Her shoulders sagged, and she shook her head. "Well, go see if you can find me one of them."

"What are you gonna do, terrorize him?"

"Of course not." She dumped the dishes into the sink and turned on the water. "But I might need it to chase away those so-called friends of his."

I snickered. "Yeah, when they drive in you can just stick the barrel out the kitchen window and shoot 'em."

"I'm serious. I do not want any of them in here. Go see if you can find me something."

"Okay." I pulled on a jacket and stepped out the kitchen door. The bright sunshine had melted some of the snow, exposing patches of ice in the driveway. I steadied myself on the car as I crossed to Walter's shop.

The pungent odors of varnish and paint thinner met me as I unlocked the door. I flicked the lights on and glanced around the room. Mom was right; nothing significant had been done in here for several months. Directly in front of me stood a desk Walter had started last summer, still unfinished. On top of it was an open can of varnish, its contents hard and cracked. Nearby, almost buried under a heap of dusty newspapers, stood an antique china cupboard Walter had picked up at an auction at least a year ago. On the bench lay a pile of rough planks that might have been destined for Mr. Vick's bookshelf. Stacked on them were three new cases of beer. No wonder Walter couldn't get anything done.

I shoved an overflowing trash can out of the way and ran my hand along the high shelf above the window where he used to keep his rifle. Dust showered down upon me, but otherwise the shelf was empty. This was going to be harder than I had expected.

Starting near the door, I searched every drawer and shelf and piece of machinery in the room. Last of all, I pulled myself up onto the bench and checked the cobwebby space between the top of the highest shelf and the ceiling. My fingers brushed something smooth and cold – the barrel of his old .22 rifle. I grinned in triumph as I lifted it down. Mom would never have found it up there.

As I crossed the shop with the rifle, an odd gap in the stack of folded rags on the utility shelf caught my eye. I reached in and withdrew a black .45 pistol about eight inches long. A strange mixture of terror and fascination gripped me as I stared at it. This was the gun Walter had threatened me with. I was sure of it.

Maybe one of these days it'll be my turn. I pointed the gun toward the door and tried to aim it one-handed, but I couldn't hold it steady. *She's some heavy. But hey, maybe it doesn't matter how well I can aim.* I grinned, picturing the fear in Walter's eyes if he saw me wielding this thing. I'd have to pay close attention to where Mom put it.

Carrying a gun in each hand, I returned to the house. Mom met me at the door. "Wow, you are well armed. Keep them pointed down, Tessa."

"Oh, yeah." I quickly tipped the rifle down. "I guess they're probably loaded."

Mom took the pistol first and examined it. "Nice gun. Yep, she's loaded. I think I'll just take that out."

Watching her remove the bullets, I realized how stupid I'd been to point the gun toward the house. Suppose it had gone off?

The rifle seemed to be empty. Mom dusted it off and laid it on the table next to the pistol. "I'll find a good place to hide these. Say, one more thing. You don't still have the keys to that old house, do you?"

"Not anymore. He made me give them back."

"I thought so. I've been looking everywhere, but I can't find them. They're probably with him. Which reminds me, I need to go get him. Want to come?"

"No thanks. Maybe you can conspire to crash into something on the way home."

"Tessa!"

My face burned. "Well, you know what I mean."

"Listen, I know he's been a real jerk. But we're not gonna take him out, okay?"

"How about accidentally?" I tried to hide my smirk.

"Absolutely not." Mom slid the rifle onto the top of the refrigerator and then stood back critically.

I had to laugh. "That's kind of noticeable."

"I'd say." She took it down and tried it on the shelf in the coat closet, with much better results. Then she slipped the pistol into her purse and prepared to leave.

"Don't you need some kind of permit to carry a concealed weapon?" I had to give her that jab.

"To tell the truth, I don't remember." She pulled on her gloves and picked up the purse. "See you later."

29

Left alone, I retreated to my bedroom, where I flopped down on the bed and tried not to think what it was going to be like having Walter around twenty-four hours a day. I closed my eyes, and I was back at Heather's house, watching Tom wrestle a huge Christmas tree into the house. Patty was laughing as she playfully scolded him for selecting a tree that would "never in a hundred years" fit in their tiny living room. Heather was plugging in strings of colored lights while I swatted at Sadie for barking at them. Then all four of us were decorating, Tom giving advice from the couch while the rest of us hung the ornaments to the joyous accompaniment of "Silver Bells" and other Christmas songs on Patty's CD.

But the music faded, and suddenly I was back in my own dreary bedroom, staring up at the huge crack in the ceiling. A terrible ache filled my heart. I had to go back. I had to see Patty and Heather and Sadie again. I longed to walk into the warm kitchen and breathe the spicy aroma of the gingerbread Patty had baked. I yearned to feel Sadie's rough fur under my hand, hear Patty picking her guitar, and snuggle under a blanket with Heather as we watched a movie together.

The ache grew so intense I could not bear it. I groaned and clutched my pillow to my chest in an effort to ease the pain, but it didn't help. Something inside of me desperately needed Patty. I felt like I couldn't survive without her. Yet, I would have to.

There's God, I thought. *Patty says he loves me and cares about me just like she does. But I can't see him! How can he possibly hold my hand or tuck me into bed or give me a hug?*

Tears ran down my face. *That's what I need, God! Not some person way off up in the sky that I can't see or feel. Please, I wanna go back and stay with Patty. If you'll do that, then I'll believe you love me.*

I was so sincere I almost believed something would happen. But I waited in vain. No voice spoke from heaven. The disconnected phone didn't ring with Patty on the other end. Mom didn't come back and say she'd decided to let me stay with Ericksons again. The silence was deafening. Even God didn't care.

"Okay. Screw it," I muttered. "You're not going back, Tess. As selfish and mean as you are, nobody could love you anyway. Get used to it!"

I thought this would end the pain, but it grew worse. Sobbing, I cursed myself for having ever gone to Patty's in the first place. All that talk about love seemed a cruel joke now. There was no love for me. I might as well swallow the pain and learn to live with it, as I had done for most of my life.

The trouble was, I couldn't get my thoughts to cooperate. Things Patty had said about God and his love for me kept swirling around in my head. Things I wished I could believe. *God loves you, Tessa. You're very special to him.*

But the words grated on my bleeding heart. "No! No one loves me! No one!" I screamed.

Try as I did, I couldn't drown out Patty's gentle voice. *God loves you. That's why we love you. You've just got to open your heart . . . God loves you, Tessa!*

I couldn't hide from it. Deep inside, something told me Patty was right.

Okay, fine. So maybe God does love me. But what's this thing about opening my heart? How am I supposed to do that? It all seemed too vague and difficult.

My thoughts kept returning to the time Patty had spent with me that morning. Something had happened inside of me – something good. All I had done was let go. I had let myself trust her. By letting go and trusting her, I realized, I had opened my heart to her love. Maybe I could do the same with God.

My voice was so thick I could hardly speak. "God," I whispered, "I'm gonna trust what Patty told me about you. She says you care, and that you love me just like she does."

I felt an inexplicable warmth come over me, as if the sun were shining on me. In that instant, I knew beyond a doubt that God really did love me. I could sense his arms around me, holding me close. Overwhelmed, I began to cry. *God, I really do believe you love me! I don't understand it, but I do.*

Time passed. I heard Mom come home with Walter, then Walter out in the living room complaining about something, but I was in another world. Evening came on, and with it the amber glow of a sunset. I moved to the window to catch the fiery rays on my face.

God's love is something like this, I thought, *warm, magical, special. Only it doesn't fade.* I watched the sun dip beneath the horizon in a splash of coral and magenta. Little purple clouds floated just above, their edges taking on hues of brilliant pink, then fading to steel blue. I stayed at the window a long time, letting the darkness envelop me and the silence seep into my soul.

30

Walter's first day at home passed uneventfully. Mom had settled him in the easy chair in front of the TV, and except when she forgot to dispense his pain medication, he was quiet. He paid me no attention. I had the feeling he was embarrassed and would rather I wasn't around. I couldn't blame him. He looked pathetic, with numerous scrapes and bruises on his face and a wide bandage across his forehead. Another much thicker bandage covered his left arm from the elbow to the wrist. A third encased his right leg and foot.

I was glad when Monday came and I could return to school. Heather met me coming in and gave me a big hug. "How's it going?"

"Okay, I guess. Better than I expected." Then, feeling a bit silly, I told her about believing God loved me.

Heather's face lit up. "Tess, that's great! Do you have a Bible?"

"A Bible?" I frowned. "Why do I need that?"

She laughed. "It's God's book. You can learn more about him by reading it. If you want, tomorrow I'll bring you a New Testament."

"Okay, but I'm not any good at keeping rules."

"Keeping rules?"

"Yeah. You know, the ten commandments, stuff like that."

"Well, it's not about keeping rules, it's…" Heather paused. "When you saw how much God loved you the other night, did it make you act any different?"

"Sure. I was happy. I didn't even mind washing the dishes for once."

Heather grinned and nodded. "See, that's what being a Christian is all about. It's not following a bunch of rules; it's just living out of that love." She gave my arm a quick squeeze. "We can talk more later. Just stick with what you've got, okay?"

I nodded. I knew I'd never give up what I had experienced. It was too precious.

But as the days went by, my happiness over God's love faded. Heather gave me a Bible, and we talked every day, but I was afraid to tell her of the change. I knew she'd be disappointed in me.

The weekend came again, and with it, a shift in Walter's disposition. Sullen and silent most of the time, he'd go into a rage if Mom didn't do what he wanted. He'd slam his fist on the end table, yell, and curse her. Mom would yell right back, adding an insult or two for good measure. Thus a disagreement over something as trivial as a TV show would escalate until I felt like screaming. Even when things simmered down, the atmosphere remained tense. I couldn't relax enough to even read a novel.

I fought to keep my thoughts off Christmas, which was now only a week away. Mom never discussed money with me, but I knew our finances were tight. I dreaded what she'd say if I mentioned Christmas. "I'm sorry, Tess. We can't afford it."

But my heart ached. Every time I turned on the radio, they were playing their stupid songs about how bright and jolly everything was. Even the commercials reflected the so-called holiday spirit. At mealtimes, the trashy magazines scattered on the table taunted me with glittering headlines such as "Celebrity Tips for Surviving the Holidays in Style" or "151 Fabulous Gift Ideas." I felt like ripping them to shreds. All they did was remind me of what I couldn't have.

Early Monday morning, I awoke to yet another fight. I pushed my head under the pillow in an attempt to muffle the harsh voices, but they kept getting louder. Then something heavy crashed against the wall.

"I said give it to me!" Walter screamed.

Fear tightened my chest. I shoved the pillow aside and propped myself up on my elbows, listening.

"Julie, please." Walter's voice was softer now, a thin cover for his obvious exasperation. "You gotta give me something. This stupid leg is killing me!"

"I don't care!" Mom shot back. "You heard what the doctor said. No drinks til you're better."

Walter slammed his fist down. "To hell with the doctor! Where's my pills? Some nurse you are, forgetting my pills."

"I didn't forget. The bottle ran out."

"Well, get a refill! And hurry up. I should've had them an hour ago."

"I can't do that. There's no refills on this."

Walter cursed. "What! You're lying. Now get going, or I'll find a way to make you."

"Forget it. There's no druggist in town gonna fill this. See here? *No refills.* Even you should be able to read that!"

For a second there was dead silence. Then Walter let loose a torrent of angry, abusive language. "What you trying to pull on me? This is impossible. The doc said–"

"That more drugs is the last thing you need," Mom cut in. "I talked to him myself."

"You sneaking–" Walter stopped. His voice took on a tone of defeat. "Julie, look. Just get me a refill, okay? Tell the doc I need it."

"Not a chance, big guy. You can just do without. It'll be good for you."

"Good for me!" he exploded, crashing his fist down again. "How would you like to have all these broken bones and then have some jerk tell you it's good for you!"

"Well, nobody gave me any painkillers after you busted that chair on my leg and slugged me in the face. Nobody gave Tess any painkillers after you mostly beat her to death. Nobody–"

"Stop it!" he roared.

I groaned as I dragged myself from the warm bed. Mom had better be joking about not getting him a refill. Listening to this for the next couple of weeks would drive me insane.

By the time I ventured out of my room, the fighting had subsided. I could hear Mom in the kitchen buttering toast. As I hurried past, Walter called to me.

"Tess, get me the phone. I've got to call my doctor. I think I'm infected or something."

He sounded desperate – pleading, almost. I stopped in surprise.

Walter gestured with his good hand. "C'mon, kid. What you waitin' for? Get me the phone."

I probably would have obeyed if Mom hadn't yelled from the kitchen just then. "Don't you dare, Walter. You've cost me enough already."

The only answer was a fist slammed on the table and a muttered curse.

In the kitchen, Mom handed me a bowl of warm applesauce and a piece of toast. "I hate to say it, but I can't leave with him like this. And the bus already went past, so I'm afraid…"

"Maybe Patty can take me to school," I said. Anything to avoid having to stay home.

"Good idea. Why don't you call her."

Patty said she'd be more than happy to drive me to school. I waited for her with a mixture of anticipation and dread. I hated to let her know how bad things were.

"So you got your phone fixed," she greeted me, as I settled into the front seat of her car.

"Yeah."

"Heather tells me you're doing well."

"Yeah. I guess."

She turned to look at me. "So, how's it really going?" she asked.

Tears pricked my eyes. "It's a mess. Mom and Walter…" I shook my head in frustration. "They fight about everything! I think they'd kill each other if they could."

"Oh honey, I'm sorry."

"And now he's dragging me into it too," I went on. "It's crazy. I think Mom's being extra nasty to him because he's hurt and can't do anything about it."

Patty reached to adjust the heat. "What do you think about that?"

"Well, I guess I don't blame her. I mean, he deserves it. But for some stupid reason, I feel a bit bad for him too."

"Heather tells me you were able to believe God loves you."

"Yeah, I did, but now I'm not sure." I twisted my hands in my lap.

"God does love you, Tessa. It's the truth, and the truth is true whether you feel sure about it or not. When God's love gets inside of you, one of the things that happens is you start to love other people. The compassion you feel for Walter isn't stupid. It's how God feels toward him."

I turned to stare at her. "You mean to tell me God cares about him? How could he?"

Patty slowed the car as we approached the bridge into North-ford. "Suppose you had known Walter when he was a baby. Would you have hated him then?"

"Of course not. He wasn't bad then."

Patty continued. "But since then, he's grown into a very bad man. We don't see how to separate the badness from the man, but God does. He hates the badness, but he loves the man."

"But what good does it do for God to love him, when he's so evil?" I protested.

"Remember when I told you about Jesus dying on the cross?"

"Yeah, sort of." I recalled hearing something about it during one of her bedtime talks.

"Well, when Jesus died, he took on all of our evilness and got rid of it. That's why he forgives us. When we accept him – his love, his forgiveness – into our lives, spiritually we get born again. It's like starting your life all over. Your old, bad life is all gone, and in its place you have a new life that Jesus gives you."

The things she was saying felt strangely familiar. "So, maybe that's what happened to me when I believed Jesus loved me," I mused aloud.

Patty pulled over and parked in front of the school. "If you accepted his love, then you accepted him. God is love."

A tingle of excitement ran through me. "You mean . . . I'm a Christian?"

Suddenly we were both laughing. Patty reached over and gave me a hug. "You're a Christian, you're born again, whatever you want to call it. Yes."

"Cool! Wait til I tell Heather."

I felt like telling the whole world as I skipped up the sidewalk. *I'm a Christian. I really and truly belong to God!* Never in my life had I felt so much joy. Why would anyone not want to belong to God?

31

Wednesday was the first day of Christmas vacation. I would have liked to sleep in, but it was impossible with the arguing that commenced about six thirty. I felt like screaming at both my parents. *Just give it a rest! Why'd you bother getting together in the first place if you hate each other so much?*

In disgust, I pulled on my clothes and strode out to the kitchen for an early breakfast, ignoring the yelling and banging coming from Walter's corner of the living room.

Mom was at the table, spooning up a bowl of cornflakes. She was also ignoring the noise, or pretending to. Before I sat down, I reached over and flipped the radio on. While I didn't care for the mix of commercials, news tidbits, and jokes that comprised the morning show, it did help drown out the racket Walter was making.

Toward the end of breakfast, Walter's temper cooled off. He inched his wheelchair across the living room until he could see us sitting at the table. "Hey. Give me some food."

Mom went to the counter to refill her coffee mug. "No way. You're on your own. You don't want my help, remember?"

Walter cursed. "Do what I say. Get me some food."

"Listen to you begging. Come on, Walter, if you're really such a big tough guy, get it yourself. Quit sitting there like a helpless invalid."

"I said, *get me some food!*" Walter's voice shook with fury. "Don't make me have to do something to you."

"Yeah? Like what? You can't even–"

"Shut up, woman!" He bit out the words through clenched teeth.

Mom thumped her mug of coffee down hard, slopping some of the liquid. "Fine! But just so you know, you're getting nothing til you apologize to me!"

"I said shut up!" Walter hissed.

Something in me snapped. Standing up, I grabbed the radio and dashed it to the floor. A piece of plastic broke off and skidded under the refrigerator. From the speakers came a loud crackle, then silence. I ran out of the room.

"Tessa! Get back here! What's the matter with you?" Mom's voice carried down the hall after me.

What's the matter? Man, if she doesn't know by now, she's crazy. I slammed my door, shoving a book against it to make it stay shut, and threw myself onto the bed. I felt bad about wrecking the radio, but what was I supposed to do?

In the kitchen, I heard talking, then arguing. Were Mom and Walter at it again? I shoved a CD into my player and cranked up the volume until the window rattled. How I would survive eleven more days confined to this loony bin I had no clue. Maybe I should just check out. I still had the marijuana joints Lorraine had given me, hidden in my top dresser drawer. But since there were only two, I would wait until I really needed them.

My parents eventually reached some kind of truce, and things quieted down. Around noon, Mom stopped by my bedroom to tell me she needed to run over to the farm market and get some potatoes.

"I'm counting on you to keep an eye on Walter," she said. "He's in his wheelchair and he's trying to move around a bit, but I don't trust him. I set up some ironing in the kitchen, and I want you to stay out there and work on it. I shouldn't be long. Keep him away from the phone, and do not give him any alcohol or medications. Understand?"

I nodded.

"I'm gonna try to sneak out of here. Hopefully he won't know I've left."

But Walter was more perceptive than she'd judged him to be. As I walked to the kitchen a few minutes later, he called to me. "Hey Tess, where's your mom?"

I kept walking. "What do you mean?"

"Don't try that on me. I know she's gone. Listen. I want you to do a job for me tonight. We could sure use the money."

My heart rate doubled and my hands started to shake. I leaned on the kitchen counter. What could I say? If only Mom were home!

"Did you hear me, Tess?"

"I-I don't think I can do it," I stammered.

"Aww, sure you can. You're good at it. Heck, you're even better than me. Never told you that, did I? But you gotta stay in practice, or you'll get rusty."

I didn't answer. I had no intention of doing the job, but I was scared what he might do if I said no. Grabbing the iron, I tackled the pile of shirts. If I put him off long enough, Mom would come back, and that would be the end of it.

In the next room, Walter groaned and muttered as he strained to move his chair. After a short time, he appeared in the kitchen doorway. Desperation lined his face.

"Tessa, please. Just this once? We really need the money. The rent's so far behind, we could get kicked out any day. And there's nothing to eat except that stupid canned soup. Do you wanna starve?"

I hesitated. He was right about the money. Mom had cut the grocery list down to the bare necessities, and then some.

"Your mom doesn't ever have to know. She'll be so busy with me she won't even notice you left. Please, Tess, say you'll do it." Walter shifted in his chair, grimacing at the pain.

I stood silent. How could I say no with him sitting right there? Especially when he was being so polite. Maybe it would be okay. It would be scary, yes, but I could handle it. And it would help out a lot.

I nodded. "I suppose."

Walter's face broke into a sort of grin. "Thanks. You're a good partner. I knew I could count on you."

A lump filled my throat. Never in my life had Walter spoken that respectfully to me. In fact, I wasn't sure anyone had.

"Hand me the phone, and I'll set things up," he said.

"Set things up?" I felt a stab of apprehension.

"That's where the money is, kid. Don't worry, I do this all the time. Hand me the phone."

So, contrary to Mom's specific orders, I got him the phone. What else could I do? Then, like a good partner, I positioned myself at the kitchen window so I could warn him if she drove in. But I could not push away the nagging thought that I was turning into a criminal, just as Mom had predicted.

32

By the time Mom returned from the farm market with her potatoes, Walter had made half a dozen phone calls and changed my job description considerably. Not only was I supposed to return to the farmhouse the next night to finish the job – a necessity he had failed to mention in the beginning – but after that, I was expected to drive out to the dog park at the far end of town and deliver the finished product to two of his buyers. Of course, I had to bring some home for him too. I couldn't help but notice the gleam in his eyes when he said that.

I swallowed my disgust and promised I would. I had expected as much. But that part about selling it had me scared. I knew the sort of characters Walter dealt with. I was pretty sure they wouldn't hesitate to kidnap or even murder me, if it suited their interests. Having a gun in my pocket that I didn't really know how to use wouldn't make things any safer. But Walter assured me everything would go fine. I hoped he was right.

Mom did question why I hadn't finished the ironing. I told her I had a headache, an explanation she seemed to accept. It also doubled as an excuse to stay out of sight the rest of the afternoon. I knew Mom too well to take her intuitive powers lightly. But supper came and went with no sign of suspicions on her part.

Late that evening, while Mom was helping Walter in the bathroom, I slipped the ring of keys he'd given me into my pocket, pulled the biggest kitchen knife from the drawer, and stole out the back door. Walter had instructed me to take the pistol, but I didn't know where Mom had put it. The knife would have to do for tonight.

Trembling with excitement and fear, I got into the car and softly closed the door. I turned the key, holding my breath as the engine started. Was the car always this noisy? I shifted into reverse and backed down the driveway, leaving the headlights off. I didn't want to think what would happen if Mom caught me.

As I swung the car onto the road, I glanced back at the house. No lights had come on. Everything was quiet. A sudden thrill ran through me. *I finally did it! I ran off with Mom's car, and it wasn't even that hard.* I groped in the dark for the headlight switch, then hit the gas and tried to remember the things Walter had taught me about driving. *Look ahead on the curves, don't hug the center line, and don't poke along, they'll think you're drunk.*

I tried my best. But I hadn't driven for some time; and at forty-five miles an hour, with a light wind drifting loose snow across the blacktop, it took a great deal of concentration just to stay on the road. Passing the tavern at the corner of Kruger and East Bluff Road, I glimpsed a sheriff car parked at the edge of the lot. My stomach knotted. *Just what I don't need. Suppose he recognizes the car and follows me?*

I forced the thought away. No doubt he was watching for drunks. But as the road narrowed and began to wind back along the ridge, I realized I had a lot more on my mind than the fear of being stopped. Deep inside, I knew I was doing wrong. I also knew God wasn't happy about it. I dreaded what might happen if I continued on. Would he punish me? What if he let the place blow up with me in it?

As I rounded the final bend and steered the car into the narrow, snowy field lane, I broke out in a cold sweat. I hadn't been this nervous since the night Walter drove me back into the forest to punish me for running away. But I couldn't let fear stop me. Walter had already set things up. I had promised, and everyone was counting on me. I had to go through with this thing.

Or did I? Uncertain now, I shifted the car into park and switched off the lights. "God, I need help. I don't know what to do. Walter's gonna kill me if I don't go through with this."

I waited, but there was no answer. The car engine vibrated beneath me. *I might as well drive on to the farmhouse,* I thought. *If I sit here too long, I'm gonna totally freak.*

But I decided to hold out a bit longer.

"I don't wanna be a criminal, God. You know that. But I feel like I gotta do this, and in some ways, I guess I want to do it too. I want Walter to think I'm good at something."

But even as I said it, I realized the foolishness of supposing I could earn Walter's respect. It had never worked before.

I continued. "God, I'd get out of this if I could. But I can't. Walter will throw a fit and do something really mean to me."

The answer this time was clear. *No matter what Walter does, I'll be with you. It's going to be okay.* Suddenly, I could sense God's arms around me. He really was here, talking to me! The fear drained away, and I realized I didn't have to do what Walter said. I was free to make my own decision.

I backed the car onto the road and pointed it toward home. Facing Walter would be difficult, but at least I knew God would be with me.

The car clock read ten minutes past midnight when I pulled into the driveway. I parked in the usual spot, sent up a final prayer, and stole into the dark house.

Walter didn't stir as I tiptoed past him to my room. I closed my door, pulled off my wet shoes, and collapsed on the bed. I couldn't believe how exhausted I felt. But there was a sense of relief as well. I was glad I'd made the right decision.

Five minutes later, there came a sharp knock on my door. I bolted upright, nearly falling off the bed in fright. "What? Who's there?"

"I want to talk to you," said Mom.

Lightning struck my soul. *She knows.* I grabbed my pajama top and yanked it on over my sweatshirt in a frantic attempt to disguise the fact I was still dressed. Mom pushed the door and flipped on the lights. For a long moment, she stood there with folded arms and scrutinized me. I hung my head, my confidence melting like snow in a July sun.

"Where were you?"

From her tone of voice, I knew it was no use trying to lie my way out of this one.

"I . . . well, it was Walter's idea," I faltered. "I don't know what got into me. I..."

"Go on," she said. "You what?"

I wished I could drop out of sight. How would I explain this?

"I-I was on my way to do a job. Walter told me to. But I got so scared I had to turn around. I didn't even get there."

The fury on Mom's face changed to scorn. "Tessa, I honestly don't know what to do with you anymore. You're just like your father. I know a lie when I hear one."

"You gotta believe me," I pleaded. "I turned around because I knew God didn't like what I was doing. He helped me decide to turn around. I'm never going back there again, I promise."

"Yeah. I've heard that before too. If you mean it, you can start by giving me that key."

"It's Walter's. He'll be mad if I don't give it back."

Mom held out her hand. I gave her the keys, and she pocketed them. But she wasn't done with me.

"You should know I was on my way over to Ericksons' to hitch a ride out there and stop you."

Another bolt of lightning struck me. "What?"

"You really don't get it, do you." She gripped me by the shoulders and shook me. "Listen," she hissed, her breath hot on my face. "I'd rather end up in prison than see you go anywhere near that cursed stuff. Do you understand?" She shook me again, harder.

"Yeah. I-I won't do it again." Her uncharacteristic severity frightened me.

"I hope not." She gave me a final shake, then left, bumping the door shut behind her.

I cast myself onto the bed and buried my head under the blankets. *You're no Christian. You're nothing but a miserable, worthless failure. No wonder Mom doesn't believe you. Why should she?*

That night I cried myself to sleep.

33

i awoke feeling lower than I'd ever felt in my life. *I knew it was wrong to go along with Walter,* I mourned. *But for some reason, I didn't care. Why couldn't I have been born into a family like Heather's? Here I don't stand a chance.*

I wondered what Patty would think if she knew what I'd done last night. Would she still hug me and say how much God loved me? Did God still love me? Or did he only love people like Patty and Heather who had it all together?

Dragging myself out of bed, I crossed to the window and pulled up the shade. Outside it was snowing, the fine-textured, heavy kind of snow that meant it wasn't planning to stop. Maybe later I could shovel the driveway. It would give me an excuse to get out of the house.

Walter didn't look up as I walked past on my way to breakfast. But when Mom slipped down to the basement a few minutes later to wash a load of towels, he called me.

"Say, Tessa. Would you do something for me?"

I swallowed my mouthful of cereal and growled, "Why should I?"

"Hey, don't get all mad on me," he said in an injured tone. "You're the one who broke your promise."

I didn't try to answer that.

"Look, I know it was a big order. I guess I was asking too much of you. If you just get me a beer, we'll call it even, okay? We'll forget it happened."

I was disgusted with him. Was he so desperate for a drink that he'd resort to pleading like a child?

"Walter, you need Jesus, not a can of beer."

He tried to laugh. "That's so cute, Tess. Now be a sport and get me that beer. Please."

"Ask Mom." I lifted my cereal bowl to my mouth to drink the rest of the milk.

Walter slammed his fist on the end table so hard I jumped. Milk dribbled down the front of my sweatshirt.

"Who's in charge here, anyway?" he yelled. "You're not gonna get away with treating me like this. I'll see to that!"

I shoved back my chair. "You know what? You're not in charge." I grabbed my dishes and carried them over to the sink. I was shaking, but inside I felt good. For the first time ever, I had stood up to him. I didn't care that he was calling me every dirty name he could invent.

The snow let up mid-afternoon. I put on my coat and boots and went outside to shovel. As I worked, scooping and throwing in rhythm, I began to relax for the first time in days. Except for a family of crows in the pine tree and the occasional car on the road, the world around me was silent and incredibly beautiful. If only I didn't have to go back inside when I was done.

I stopped to rest before tackling the last ten feet of the driveway. Here the snow lay deeper and heavier because of the plows. As I stood leaning on my shovel, a red SUV slowed and then stopped in front of the driveway. Tom rolled down the window. "Hey, you need some help?"

"Sure."

"Got an extra shovel?"

"Yeah, up at the house. I'll get it."

By the time I returned with the second shovel, Tom had cut a path through to the road. "You start on this side, and I'll work in from the road," he said.

In about fifteen minutes, the shoveling was done.

"Thanks," I said.

"Not a problem. I can use the exercise. So, how's Walter doing?"

"He's horrible."

Tom laughed at my matter-of-fact tone. "Okay. How's Tessa doing putting up with him?"

"I wish I didn't have to be here."

"I see." His face grew serious. "You're welcome to come over, you know, if your mom is okay with it. Maybe you could even go to the Christmas Eve service with us tomorrow night."

I shook my head. "I'd be crazy to even ask. She doesn't trust me out of her sight."

"Do you have a radio?"

"Sure, why?"

"Because there's this program I think you'd like. Here, I'll write it down for you." Tom pulled a pen from his pocket and scribbled something on a scrap of paper, then handed it to me. "It'll be on in about ten minutes. Check it out."

I promised I would, even though I knew I wouldn't. If I could judge from the week I'd spent at their house, Tom's music tastes were outdated by at least fifty years.

Back in my bedroom, though, curiosity got the better of me. I pulled the crumpled paper from my pocket. "Set Free, 92.5 FM," I read. "Weekdays at 4:30. Oh, what the heck. I can always turn it off."

I set the radio on my bed, adjusted the antenna, and tuned in. After a brief commercial, the program announcer came on.

"How do you do, friends? Few people set out to ruin their life on purpose. Often it happens through a series of small and seemingly unimportant decisions, decisions that once made are difficult to reverse. The man in our story learned this the hard way. He thought he was stuck with the mess he'd created, until the day the grace of God set him free."

Intrigued, I turned up the volume and listened as the dramatized story unfolded – the story of a young man who, although raised in a Christian family, turned his back on God at the age of sixteen and began using alcohol and heroin to cope with his heartache over his father's death. After two failed marriages, three treatment programs, and innumerable stints in jail, he concluded suicide was the only way out of his terrible addiction.

That night, as he was on his way to jump off a bridge and end his life, he stumbled into a rescue mission and heard about Jesus. He got down on his knees in front of everyone and gave his life to God. From that night on, he was a changed man. He reconnected with his family, attended a Bible college, and dedicated the rest of his life to helping other men like himself.

When the story ended, I sat deep in thought. Although my circumstances differed, I could relate to the story. I too felt stuck in a situation from which there was no escape. Time and again I had tried to escape, only to find I couldn't. I had even wondered whether suicide might be an answer. The main difference was that, for the man in the story, things had straightened out when he became a Christian. For me, they hadn't. Not yet, anyway.

***

Supper that evening consisted of cabbage and potatoes boiled with ham to make a chunky soup. I didn't like it, but at least it was warm and nourishing. Clearly we were not about to starve, regardless of what Walter said.

After the meal, Mom went to help Walter into his wheelchair. I was clearing the table when I heard the unmistakable sound of the front door being opened. I assumed Mom was doing it, until I heard her agonized yell. "Hey! You can't come in here!"

A commotion followed. Hurrying around the corner, I saw a large bearded man in a dark jacket and orange stocking cap. I recognized him as one of the guys Walter hung out with at the tavern. He pushed his way past Mom and plopped down on the couch beside Walter's chair.

"Hey buddy, how's it going?" he said.

"What are you doing in my living room?" Mom demanded, her hands on her hips.

Walter waved his hand as if to dismiss her, but the stranger flashed her a smile. "Hey, little lady, get me a beer. We're gonna be a while."

"Make that two," Walter said.

Mom's face turned a deep scarlet. She opened her mouth as if to say something, but then shut it again. She wheeled and headed for the kitchen, leaving both men hooting.

"Good girl," Walter yelled after her. "That's the way you do it!"

Mom marched straight to the corner cupboard, pulled the pistol from underneath a stack of tablecloths, and began to load it.

Fear clawed at my heart. "Mom, don't!" I grabbed her sleeve. "What're you doing!"

She gave me a shove. "Get outta here."

I watched in horror as she finished loading the pistol and pulled back the slide. How could I just stand here, when she was going to kill somebody?

I grabbed at the gun. She yanked it away from me, then swung hard, slamming me over the head with it. I cried out and staggered backwards against the pantry door, my hands pressed to a rapidly forming lump on the side of my head. There wasn't any blood, at least not yet, but it hurt like she'd cracked my skull. I slipped down the front of the pantry to the floor, still cradling my head.

Through the blur of pain, I heard Mom walk into the living room. "You! Get out of here!" she ordered.

"Hey! What're you doing with my gun?" Walter demanded.

The man tried to laugh her off. "Ah, lady, you wouldn't shoot a nice guy like me, now would you?"

"I certainly will. Get out – now!"

"Hey, stop pointing that gun at people. Somebody might get hurt."

"Get moving. You have fifteen seconds. Fourteen . . . thirteen . . ."

"Stop it!" Walter screamed. "Charlie, wait . . ."

Charlie didn't wait. I heard scuffling noises, then the screen door banged.

"Don't you ever come back!" Mom yelled after him.

"You rat!" Walter's voice was strangled with fury. "I'm gonna kill you!"

"That'll be hard to do, being as I'm the one with the gun."

"How dare you touch my gun! You just wait til–"

Mom interrupted him. "Don't you ever let me find that door unlocked again."

There was still no blood coming from my wounded head. I rose and stumbled to my room, where I curled up on the bed in the dark and fumed at Mom.

She had no cause to hit me like that! I was trying to keep her from killing the guy. What was I supposed to do? The pain in my heart kept getting worse. I wanted to scream and beat my fists on the mattress, but my head hurt too much. *Mom, I hate you,* I thought. Then aloud, I repeated it. "I hate you!" Deep sobs shook me. Wasn't there anyone I could trust not to hurt me?

"Please, God," I sobbed. "I've had it. I can't stand this anymore. Please let me go back to Heather's!"

It must have been two hours later when I heard a soft knock at my door. I had stopped crying, and the pain in my head and heart had numbed to a dull, hopeless ache.

The knock came again. "Can I come in?" Mom asked, nudging the door open. Yellow light spilled into my room from the hallway. Mom stood near the partly open door, toying with her hair.

"I'm really sorry," she said. "I wasn't thinking. You were afraid I was gonna shoot somebody, and I guess I can't blame you. Are you okay?" She moved closer to the bed.

I didn't reply. Why did she always ask that dumb question? Of course I wasn't okay.

Mom sat down on the edge of the bed. "Tessa, I'm so sorry. Nobody should have to live in a family like this."

"Can't I go back to Heather's? Please?"

"Oh Tess, I wish you could. But I need you here. There's no way I can watch Walter by myself. He's getting worse by the day."

"Why do you even bother with him? He'll probably pay you back with a gun in your face the day he's well."

"Don't be dramatic, Tess. Somebody's got to look after him. He's in a lot of pain. I'm sure he'll settle down once he feels better."

"Yeah right." I turned away. How could she be so blind?

Mom stood up. "So are you gonna be okay? Do you need anything?"

"Just leave me alone."

"How about some aspirins for your head?"

"I can get 'em myself."

"Okay. Well, goodnight." She left the room.

Moving slowly so as not to worsen my headache, I reached down and pulled a half-empty bottle of Nyquil from under the bed. I took a good swig and lay back on the pillow. Gingerly I ran a hand over the painful lump on the side of my head. At least it wasn't getting bigger. I hoped that was a good sign.

34

When I awoke in the morning, my headache was almost gone. To my relief, the lump on my head seemed smaller as well. Although Mom didn't ask how I felt, I could tell she was relieved to see me up and walking around. She even made me pancakes and scrambled eggs for breakfast.

"What's the occasion?" I asked, as I sat down and forked two pancakes onto my plate.

"It's Christmas Eve, silly." Mom passed me a bottle of syrup. "Don't tell me you didn't know that."

I shrugged. "I haven't paid much attention. What's the point, if you're not gonna celebrate anyway?"

"Who said we're not gonna celebrate Christmas?"

I laid down my fork and looked at her. "Really, Mom. I'm not a little kid. You don't have to sugarcoat things for me."

"Okay, then I won't. I made the pancakes because we're out of bread. I really need to run into town and get some, but I don't trust either of you enough to leave."

"Great. I guess we'll starve then." I slathered the hot pancakes with butter, then added just enough syrup to make them sweet but not soggy.

"Actually, I've half a mind to ask Ericksons to stop over for an hour and keep an eye on you guys."

"Mom, seriously. I'll behave, okay? How many times do I have to tell you that?"

She raised her eyebrows and continued eating. I knew she had good reason for not trusting me, but still, it stung. Too bad Walter hadn't overheard the proposal. He'd make a proper fuss about it. But he was sitting in the easy chair with his leg propped up, picking at his food while he watched the morning news.

Finishing off my pancakes, I retreated to my bedroom. I couldn't stop Mom from calling Tom and Patty, but I could hide out in here the whole time and pretend I wasn't home. I was way too old to have the neighbors coming over to look after me.

I should've known Mom would spoil my plans. She stopped by my room a short time later to tell me the dishes needed washing.

"That's not my problem," I retorted.

"Now, Tessa."

"Okay! Just give me a minute."

I had barely started the dishes when the red SUV pulled in. Glancing around for Mom, my eye fell on the pistol lying next to the microwave. What would Tom and Patty think? I quickly shoved it into the corner and tossed a dish towel over it.

Mom let Tom and Patty in the kitchen door and took them straight to the living room. She clicked off the TV and said, "Walter, you've got visitors."

"Get them outta here!" Walter bellowed. "I don't want no visitors!"

"You did last night."

Walter swore. "I said, get them outta here! And be quick about it!"

"Just make yourselves comfortable," Mom told them. "There's coffee in the kitchen."

"Julie!" Walter yelled. "What did I tell you about people in the house! You're gonna pay for this! Now get them outta here before I do it myself!"

"Forget it," she yelled back. "You're nothing but a brat. I can't trust you, so I got you some babysitters. You better get used to it."

"Shut up!" he screamed, adding a string of curse words.

Mom didn't stay to listen to him. She grabbed her purse off the kitchen table and left, slamming the door behind her.

In her absence, Walter turned his sights on Tom and Patty. "All right, you two. Get out of my house right now, or I'm having you arrested."

"Sorry, but we're staying." Tom's quiet voice carried a surprising amount of authority.

"No you're not. Tessa!" he yelled. "Where's my gun?"

I covered my mouth to keep from laughing out loud. Did he really expect me to bring his gun? Not that I could do it anyway. I was pretty sure Tom would intercept the thing long before it reached Walter's hands.

In the living room, someone switched on the TV. Patty started coughing. Then she came out to the kitchen. "Hi, honey. How's it going?"

"It's going."

"Is he always like this?"

"Yeah, more or less. Since he got hurt."

"That's too bad. You want to finish washing these dishes, I'll dry them for you." She reached for the dish towel in the corner.

"Wait..."

My warning came too late. Patty jumped as if she'd uncovered a huge spider. "Oh!"

"Sorry." I grabbed the gun and shoved it on top of the refrigerator. "That was ... ah ... not supposed to happen." I laughed nervously. "Mom had it out last night and forgot to put it away."

Patty nodded. "Okay. Any other land mines I need to know about?"

"I don't think so."

With Patty's help, the dishes were cleaned up in about fifteen minutes. Patty poured herself a cup of coffee, and we sat at the table, talking some, but mostly listening to the conversation in the next room. How Tom had managed to get Walter talking I could not guess.

"Don't you ever wish you were a good person?" Tom was asking him.

"A what?" Walter choked. "Of course not. Is that why she dragged you in here? So you can reform me? Well, forget it. I like the things I do. If I didn't, I wouldn't do them in the first place."

"So you like yourself the way you are? You're happy and content with how your life's going?"

"Yeah. Sure. Couldn't be better."

"You could've fooled me. You look miserable."

"Look, Mister Know-It-All. If you was stuck here with a bunch of broken bones and that stupid woman driving you crazy all day long, you'd be miserable yourself. But she's gonna pay for it."

"That's not what I was talking about. When you've got your freedom and you can do whatever you want, it's easier to cover up what you don't like about yourself. But it's still there, isn't it."

"Leave me alone! My life was fine until that stupid accident."

"What if you knew God could change your heart and make you good?"

"Don't you talk to me about God. He hates me."

"No. If God hated you, he sure could've let you get killed in that accident. God cares about everybody, even real bad people."

"That's the stupidest thing I ever heard. God cares about people who care about him. Which I don't."

"Walter, that's not true. Jesus hung out with bad people all the time because he cared and wanted to help them. He even picked some of them to be his disciples."

"You really believe all that stuff?" Walter tried to laugh, but his throat was tight with anger. It came out more like a cough.

"Have you ever read the Bible for yourself?" Tom asked.

"No! I don't wanna, either."

"Walter, God loves you so much that he sent his Son to die for you. He wants you to repent and believe the good news."

"What?"

"To repent means you feel so bad about the wrong things you've done that you're willing to give them up. It also means you're willing to give your life to God, which is the only way you can stop doing what's wrong."

"I said, leave me alone! Can't you hear me? I don't wanna talk religion! So beat it!"

Tom waited until Walter's wrath was spent. Then he said, "Do you know what will happen to you if you don't repent?"

There was a long silence. "'Course I know," Walter muttered. "You don't hafta tell me. I'll sink straight down to hell, and everybody will say good riddance."

"That's a very honest statement you just made," Tom said. "Are you content with that kind of future?"

Walter swore. "There's no way out. I've got to take it."

"You don't have to take it if you'll repent and believe in Jesus."

"I said, I don't wanna."

"All right. I'm not going to try to make you. But if you ask him, God can make you want to do it. It's entirely your choice: death or life."

Walter was silent for a very long time. When he spoke, his voice was so low I had to slip over to the doorway to hear him. Patty followed a step behind me.

"I had a dream the other night," he was saying. "It was horrible. I was being dragged toward hell, and I couldn't stop. I begged and begged to stop, but I just kept going toward that awful blackness. Finally I stopped, right there on the edge."

He paused, breathing heavily.

"It was Judgment Day, and I knew I deserved to go to hell. It was terrifying, no way to describe it. If Julie would forgive me, I could go to heaven, but I didn't think she would. I've never been so scared in my life. All of a sudden I knew I was gonna be forgiven, and I was so happy I started laughing and crying. But then it hit me that I didn't belong in heaven. It would never work. I cried out and said, 'God, give me another chance!'

"Believe me, it was real. I can't say how terrible it was, knowing God was gonna throw me in hell forever, and there was no second chance. But if that wasn't bad enough, I had the whole cursed dream over again last night. Only this time, as I was waking up, something said to me, 'If you don't turn today, it will be too late.'"

Walter's voice trembled. "What do I do?"

35

I listened in stunned disbelief as Walter followed Tom in a simple prayer, asking Jesus to forgive his sins and come into his heart and life. Patty threw her arms around me and cried. It was an emotional moment for me also, although I didn't know whether to be joyful or indignant. How could God even think of forgiving someone like Walter? Shouldn't he have to pay for the evil things he'd done?

Walter finished praying. "Something happened," he said, his voice full of wonder. "I-I don't know how you say it." Then he began to laugh. But it wasn't the old sneering laugh I so despised. It was so happy and genuine that Tom joined in. Patty pulled me around the corner into the room and joined in too.

I hung back and stared at Walter. Was this for real? Was he really a changed man? He certainly looked the part as he sat with tears streaming down his face, laughing for joy.

Behind me, the back door opened, and I heard a rustle of plastic shopping bags as Mom hurried into the kitchen.

"Tessa?" She got as far as the doorway and stopped dead. Her mouth fell open as she stared at Walter.

He grinned back at her. "I let Jesus come into my heart," he said. "Julie, it's awesome. You gotta do it too."

Mom looked from Walter to Tom. "Did you give him some kind of drug?"

"No, ma'am. Just preached the gospel to him."

"Well, that's fine. Just don't turn him into a fanatic like yourselves."

"It's too late," Walter said. "You can't go halfway with something like this."

A worried expression crossed Mom's face. She turned back to Tom. "Well, I'm back, so I guess you guys can leave now."

Tom nodded. "Just give us a couple more minutes, okay?"

"Yeah," Walter chimed in. "Don't throw my new friends out already."

Mom threw up her hands in mock dismay. "Okay, you win. I've got to get my groceries put away." She turned back to the kitchen. I followed.

"So, how'd this happen?" she asked in a low voice.

I shrugged. "Tom got him talking and asked if he was happy with his life. Walter was pretty mad and yelled at him to shut up, but eventually he gave in and prayed with him."

"Wow. I never would've guessed it." Then she looked hard at me. "You're a Christian too, aren't you."

I nodded. Was she accusing me of it, or simply asking a question?

"I kind of thought so." She paused. "You know, I prayed the sinner's prayer myself once."

"The sinner's prayer?"

"Yeah. You know, when you ask Jesus to come into your heart and all that." Her face flushed, as if she was ashamed to talk about it. "I was six years old. I had pneumonia real bad, and Dad thought I was gonna die. He told me I had to get saved or I'd go to hell."

"Oh."

"So, I prayed the prayer. Don't think it did me much good, though." A cynical smile crossed her lips. Then she shrugged. "But hey, if it works for you, great." She lugged a grocery bag over to the pantry and began stacking cans of soup on the shelf.

I wished I could say something to change her attitude about it. But I didn't want to start an argument. I was afraid she'd try to talk me out of what I believed. It would be better to let the subject drop.

I turned to leave the kitchen, then remembered something. "Say, do you think I could go to a Christmas Eve service with Tom and Patty? They'd give me a ride and everything."

"That's tonight?"

"Yeah. Seven o'clock."

"Fine. I don't see any harm in that. But don't be gone late."

It was all I could do to keep from jumping up and down. She'd said yes to something! Before Patty left, I told her the good news. She pulled me close and gave me another hug, then promised they'd pick me up around six thirty.

The afternoon passed in a strange blur. Walter kept telling Mom about Jesus, and he even tried to preach to me. Mom alternated between playing along and totally ignoring him. I avoided him as much as possible. As remarkable as the change in him was, inside I was still bitter and afraid of him. I didn't trust him. I doubted I ever would.

***

The church was already packed when we arrived for the service that evening. I sat between Heather and Patty in the fourth pew from the front, clutching an unlit stub of a candle and listening as a group of grade school kids took turns reading the Christmas story from the Bible. The beauty of the story gripped my heart. I'd never heard it before.

When the reading ended, the organ began to play, and everyone stood up to sing. I tried to follow along with the words projected on the screen, enjoying the rich sounds of the organ and the blended voices.

After three or four songs, the lights dimmed way down, and a curtain up front parted to reveal a live manger scene. Around me, candles flickered to life one by one. Heather lit hers, then touched the flame to mine. Everyone sang "Away in a Manger" as a procession of children portraying the shepherds and the three wise men joined the manger scene.

I glanced around the darkened room at the hundred or more tiny flames, each one illuminating a face. The scene was lovely and strangely moving. I blinked back tears as we sang the final carol.

"How'd you like it?" Heather asked, as we waited for her grandparents by the coat rack afterwards.

"It was awesome, especially the manger scene. I'm glad I got to come." I took my coat from its hanger and thrust my arms into the sleeves. Then I glanced back to see whether Tom and Patty were coming, and my heart stopped.

No. It can't be. There, stylishly dressed in a maroon sweater, scarf, and short black skirt, stood Pat, the police officer. She was talking to Patty.

"It's okay," Heather said, following my gaze. "Pat's a good friend of ours."

"Oh great." I turned my back and concentrated on zipping up my coat. I hoped they weren't talking about me. I didn't want Patty to know I'd been arrested. But when I dared to glance behind me again, Patty was hugging a frail, white-haired lady in a purple dress. Pat had disappeared. I breathed a sigh of relief.

"Let's drive around and see some Christmas lights before we go home," Heather suggested as the four of us stepped out into the slushy parking lot a few minutes later. "We haven't done that yet."

"Do you think your mom would mind?" Tom asked me.

"She won't know. She'll figure I'm still at church."

"I'm sure you're right. But if she did find out, would she care?"

I was silent. Why did he have to be so particular about everything?

"She might," I muttered. "How do I know?" I followed Heather into the back of the SUV and slammed the door.

"I know what," Tom said, as he started the engine. "We'll drive up through town and go home the back way. I think there are some good displays along Washington."

"Sounds good," Patty said. "I'm really tired."

The light displays were only mediocre, but it was still more Christmas lights than I'd seen all season. I arrived home in a buoyant mood.

I found my parents sitting together in the living room – him watching TV, her reading a magazine. It had been months since I'd seen them getting along this well. With a prayer of thanks, I slipped away to my bedroom, fearful lest my presence upset the fragile peace.

36

i awoke Christmas morning with a happy heart. The house was quiet. *Today is going to be a fantastic day,* I thought. It didn't even matter if there were no gifts. The peace wrought by the change in Walter was more precious than any gift.

I reached for the Bible Heather had given me and paged through it until I found the book of Luke. It would be fun to read the Christmas story for myself. I began reading, then stopped short.

Read it to Walter. The thought was so clear it was almost audible. I knew it was God. Although it was the last thing in the world I wanted to do, I pulled on a pair of jeans and a sweatshirt and tiptoed out to see whether Walter was awake.

"Hi," I ventured.

He yawned. "Good morning!" He still looked happy.

"Uh, it's Christmas, and I thought maybe you'd like to hear the Christmas story," I blurted.

I hoped he'd say no. But his eyes brightened even more. "That'd be great."

Sweat trickled down my back as I returned to my room to get my Bible. My hands shook. What had I just offered to do? I stripped off my sweatshirt, but still I was sweating.

I can't do this, God. I just can't. I don't even want to be in the same room with him. You're really gonna have to help me.

I forced myself to walk out to the living room. I sat down at the far end of the couch and, fixing my eyes on the page, began to read in the second chapter of Luke. As I read, some of the nervousness faded. My voice grew stronger.

Partway through the reading, I heard Mom's bedroom door creak open. Moments later she walked into the room, tugging a bathrobe around her. I paused, half expecting her to scold me.

"Go on," she said. "It's been a long time since I heard that." She lingered in the doorway to hear the rest of the story, then withdrew to the bedroom again.

Walter sat quietly while I read the remainder of the chapter to myself. At length he spoke.

"That was real nice. There's something I gotta say though." He cleared his throat. "I wanna ask you to forgive me. I've treated you bad and caused you a lot of pain. I feel terrible about it all, especially . . . that one night. . ." He broke down and couldn't finish.

I sat with my head bowed. How could I forgive him! I could not. But as I listened to his sobs of genuine remorse, the resentment in my heart began to break up like ice on a river. It wasn't that he hadn't hurt me. And I certainly wasn't ready to trust him. But somewhere inside me, I felt a glimmer of forgiveness. It could only have come from God.

"I forgive you," I whispered. And then I started to cry too.

"How could you!" he sobbed. "Tess, I never saw before how rotten I really was. There's one thing I have to tell you. I really meant to kill you that night, but . . . somehow I couldn't. Are you sure you really forgive me?"

I nodded and said, "I guess so. I don't know why." Then I closed my Bible and returned to my room, where I broke down crying all over again.

By and by I heard Mom come out of her bedroom and head down the hall. "Well, do you want to get up today?" she greeted Walter.

"I sure do," he replied. "Julie, I feel so good today. Like I'm really alive for the first time in my life!"

"That's nice. Feeling good doesn't pay the bills, though."

"I know. But it does mean we don't have to spend all that money on beer and cigarettes."

"Huh?"

"Yeah. I woke up this morning, and I was so happy. I don't need any of that stuff. I don't even want it."

"Well, that's great. But you can speak for yourself. I have no intention of quitting."

"I haven't said anything about you, have I?"

"You're being very nice, so far. I hope it lasts. Now let's get you into your chair."

Listening, I marveled at the confidence Walter already had in his new life. Maybe he really had changed, like the man in the radio drama. If he didn't want to drink or smoke anymore, did I dare to hope he wouldn't cook meth either?

At breakfast, Mom presented each of us with a small, neatly wrapped package. "It's not much," she said.

I tore the paper off mine, uncovering a Christmas album of Alan Jackson. "Hey, thanks. I've been wanting this one," I said.

Mom nodded. "I thought I remembered you liked Alan Jackson."

Walter worked away at his gift with his one good hand and soon drew forth a bag of roasted peanuts and a Snickers bar.

"You can chew on that instead of yelling at me now," Mom said.

Walter smiled. "Thank you, Julie. I wish I could've gotten you something."

"You can," she said, with a hint of a sparkle in her eyes. "Keep being nice like you are right now."

The remainder of the day passed pleasantly. Mom made potato soup and buttered toast for dinner. I played my new CD through twice. Walter said little, but he radiated a thankfulness and joy which lightened the atmosphere of the whole house. Mom kept gazing at him in bewilderment, and whenever he caught her doing so, he'd smile at her.

After dinner, Mom helped me mix up a batch of sugar cookies. I spent several hours cutting them out and decorating the various shapes with bright frostings and colored sugar. *This is how Christmas is supposed to be,* I mused. *Lois and Sandy, with all their gadgets and fancy presents, have nothing on me this year.*

As I worked, I hummed songs from my new CD as well as a few carols I remembered from the service the night before. I'd enjoyed the service so much. Too bad I couldn't go again tomorrow morning. Or could I? When Mom stopped by to check on my progress and eat a cookie, I presented my request.

"Say Mom, do you think I could go to church tomorrow? I know Ericksons wouldn't mind taking me."

"Why…" She gazed at me in surprise. "You're gonna start going to church now?"

"Only if you don't mind." I picked up a teddy bear shaped cookie and spread yellow frosting on it. "I wanna try it."

"All right. I'm sure Walter won't care. But if you leave early, you have to make your own breakfast."

"That's okay."

It wasn't until after I'd made arrangements with Patty that I remembered the possibility of running into Pat. That could ruin everything. As I decorated the last cookies, I prayed she wouldn't be there.

37

I kept a sharp eye out for Pat as we walked into church the next morning, but I didn't see her. I attended Sunday school with Heather, where we watched a short video with the other young people. Afterwards, Heather made a few introductions, and then the two of us stood around nibbling doughnuts and watching people until it was time for the service.

I was enjoying myself until we walked into the sanctuary. There was Pat, sitting with some other women on the far right side of the room. Today she wore hoop earrings and a flashy black and gold blouse with butterfly sleeves. How had I missed her coming in?

I did my best to forget about her as the service began. I listened as the pastor read from the Bible and talked about the importance of treating God with reverence. I partook of communion and passed the collection plate. And I did my best to follow along with the songs, none of which I knew. But a gnawing uneasiness in the pit of my stomach kept me from relaxing and enjoying the time.

As we walked out of the sanctuary, I tugged Patty's sleeve. "I'll go wait for you guys in the car."

A look of surprise crossed her face. "Why? Don't you want to stay and meet some more people?"

"She's afraid of Pat," Heather cut in.

I jabbed her with my elbow and said, "I am not."

Heather gave me a look and then sauntered over to the counter to eat the last doughnut.

Patty glanced across the crowded room to where Pat stood, deep in conversation with a group of ladies. "What have you got against Pat?"

"She . . . well, she's a cop." I felt my face flush. How could I admit to the embarrassing circumstances under which I'd first met Pat, or explain the nervous fear and hate that rose up in me every time I saw her?

Patty steered me into an empty Sunday school room. "Now look, Pat is just an ordinary woman who happens to have a job as a cop. She won't bother you, I promise. You need to get over your anxiety about her."

"What do you know about it?" I muttered.

"You're pretty mad at her, aren't you? How come?"

"Will you quit bugging me? You're as bad as her. You won't keep your nose out of everybody else's business!"

"Tessa," Patty reproved me, "you must get to the bottom of this. Grudges will hurt you." She turned and walked out of the room.

Get to the bottom of this? What's that supposed to mean? I plunked down in a folding chair and rested my chin on my fist. *I'm never gonna make up with her, if that's what you want. She's so disgusting, so annoying, oh, I don't know. I can't stand her.* I chewed harshly at my fingernails as my thoughts ran on.

She had no right to scold me that night. I had to get food or I'd starve. Anybody can see that. Shame swept me again as I recalled the events of that night, and the reprimand Pat had given me.

"Stealing is wrong, Tessa," she'd said, with a look that would make a stone hang its head. I winced at the memory.

But what if Pat was right? Tom and Patty would surely agree with her. So would Mom, I realized. With a growing sense of guilt, I began to recall all the things I'd stolen in my life. Small things, like the dessert from another kid's lunchbox in elementary school, a candy bar slipped into my pocket during a grocery trip, a card of stickers from Mom's dresser drawer. Money, stolen a few dollars at a time from Mom's purse. A necklace of glass beads, taken from a girl in third grade. Cigarettes. Two CDs I'd smuggled out of the department store. The list was endless. Overwhelmed, I bowed my head.

"Okay, God," I whispered, as the tears trickled down my cheeks. "I guess Pat was right. I'm sorry. I was wrong to steal that food, and all the other stuff, and . . . and I accept the scolding she gave me. I still don't like it, but I guess I needed it. I don't wanna be a thief."

When I had finished, I felt better – more secure and less ashamed of myself. Though still unpleasant, the memory of my arrest and Pat's scolding no longer filled me with rage.

"Tessa, it's time to go," Patty called from the doorway.

I stood up. "Okay. Hey, I'm awful sorry for talking to you like I did."

"All right." She smiled. "How are you coming on your problem with Pat?"

"I still don't like her, but I guess I don't hate her anymore."

"That sounds better," Patty said with relief, as we walked out together into the nearly deserted hallway.

38

i returned to school on the third of January, this time riding the bus with Heather. Thanks to the relative quiet at my house, I'd made significant progress catching up with my schoolwork during the vacation. But I quickly discovered I had made no progress at all in some other important areas.

Lois greeted me with her infamous question. "Well, what did you get for Christmas?"

"A CD I've been wanting. How about you?"

Behind me, Sandy groaned. "Still no cell phone?"

Lois's plump face twisted in disgust. "Come on, that's just pathetic. What are you, Amish? You should see what my dad got me." She pulled a pink tablet computer from her knapsack and held it up.

"Hey, that's a nice one," said Sandy.

"Don't drop it," I said, squelching the impulse to knock it out of her hand.

"But that's just the teaser." She grinned as she tucked the item back into her knapsack. "I also got two all-expenses-paid, round-trip tickets, to . . . well, you guess."

"Disneyland?" Sandy proposed.

Lois shook her head. Her eyes danced with glee.

I swallowed hard and said, "Mall of America." Lois loved to shop. But she again shook her head.

"It's tropical, sand and seashells, palm trees waving in the breeze..."

"You're kidding," Sandy said.

"Am not." Lois pulled out a glossy travel brochure with *Jamaica* printed in a fancy script at the top.

"Wow! I don't believe it. Do you know somebody there?" Sandy asked.

"Not exactly." Lois grinned again. "But I hear those Caribbean boys are really cute."

Sandy laughed and made a couple of crude comments. I saw my chance and headed down toward my locker. My mind churned. *Why does Lois have to boast until she makes everybody jealous? Even if I had gotten a cell phone, you can bet she'd tell me it wasn't as good as hers. I am so sick of that girl!*

At lunch that day, I stepped in line just ahead of Lorraine and Brittney.

"Where's Crystal?" I asked over my shoulder.

Lorraine just shrugged. "Who knows. She probably ran away again. Can't say I blame her."

"That's too bad." Lorraine had told me Crystal was staying with a foster family, but what had led up to that, I could only guess. Had she been in a situation like mine? I decided to change the subject.

"So did you get something nice for Christmas?"

Lorraine flipped back a lock of long black hair so she could see me better. "Don't know. What'd you get?"

"Just a CD."

She appeared relieved. "Well, I got this hoodie. Pretty, ain't it?"

"I love it," I told her, even though the image on the front of the thin black garment portrayed a vampire with blood dripping off his fangs.

"And a new video game," she added. "You should come over sometime, Tess. I'd love to get to know you better."

"Hey, I'd like that," I said, though I had no idea how I'd really get there. "Maybe some evening?"

Lorraine assumed a thoughtful expression as she chipped black nail polish off one of her fingernails. "Sunday," she finally said. "That would be the best day. Britt can come over too, and we'll have the place to ourselves."

"Yeah right," piped up Brittney. "Last I heard, Tess is permanently grounded. Aren't you, Tess?"

Permanently grounded? I did a double take. Did Brittney somehow know about my midnight trip to the farmhouse? No, that was impossible. She must have overheard something I'd told one of the other girls.

Lorraine was staring at me. "Good grief, Tess, what'd you do?"

"Nothing," I declared. "It's just that my mom can be really unreasonable." I stepped forward and took a tray, then a foam plate and a napkin.

Lorraine nodded as if she understood perfectly. "Well, I'll call you sometime, and we can talk awhile."

"Thanks." I picked up a roast beef sandwich. "But I don't have a phone, so..."

Lorraine laughed. "Don't worry. Man has lived millions of years without those stupid toys. But don't tell anyone I said that. Most of these kids think their life has ended if their iPod falls in the toilet."

All three of us laughed. Inside I felt warm. Lorraine accepted me. It didn't matter what I had or what I could do. It would be fun to get to know her better.

"Gonna sit with us?" Lorraine asked me.

"I, uh..." I scanned the crowded cafeteria until I spotted Janet and Heather sitting at Lois's table. "I'd like to, but I really need to talk to Lois about something."

"Hypocrite," Lorraine teased.

"Hey, I just wanna hear the rest of the story she was telling this morning. Maybe another day." I hurried across the room toward the one empty chair left at their table.

Lois reached over and clamped a hand on the chair before I could pull it out. "What's up with you and Lorraine?" she demanded. "Everybody knows she's a pothead, and there's rumors she's into the hard stuff too."

"So what! We were just talking."

Lois rolled her eyes, but released the chair. "Like old friends," she added. "I hear Crystal's in the hospital. Bet she didn't tell you that."

"What's wrong with Crystal?" I asked, curious, even though I didn't want to feed this conversation.

"She overdosed."

My blood ran cold. "You're kidding. What on?"

"Meth and alcohol." Lois shrugged now. "At least that's the rumor. They say she could've died."

I felt like somebody had slugged me in the stomach. Was it some of Walter's meth? Had I helped make it? No, that was impossible. It was all just a rumor.

"How do you know all this?" I asked, struggling to keep my voice steady.

"My aunt works with her foster mom at the hospital. They're pretty good friends."

"Oh." My stomach was still churning. "So is she gonna be okay?"

"I guess so, this time anyway, but they say she really needs to get some help."

"Well, I hope she does then."

The conversation turned to other subjects after that. I was relieved. But on the bus on the way home, after most of the other kids had been dropped off, Heather broached the question again.

"So tell me, are you and Lorraine really friends?"

I shrugged. "Like I said, we were just talking. Got a problem with that?"

"Not really. It's just . . . if you're gonna hang with kids like that, you better have standards. Do you?"

The question irritated me. "Look. I know a lot more about this stuff than you ever will. So get off my back."

Heather studied me, her brows knit. "What are you saying?"

Shame hit me. What *had* I just said? A simple denial wasn't going to get me out of this one.

"Well, I just meant, it's not the kind of thing they teach you about in Sunday school, where you seem to have spent most of your life."

Her face flushed. "Will you quit labeling me as the good little church girl? I've been around a lot more than you think."

The bus screeched to a halt in front of my driveway. I stood up and grabbed my knapsack. "Yeah? Well you haven't seen anything yet," I tossed over my shoulder as I stepped off the bus.

I got the mail, then trudged up the driveway to the house. Tomorrow I'd apologize to Heather and tell her I didn't mean to pick on her. But really, what right did she have to lecture me on my choice of friends? Not that anything significant was likely to happen between me and Lorraine anyway. I dreaded the teasing I'd face if I publicly befriended her. But she was fun to talk with on occasion, and I was quite sure she didn't use meth.

39

ife settled into a routine over the next few weeks. Mom took a job with a cleaning company, working afternoons five days a week. Sometimes she worked until six o'clock or later. When I got home from school, there'd be a casserole in the refrigerator with a note directing me to put it in the oven for a certain length of time. I'd follow the instructions, and by the time Mom came home, I'd have the food hot and the table set. Often I had part of my homework done as well. It would have been an ideal setup, except that Mom usually returned in a foul mood.

"I go out and work all day, and what do you do? Sit there," she'd fume at Walter. "And then I come home and you expect me to do your laundry and make you supper and take care of you. I don't know why I put up with you all these years."

"When I can work again, I sure will," he'd say. "But it'd be stupid for me to even try right now."

"Yeah, I bet you will." And then she'd remind him of the unfinished furniture in his shop, the customers he'd cheated, the mounting medical bills, his newest court summons, and a dozen other embarrassing things. Before long, Walter would start yelling back. I spent many evenings in my bedroom with the door closed, just to maintain my sanity.

Despite the unpleasant arguing, though, I thought Walter was doing well. Every day he pestered me to read to him from the Bible, and when I returned from church on Sundays, he begged me to reconstruct the sermon for him. A couple nights a week, Tom came over to visit and pray with him.

Walter's mobility also continued to improve. After two full months of confinement, he had been outfitted with a set of crutches. It was clumsy, but by using a strap to fasten his newly healed left arm to a crutch, he could hobble around the house.

Then one afternoon in mid-February, I came home to what smelled like a brewery. Walter was sprawled on the couch in a half stupor, with at least a dozen beer cans scattered around him. From the looks of the carpet, some of them hadn't been completely empty when he discarded them.

I tiptoed past the mess to my bedroom, sick with disappointment. Was this how things were going to end? What about the announcement he'd made Christmas Day that he didn't need to drink anymore? Or was that no longer in effect now that he had access to alcohol? Next he'd probably go back to the farmhouse and start cooking meth again.

Mom was equally put out by his behavior. "Some Christian you are!" she scoffed. "I knew that religious kick you got off on wouldn't last. Too bad Tom isn't here to see you like this."

Walter mumbled something about still being a Christian, which only made her laugh.

"Yeah, right. A Christian drunk, that's a new one. Maybe you should start a church. It would be popular."

After that incident, Walter became depressed for days. He stopped asking me to read to him, and even Tom's visits failed to cheer him. Although I did not find him that drunk again, the regular trickle of crushed beer cans in the kitchen garbage told the tale of how he spent his afternoons. I mentioned it to Tom as we were driving to church the next Sunday.

"Yeah, I know he's been drinking," Tom agreed. "God doesn't hold it against him, but all the same it's not good. He has some tough issues he needs to deal with. But as long as he thinks he can cover them up, he's not going to face them, and things won't get better."

"He won't go back and be like he used to, will he?" I hated to even ask the question.

MELISSA WILTROUT

"We're praying he doesn't. But God won't force his life on us. We have to want it and work with him to receive it. Sometimes that process is scary and painful."

At church that day, the pastor preached on forgiveness. I tried my best to pay attention. But instead, I found myself pondering a single verse he had read at the beginning.

"If we confess our sins, He is faithful and righteous to forgive us our sins and to cleanse us from all unrighteousness."

As I read the passage over and over in my Bible, I began to grasp a fantastic truth.

I know God forgave me, but I didn't know he'd cleaned all the sin and badness off of me. But that's what it says here! According to God, I am not a thief. I'm not a criminal. I'm as good as anybody here!

I lifted my head and gazed about me with a sense of wonder. My eye settled on Pat, and for a moment I felt the old familiar chill. But I shoved it off. *I'm not a criminal. I have nothing to be ashamed of anymore. I'm never ever gonna be arrested again!*

Joy began to fill me. I knew it was all true. But there was still one step I needed to take. With a mixture of eagerness and anxiety, I awaited the end of the service.

As the final notes of the closing song died away, I leaned over and whispered to Patty. "I'm ready to meet Pat."

She smiled and put an arm around my shoulders. "Well, come on then."

I tried to squash the butterflies in my stomach as we crossed the room. Pat was chatting with an older lady, but she paused and greeted us. I managed a nervous smile. To my relief, Pat paid me no further attention, but instead asked Patty what she'd put in the macaroni salad she'd brought to potluck the previous week.

"Not as bad as you thought, huh?" Patty whispered to me, as we stepped back into the line of people leaving the sanctuary.

I shook my head. I felt as light as a swallow. Smiling at people was easy now.

Mom was not at home when Tom and Patty dropped me off some time later. I found Walter in the easy chair with his leg propped up, eating a peanut butter sandwich.

"Your mom said to tell you she'll be back in a little bit," he said. "She made you a sandwich. It's out there on the cupboard, I think. So tell me, what did you learn today?"

"Something you might not like." I rubbed my damp palms down my jeans. Talking with Walter made me nervous.

"What was that?"

"Well, I learned I don't have to be afraid of Pat anymore."

"Who's Pat?"

"That lady cop. You've met her."

"Oh, yeah." He frowned, but he didn't look angry. "How'd you get that idea?"

"I was reading these verses." I opened my Bible to chapter one of First John and read him the key verses from the sermon that morning.

"If we say that we have fellowship with Him, and yet walk in the darkness, we lie and do not practice the truth."

"If we confess our sins, He is faithful and righteous to forgive us our sins and to cleanse us from all unrighteousness."

"Let me see that," Walter said.

I crossed the room and held the Bible in front of him, pointing out the verses. He took the book and stared hard at them, but after a few moments he shook his head in frustration. "Read it again."

Standing beside him, I read the entire short chapter aloud.

"Keep going," he urged me when I reached the end. He drank in every word of the next chapter. "That's good," he said then.

I reached for the Bible, but he held onto it. "Leave it here. Just warn me if you see Julie drive in."

"What're you gonna do?"

He waved me away. "I just wanna try something."

As I sat at the table eating my lunch a few minutes later, I heard him trying to sound out words in a halting monotone. "If . . . we say . . . that . . . we have . . . we have…"

A fist slammed on the end table. "God, you aren't helping!"

I choked on my milk. Did Walter really think God would teach him how to read? It was a good idea, though. Based on what I'd overheard, God was the only one with enough patience to do it.

Despite his initial failure, Walter persisted in trying to read. He had plenty of time to practice in the long afternoons while Mom was at work. Every day I'd come home from school to find my Bible in his lap or lying on the end table next to his chair. Though I resented him taking my Bible without asking, at least I didn't have to read to him anymore. I had never enjoyed that. Simply knowing Walter had changed wasn't enough to ease the discomfort I felt in his presence.

One evening I overheard Walter demonstrate his reading skills to Tom. He stumbled over a few of the longer words, but otherwise he did well. I was amazed how fast he'd learned.

"That's great. I had no idea you couldn't read," Tom exclaimed.

"Well, I can now. Tess probably wants her Bible back, but I don't wanna give it up. It gives me something to do."

Tom laughed. "With all that hard work, I dare say you've earned a Bible of your own. I'm going right home to get you one."

"No, no. You don't have to do that. I'll buy one for myself."

But Tom was already on his way. "I'll be back in five minutes with your Bible."

Mom, who always holed up in her bedroom during Tom's visits, heard the excitement and went to see what was happening. "It sounds like you're having a party out here. Where's Tom?"

"He'll be right back. He's getting me a Bible."

"A Bible? Whatever for? You can't read."

"You might be surprised what I can do."

Mom came back down the hallway, grumbling aloud about the crazy things men will do if left to themselves. I had to laugh.

Later that same week, the doctor removed the cast from Walter's leg and gave him the good news that he could walk with just a cane. Walter began helping out with simple household tasks, such as vacuuming the floor, and one afternoon he limped out to his shop and gathered up a huge bag of trash. But something still seemed to be weighing on his mind.

40

One Friday evening, Mom was extra late. She had left no instructions regarding supper, so Walter concluded it was up to him to make something. I stayed at the table finishing my homework while he hobbled around the kitchen. By the time Mom walked in, he had a bowl of scrambled eggs cooling on the counter while canned peas simmered in the open fry pan.

Mom hurried to the stove without even taking her coat off. "Don't tell me you're cooking again," she scolded. "You trying to ruin my good fry pan? This is no way to heat vegetables! Can't you wait til I get home?"

"I didn't burn anything," Walter defended himself. "And I'm sure your fry pan is just fine."

Mom tossed her coat and purse onto a chair. "Tess, set the table." She drained the peas, then tried to pick the soggy bits of egg out of them. "I swear I've never seen the likes. Why not just fry the egg and peas together?" She continued to mutter as she examined the bowl of cold eggs. "Tess, put some bread on. If Walter's eggs are as bad as they look, we're gonna need it."

Walter retreated to the living room, where he hunched on the end of the couch. I felt sorry for him. Hardly a day passed that Mom didn't find a way to put him down. Even when he did something nice for her, she reacted with criticism. Lately, however, Walter had been taking it quietly.

"So how was work today?" Walter ventured, as we sat down to supper.

Mom glared at him. "Terrible. If it wasn't for you, I would've quit that stupid job a long time ago."

"What happened?"

"Oh, more of the usual. Kathy's got the flu, or so she says, so she's been off since Wednesday. That leaves me and Denise to do all the cleaning, and she's a pretty shoddy worker. Managed to break one of the lady's porcelain dolls, and then she's got the nerve to turn around and tell the boss I did it."

Mom thumped her empty glass down on the table. "She seems to think just because she's worked there a couple years and I'm new, she can shove all her mistakes off on me. I won't take it."

"Won't the company pay for the doll?" he asked.

"Yeah, but if this keeps happening, I'll lose my job. And it's gonna be fun trying to get another one." She took a piece of bread. "Tess, didn't you put the butter on?"

"Oops." I jumped to get the butter.

"Guess what," Walter said. "I got the first coat of varnish put on that desk in my shop today."

Mom shrugged. "Well, good. I suppose next you're gonna call up your old customers and tell them you've got their work done."

"I haven't thought about that end of it yet. I just think I ought to finish the stuff."

"That would be remarkable in itself," Mom agreed.

Later that evening, after the dishes were done, I was sitting on the kitchen counter paging through a seed catalog when Walter hobbled out for a drink of water.

"You gonna order something?" he asked.

I looked up in surprise. "No. I'm just looking."

"There's a whole garden out there that's gonna need planting," he said. "We might as well grow something good in it for a change. If you want to, that is."

"I-I haven't thought about it," I stammered.

Walter set down his glass. "You should. I dare say you'd grow a lot nicer things than I did. If you want, we can order some seeds."

I stared down at the page, unsure what to say. Walter was the one who knew how to grow things. Would I have to work with him? If so, I wasn't interested. I'd done enough of that for a lifetime.

"Aww, come on," he coaxed. "You're gonna need something to do this summer."

"Mom says we don't have any extra money," I stalled.

"Oh, I think I can get her to agree. Especially since it'll save on the grocery bill. How'd you like to grow some green beans?"

"Is it hard?"

"Nope. Only trick is to pick them every other day, no matter what. That way they're always tender. Let me see what kinds they've got in that catalog."

I handed it over. "How do you know so much about growing vegetables?"

"We grew them when I was a kid."

The comment piqued my curiosity. "I never heard you say anything about when you were a kid."

Walter thumbed through the catalog until he found the right page. "There's a lot of trouble back there, Tess," he said. "My father was a lot like I used to be. We got along like a couple of pit bulls."

"That's too bad."

"Yeah. There were four of us boys," he continued. "I was the oldest. I left the day I turned sixteen and never went back."

Walter's finger settled on a picture in the catalog. "Blue Lake. That's the best kind. The plants don't fall over, and they make a lot of beans. You want to mark it?"

I pulled a highlighter from the desk drawer and circled the name. Walter turned the page and began to study the sweet corn section.

"Say, Dad..."

"Yeah?"

I hesitated, my courage running out like water from a sieve. I wasn't sure it was okay to ask this question. But it might be my only chance.

"I've always kind of wondered . . . what happened to my sisters? Mom won't tell me anything, except how old they are."

Walter's face tightened and he shook his head. After a moment of hesitation, he laid down the catalog and reached for his wallet. He slipped out a color photograph of Mom sitting in the grass with two smiling little girls perched on her knees. "That's Sarah, and Megan," he said, pointing them out. "They're about seven and five here."

I took the old photo and studied it. Both girls looked so innocent and happy. Sarah had light blond curls tied up with a pink ribbon, while Megan's hair was dark and straight like mine. How would they look now, I wondered?

I didn't press my luck by asking further questions. But the mystery continued to haunt me. Why did I not remember them? What really had happened to them?

Mom hedged a bit about the seed order, but to my surprise, she gave in and signed a check for me. I sat at the table and filled out the order form. Then I paged through the catalog some more, looking at the pictures of sunflowers and snapdragons and dreaming about the flower garden I hoped to have someday. Walter's deep voice drifted in from the living room.

"You know, Julie, if I had any money, I'd take you to see a movie one of these nights."

"What makes you think I'd go?"

"I just hoped you'd want to."

"I don't." Mom's reply was blunt. "I mean, you've got yourself quite a reputation. I really don't want to be seen with you."

"We could go after dark."

"Yeah, fine idea. I think I'll use my money to buy groceries and pay the rent."

Walter didn't answer. I knew this wasn't the first time he'd suggested the two of them do something together. *Why does he keep asking*, I wondered, *when she always snubs him? It's like he's trying to court her, but this time she doesn't want him.*

The thought intrigued me. I tried to picture Mom the way she must have been years ago when they were dating. Did she blush when Walter first asked her out? Did she giggle at his lame jokes? Did she tear up when she said her vows on her wedding day?

It was hard to imagine, but sometime in the past, Mom must have been more tender and trusting. She must have donned pretty dresses and tied ribbons in her hair. Sometime before the disappointments of life made her harsh and defensive, she must have been worth pursuing. At least, Walter had thought so. Now he seemed determined to win her affections again. Unfortunately, Mom was having none of it.

41

At breakfast the next day, Mom greeted me with the usual Saturday-morning proposition. "I have to go shopping. Want to come along, or do you want to be dropped off at Heather's?"

Even though Walter had been no trouble for several months, Mom still refused to leave me home alone with him for long periods of time. As a result, I got to visit Heather almost every weekend.

On this particular morning, I took one look at the long grocery list and said, "I think I'll go to Heather's." I hadn't been to Allen's grocery store since the day Mom punished me for stealing the hundred dollars. Even thinking about going back made me wince.

"Call and make sure it's okay," Mom reminded me.

Tom answered on the fourth ring. "Tessa, we'd love to have you," he said. "But Patty has the flu, and it looks like Heather is coming down with it too. I don't think you should come today."

"Great," I muttered, as I slammed the phone down. I could wait in the car while Mom shopped, but it would be a long, cold wait.

Walter looked up from where he sat at the breakfast table, reading his Bible. "What's the matter?"

"They've got the flu, so I have to go with Mom."

"Is that so bad?"

Mom paused from cutting out coupons to give a scornful laugh. "Yeah, it's bad, when it's Allen's. She's got a reputation there."

I cringed. The memories hurt enough without her rubbing it in.

Walter frowned. "Tessa? What's this about?"

Mom filled him in. "Your daughter's a shoplifter and a petty thief. If you hadn't been so smashed last fall, you'd know that."

"Is that true, Tessa?"

I hung my head. "I guess. But I told God I'm sorry."

"Okay, but if you stole from people, you might have to tell them you're sorry too."

Anger sprang up in me. "Listen to you talk. Like you're some great saint now." I spun around and left the room.

"Tessa, I'm not gonna tell you what to do. But talk to God about it, okay?"

No way, I vowed. I could still see Bruce, standing behind the customer service counter with that ugly smirk on his face. *No way am I gonna tell that jerk I'm sorry. He'd just laugh.*

In my bedroom, though, I broke down and cried. *God, I know you forgave me for stealing a couple months ago. And I know I'm not a thief anymore. Why do I still feel ashamed when I think of going to that store? Please, you gotta help me!*

The answer didn't come in the form I expected. There were no words impressed into my mind, no sudden understanding. Just more tears. Uncontrollable sobs, coming from somewhere deep inside me. Ever since that day in church, I'd acknowledged it was wrong to steal. But now I *knew* it was wrong. Horribly wrong.

"I'm sorry, God. I'm so sorry," I sobbed.

Then I found myself asking forgiveness. I knew God forgave me, but still I felt the need to ask – no, beg for – his forgiveness. After a few minutes, joy and assurance flooded me. I knew in the depths of my heart that I was truly forgiven. The shame was gone.

When I had composed myself, I went and found Mom. She was in the basement, working on laundry. "I'm ready to go now," I said. "And I want to tell you I'm really sorry for all the times I stole from you." Reaching into my pocket, I pulled out a wad of bills totaling around thirty dollars. "This is yours. I'm sorry I kept it so long."

A look of mild surprise crossed Mom's face. "Okay," she said.

Walking into Allen's store that day wasn't easy, but I did it with the joyful confidence that I was not a thief, I was forgiven. The difference was amazing. I could hold my head up. I had no desire to steal anything or even think about it. When a clerk glanced my way, I was able to smile instead of flushing in shame. By the time we passed the customer service counter on the way out, I was so thankful for what God had done that I didn't care what Bruce thought. I rode home in victory.

That evening, I witnessed another miracle. Toward the end of supper, Mom went to the pantry as if to get something for dessert. She returned with a mischievous gleam in her eyes.

"Guess what I have here," she said, and tossed Walter a small paper bag. He stared at her, then slowly unrolled the top and withdrew a package of microwave popcorn and a rented movie.

A smile spread across his face. "Is this for tonight?"

"If you like," she replied, and went to the freezer to get the ice cream.

That incident marked a change in Mom's attitude toward Walter. She stopped condemning him for his past misdeeds and began spending time with him. Although their relationship was tentative, overall they seemed to enjoy being together. I couldn't believe it. Was this what marriage was supposed to be like?

42

For three incredible days, I watched in amazement as my parents did the dishes together, discussed the news, or shared a laugh over a funny movie. I'd never seen Mom smile so much. It was like a fairy tale I couldn't step out of. But like a fairy tale, it also came to an end.

Wednesday morning, I awoke to Mom yelling at Walter. Even with blankets pulled over my head to muffle her voice, I could feel the fear in it. This wasn't just the old gripe about her having to work while he sat around. I rose up on one elbow and listened.

"Aren't you ever gonna get over this religious nonsense?" Mom demanded.

Walter's reply was too quiet for me to hear. I slipped out of bed and pressed an ear to the crack along my door.

"But that's just plain stupid!" Mom exclaimed.

"Think, Julie," he said. "They're gonna find out sooner or later even if I don't tell them."

My heart thudded in my ears. He couldn't, he mustn't, be saying what I thought he was.

"How do you know?" Mom shot back. "But you can just forget it. I'm not taking you anywhere."

"Tom says he can take me."

"Oh yeah? Now I get it. Tom talked you into this. Didn't he!"

"Tom had nothing to do with it. And you can't stop me from doing what I know is right."

Mom snorted. "You are crazy. I've half a mind to use that gun of yours and drive some sense into you. Don't you know how much trouble you're in? Why don't you do something smart for once, like destroy the place first or something? Or at least hire a lawyer?"

"I know one thing." Walter's voice rang out clear and undaunted. "If we confess our sins, we'll be forgiven; but if we hide them, we'll be judged."

"That's not the way it works out there! They don't forgive, they punish."

"Even so, I'm going," Walter declared. "And don't you dare go near that place while I'm gone."

I stumbled away from the door. "No, God," I groaned. "I wish nobody would ever have to know." In my mind I could still hear Pat's verdict: twenty-five years in prison. Walter would be old and gray before he ever got out. And me – what would happen to me?

Fear constricted my throat so tightly I couldn't even cry. I crawled into bed and buried my head under the pillow. If my world was going to collapse, I didn't want to watch. Was there nothing I could do? Where was God?

I prayed frantically. *God, I'll do anything. Please. Don't let Walter do this. Please, God!* By the time Mom knocked at my door to awaken me for school, I was trembling all over.

"Go away," I muttered.

"Tessa, you're gonna be late for school. Now get up!"

"I'm not going. I'm sick."

"Yeah, I bet you are. So is everyone else around here this morning." She came in and started to pull the covers off of me. "Come on. Walter might as well see firsthand the trouble his stupid religious ideas are causing. Nothing else is stopping him."

Although I doubted it would make any difference, I gave in and followed her to the living room. Walter hunched in a corner of the couch, his head bowed.

"Can't you see what you're doing to your family?" Mom said. "You've got Tess so worked up she can't go to school."

Walter raised his head. His eyes were dark with sadness as he looked at me. "Sit down, would you?"

I perched on the arm of the chair and stared at the carpet.

"I'm sorry it's come to this," he said. "But I can't live one more day with all this stuff on my conscience. It's like a dark sickness inside of me. If I don't come clean, it's gonna spread and do me in."

"What about me?" My voice trembled. "Did you ever think about that?"

"It's all my fault," he answered. "I'm gonna tell them that, and hopefully they'll let you go."

"*Hopefully*, that's a comforting word," Mom muttered. "What if they don't?"

"Julie, just let me talk to her, okay?"

He leaned forward, and I could feel his gaze resting on me. "Tess, listen. Don't hide from the past, and don't lie about it. Not even to keep from getting in trouble. If we're honest, the Lord will take care of the rest. Okay?"

I continued staring at the floor. I didn't want to be honest. I just wanted to forget the whole mess.

Walter went on. "I've thought a lot about that one verse. If we confess, he forgives us. Remember?"

"I thought that meant, to God."

"It does. I know God forgives me. But I broke the law, and I have to face it. If I keep trying to hide it, I'm still guilty. Does that make sense?"

I shook my head. My throat was tighter than ever. Why did things have to go this way?

Walter sighed. "I don't know how to put it, I guess. All I know is I've got to go."

"Are you gonna . . . come home again?" I could hardly force the words out.

"I don't think so. They'll probably put me in jail."

"Probably us, too," Mom retorted.

"I sure hope not. I'll do my best, but I won't lie."

At that, Mom snorted and left the room. I rose to leave also, but Walter wasn't quite finished.

"Tessa?"

I paused in the doorway. "Yeah?"

"Would you pray for me?"

I felt intensely uncomfortable. How could he ask something like that?

"I'll think about it," I muttered, and slipped off to my room.

Breakfast that morning was late and tense. I managed to choke down a glass of orange juice and part of a piece of toast. Walter ate even less. Mom continued trying to reason with him, but when he went to the closet to put his coat on, she turned mean and started threatening him again. I was almost relieved to see Tom drive in.

Still muttering, Mom packed me into the car and drove me to school. "You don't wanna stay home," she told me. "They'll get search warrants, and the next thing you know the place'll be crawling with cops."

"Are you gonna get in trouble too?"

She swore. "I don't know. You ask the worst questions sometimes."

"But, you are involved, aren't you? I mean…"

"So you think I'm a criminal, huh?" She shook her head.

"Well, you sort of sounded like one," I fumbled. "Like when you were talking to Patty that day."

"Yeah, I probably did. We can talk about it another time. Right now, Tess, the less you know the better."

Mom pulled to the curb in front of the school. I stepped out of the car, then remembered something.

"Hey, I need you to write an excuse for me."

Mom opened the glove box and pulled out an old registration paper. "An excuse. Let's see, how about 'Family Emergency?' Sound good?"

I shrugged. "It's true, anyway."

She scribbled something on the paper, folded it in half, and handed it to me. "See you later."

As I trudged up the sidewalk, I couldn't help but wonder if Mom would be in handcuffs the next time I saw her. I glanced behind me, but the white car had already driven away. I wished I had said goodbye to her.

43

i arrived in time for second period. I tried hard to act normal, but I could not get my mind on my studies. Who cared which Chinese dynasty held power in 1276, when I might not have a mother to go home to after school? When I might end up spending the night in jail or an institution? Would I even be at school tomorrow?

"What's up?" Heather asked me at lunch. "You look really glum today."

I considered lying, but decided there was no point. "My whole life is falling apart, and I can't stop it. And pretty soon everybody in the whole world is gonna know about it."

"Wow, Tess, this sounds bad. Are you sure?"

I just nodded.

"Well, I'll still be your friend, no matter what," she promised.

Toward the end of sixth period, an announcement came over the intercom for several students to report to the office. My stomach knotted when I heard my name. Grabbing my things, I made my way down the hall to the office. It could be something normal, or it could be...

"I'm Tessa Miner," I told the secretary, though she probably recognized me. "You wanted me?"

She smiled. "That's right. The principal wants to talk to you. Have a seat, and I'll let him know you're here."

I bit my lip and folded my arms tightly around myself. *This is bad, really bad.* Was this how they worked it if the police showed up to arrest a student?

The principal's words were not encouraging. "Tessa, there's a police officer here to talk with you," he said. "I understand it has something to do with your father." He steered me around the corner to the guidance counselor's office and nudged me inside.

At least it's not Pat, I thought, as I sized up the officer. He was at least Walter's age, maybe older, with thinning hair and glasses. Except for the badge pinned on his shirt pocket, he looked like an ordinary businessman.

He stuck out his hand with a smile. "Hi, Tessa, I'm Chris Johnson. I'm a detective with the Northford Police Department. I talked to your father earlier today, and I need to ask you a few questions."

I couldn't bring myself to shake his hand. "Am I being arrested?"

"No, miss. Not a chance. I want to talk to you about your father."

"My father?" My breath came in short gasps. I wished I could stop shaking.

"I understand he told you he was going to make a confession."

"Yeah."

"I have to say, he showed a lot of courage today. I didn't think he had it in him." Chris gestured toward one of the upholstered chairs near the door. "Have a seat."

I sat and clenched my hands in my lap.

Chris settled into the other chair, crossing one leg in a relaxed fashion. "Tessa, your father says he's entirely responsible for the fact that you helped him in his illegal activities. He says you didn't want to do it. Is that true?"

I nodded.

"And is it true, also, that if you didn't obey and help him, he'd mistreat you?"

I nodded again.

"Would you do something for me?"

"What."

"Try to relax. You are not the one in trouble here, your father is. I'm just trying to establish some facts about his behavior toward you."

I looked up. "His behavior?"

"I understand he treated you pretty badly at times."

"Yeah."

"Can you tell me about any of it?"

It took a lot of prodding, but once I started talking, I couldn't stop. Story after story poured forth, and with each one, I grew angrier. At times I broke down and could hardly talk. Chris leaned back in his chair and listened, occasionally interrupting to ask a question.

"That is really sad," he said, when I was finished. "I can see why it makes you so angry. Anybody would feel that way."

"Yeah, but maybe some of it was my fault. I shouldn't have made him mad."

"Tessa, that's not true. You've been abused, and it is not your fault. A loving parent doesn't abuse his children, no matter what."

I shook my head, confused. *Sometimes I deserved at least part of what I got,* I argued silently. *Like when I'd be sassy, or just plain disobedient.* But I knew Chris would disagree, so I kept the thoughts to myself.

"Let's talk about something else," Chris said. "I understand you helped your father in his meth lab. What was it like working in there?"

I grimaced. "It was horrible. It stunk so bad I couldn't breathe. A lot of times it made me sick. Walter was usually there, and if I did something wrong, he'd yell at me. Or if I spilled something, or got sick, he'd laugh. In the summer it was really hot, and he wouldn't let me open the door for fresh air. A lot of times we worked late at night. I'd get so tired I couldn't stay awake. And then Mom would make me go to school the next day."

"Did you ever try the stuff?"

I shook my head. It wasn't that I hadn't considered it. I had, a lot of times. But something always held me back. Maybe it was seeing all the weird chemicals that went into making it.

"That's good. How about your mom, she ever try it?"

"I don't think so."

"Did she help your father with his drug business in any way? Getting him supplies, arranging sales, anything like that?"

"I'm not sure. I always figured she wasn't involved, but then I started to think maybe she was. I don't know."

"What made you think she was involved?"

"I heard her threaten somebody."

"Really. Tell me about it."

So I recounted the conversation I'd overheard at Patty's. Chris listened thoughtfully.

"Yeah, I can see where you'd think that, after hearing something like that."

"Is she involved?"

"She says she isn't, and so far we haven't arrested her, which is a good sign, I'd say."

As relieved as I was to hear that, it left many unanswered questions. Why had Mom been so opposed to Walter confessing, if she wasn't involved at all? Why did she think she might end up in jail? Also baffling was Mom's hateful attitude toward the police. To my knowledge, she'd only been stopped once for speeding. Nevertheless, anytime she saw a cop, her eyes would narrow and she'd cuss. It made no difference whether he was taking a cruise through the park or running a radar gun in a speed zone. She never missed one. Why did she hate cops so much?

"You look puzzled." Chris's comment broke into my thoughts.

I shrugged. "I was just thinking."

"There was one last thing I wanted to ask you. Do you know how your mom got out to the lab site back in December to get the car that was parked there?"

"Well, yeah. She got the neighbors to drive her."

"Tom Erickson took her?"

"Yeah. It was like midnight."

He nodded. "Okay, good."

"How'd you know about the car?" I asked.

Chris looked amused. "Oh, we've been watching that place for quite a while."

"You mean if one of us had gone there, we would've been caught."

"It's quite possible."

I shivered, recalling the night Walter had tried to send me there by myself. Maybe my premonitions hadn't been as foolish as I'd thought.

Chris stood up. "Well, it looks like it's time to get you home."

I glanced at my watch and gasped. It was nearly four o'clock. Had we talked that long?

"I think I missed my bus," I said.

He smiled. "That's why I'm offering you a ride."

I was glad the halls were empty as I got my things from my locker. I'd never live it down if my friends found out about this. Out in the parking lot, Chris opened the front passenger door of a small gray car. "Hop in."

A tiny smile tugged at my lips as I settled into the comfortable seat. I had been expecting another ride in the back seat of a cruiser. *This is cool.*

Chris already knew where I lived. As he drove, he asked me about school and talked a little about his job. I tried to be sociable, but I couldn't stop worrying what Mom would say when she found out I'd been interviewed. I rehearsed my answers as I rode along.

I couldn't help it. The detective came to school. I had to talk to him. But I tried to be careful, and I didn't say anything about you.

When we arrived at the house, Chris ruined any chance I had of keeping the situation a secret. Over my protests, he walked to the door with me and knocked. He explained to Mom why he'd driven me home, and then he bid us a good evening.

I dumped my knapsack in my bedroom, then gathered my courage and returned to the kitchen. Mom had the table set and was pouring the milk.

"How'd your end of things go?" she asked.

"Okay. Kind of boring, actually." I prayed she wouldn't ask for details. "Did I miss anything here?"

She shrugged. "Two cops showed up this afternoon, poked around for a while, and asked like a million questions." She pulled a green bean casserole out of the oven and set it on the table. "I should've gone to work and left them to track me down. That would've been more interesting."

"Why didn't you?"

"Because I don't want my boss to find out about this. I could get fired for all I know."

"Fired? Why?"

Mom took a helping of beans and pushed the bowl toward me. "You ask too many questions. I got a call from Walter this afternoon. Of all things, he wanted to tell me how good he felt after he'd confessed all his crimes. I asked him who he thinks is gonna pay his bail."

"Was he worried?"

"He should be. My wages barely pay the rent on this place."

"But your boss will find out anyway," I persisted. "I mean, won't it get in the papers and stuff?"

"By the time it hits the papers, neither my name nor yours will be in there anywhere. That will help."

"Yeah, I guess." I wished there was a way to keep the story out of the news. Why did the whole city have to know what my father had done?

Mom must have read the look on my face. "I'm sorry, but there's no avoiding this thing. It's gonna be embarrassing. We'll have to face it and live it down the best we can."

Live it down. Hadn't I been doing that all my life? I sighed, remembering the first time I'd felt ashamed of my connection to Walter. I had just started second grade. Walter had gotten into a fight at the bar and landed in jail, and the paper had picked up the story. As a little seven-year-old, I was so afraid someone would find out he was my father that I began abbreviating my last name on my school papers. Though I had long since stopped doing that, I continued to resent the name. It was like an ongoing reminder that no matter what I did, I could never escape the disgrace of being Walter's daughter.

44

As I had hoped, no one at school the next day suspected anything. I applied myself to studying history and algebra, glad to let the events of the previous day fade from my mind. Despite the uncertainty of everything, I felt peace. I no longer had to hide and cover things up. I could relax.

Still, I groaned when I saw Lois heading my way at lunchtime. She set her tray on the table between Janet and me and pulled up a chair. After complimenting me on my top, which wasn't even new, she cut to the chase.

"So, what was going on with you and the principal yesterday?"

I took my time chewing a mouthful of hash browns. Then I swallowed and said, "Nothing. It was a family matter."

"Oh, that figures. Did your mom kick your dad out or what?"

Heather, who had just arrived with her lunch, overheard the question. "It's none of your business, Lois," she said.

"Well, for Pete's sake," Lois exclaimed. "What is it? Fire? Foreclosure? Trust me, I won't tell a soul." Her expression became so comically grave that we all burst out laughing.

"If you've ever kept that promise, I haven't seen it," Janet said between laughs.

Lois shoved her chair back, her face red. "I was just trying to be friendly. You can laugh if you want, but you'll regret this, Tess." Grabbing her tray, she sailed across the room toward Sandy's table.

Janet shook her head. "Maybe I shouldn't have laughed, but I couldn't help it."

"She needed it," Heather asserted. Leaning close to me, she whispered, "Grandpa told us a little bit when he got home last night. I hope you don't mind."

I shrugged. I did mind, but why make a fuss about it? In a few more days, our secret would be public knowledge anyway.

"What is going on?" Janet asked. "Or is it none of my business either?"

I sighed. "I could tell you, but about that time somebody will overhear."

"You're not in trouble, are you?" A worried expression creased her face.

"Not exactly. But my dad is. He's in jail."

"In jail! I thought he was a Christian!"

"He is. That's why he's in jail. He went yesterday and confessed to what he's been doing."

Janet stared at me, unspoken questions written on her face.

"So of course they had to hear my side of things. A detective came to school yesterday, and I talked to him for like an hour and a half. You see why I didn't want to tell Lois. But I'm afraid it'll get in the paper, and then everybody will know."

Janet was shaking her head. "Wow. That's just crazy. Do you think he's in a lot of trouble?"

"Yeah. Mom's not sure he's gonna get out of jail."

"I'm sorry."

"Thanks. But it's not like I really miss him or anything. It's just kind of . . . well, embarrassing."

"I'd say. Keep me posted what happens, okay?"

"I will." I appreciated her concern. What would I ever do without my friends?

***

Saturday morning, the phone rang while we were eating breakfast. Mom picked it up on the third ring. I stopped chewing and listened. Though I couldn't make out what he was saying, I recognized Walter's voice. How had he gotten on the phone?

When Mom hung up, she filled me in. "Walter was in court yesterday. The judge set bail on him."

"Oh yeah? How much is it?"

"A lot. I guess they don't wanna take any chances, now that they finally nabbed him. But if he does get out, he's not allowed to have any contact at all with you."

"Oh."

"So. What I'm gonna do is talk to Tom and see if he'll pay it, since the whole thing's his fault anyway."

"What's this about Walter not having contact with me?"

"Just a sticky little rule we're gonna have to work around. You'll probably end up bunking with Ericksons for a couple months. I'll talk to them about that too."

Whoa. Things were moving faster than my brain could process them. Mom was going to ship me off so Walter could come home? How was that fair?

But I swallowed the protests. It was no use arguing when Mom was in this kind of mood. I'd wait and see what Tom thought about paying thousands of dollars in bail before I got too worked up about the finer details of her plan.

It was close to noon by the time Mom finished making her grocery list and doing the half-dozen other things she deemed necessary before we could leave. Though I had the option of staying home, I trailed along to see what Tom would say.

Patty answered the door and invited us in. "I'm making lunch," she said. "Would you two like to stay for a sandwich?"

Mom brushed the question aside. "Where's Tom? I need to talk to him."

"He's out for a run with the dog, but he should be back soon. Why don't you sit down."

Mom settled onto the couch. I followed Patty into the kitchen and leaned my elbows on the cupboard, watching her fry strips of bacon.

"Want one?" she asked. At my nod, she scooped a piece of crisp meat from the pan, wrapped it in a napkin, and handed it to me. I took a bite and savored the taste. Bacon was a rare treat at home. Especially these days.

The back door opened and Sadie raced into the kitchen, scattering snow across the tile floor. She skidded to a stop in front of the sink and stood panting, looking expectantly at Patty.

Tom entered more slowly, blowing on his glasses. "Oh, hi Tessa. We didn't think you were coming today." He reached into the cupboard beneath the sink and gave the dog a biscuit.

Patty gestured toward the living room. "Julie's here. Says she wants to talk to you."

"Me, alone?" Tom removed his stocking cap, causing his short gray hair to stand on end with the static.

Patty shrugged. "Want me to come in?"

"You're busy. I'll go see what she wants." He slicked down his hair with a wet hand and strode into the living room. "Hi, Julie."

I hung back in the shadow of the doorway, nibbling my bacon and listening.

"Didn't I tell you not to go messing with other people's business?" Mom began. "What's this thing you pulled off with my husband the other day?"

"You'd better ask him about it, if you haven't," Tom replied.

"Well, you've done something pretty stupid. I suppose you've heard he's in jail."

"He knew it might end that way. I'm sure he's not upset about it."

"Sure. He figured I'd bail him out, as usual. But I can't afford this time. If you want to help him so much, why don't you give me the money to get him out. It's only five thousand dollars."

"That's a lot of money. What makes you think I can afford that?"

"I guess you should've thought of that the other day."

"Look, Julie, why are you blaming me for a decision Walter made on his own?"

"Never mind. I only came here because I thought you cared about him. Which I can see you don't."

"I never said I didn't care about him."

"Then give me the money, and I'll get him out this afternoon. It's that simple."

"And I get the money back if he shows up on his court dates."

"Yeah, basically."

"There's one problem," Tom said. "I'm not willing to put up that much money under any circumstances; and furthermore, I'm not willing to hand you a single cent of it."

"Oh, come on. Just because I happen to be married to Walter, you figure I'm bad too."

"I don't mean to embarrass you," Tom said. "But you've told us an awful lot of lies in the short time we've known you. Isn't that your old Grand Am parked at that tavern next to the Chinese restaurant downtown? Looks in pretty good shape if you ask me."

I stopped chewing my bacon. My breath caught in my throat. *What?*

Mom hesitated before she answered. "Playing detective, huh? I hadn't noticed Steve got a new car. Guess those Grand Ams are pretty popular. But back to Walter, it's up to you. If you won't help, I'll tell him you're through with him since you heard what he was into."

"That would be another lie."

"Not really. What kind of Christian would leave his so-called brother to rot in jail, if he had the power to get him out? Seems pretty clear to me."

"Julie, I'm not giving you any money. And that's final."

"You can think it over," she said. "Just remember that he's not gonna get the exercise he needs to make that leg heal in a jail cell."

Then I heard her zipping up her coat. "Come on, Tessa," she called. "Let's go."

As I walked to the door, Tom called out a pleasant goodbye, but I didn't return it. I was too ashamed. When had Mom turned into such a liar? Or had she always been that way, and I'd never been sharp enough to see through her?

45

Over the next few days, Mom continued to pester Tom for the money. She'd call him on the phone or stop by after supper. Wednesday evening, she returned from her visit with a newspaper. She tossed it to me on the couch, where I sat watching an episode of *CSI*.

"Well, the story's out. You might as well take a look. Then at least you'll know what everybody else is reading."

I stared at the paper, the TV program suddenly forgotten. I didn't want to read the story. But curiosity compelled me. My hand shook as I turned the paper over and unfolded it.

There it was, in the sidebar of the front page. I felt a slow flush spread over my face as I read.

> *Charges are pending against a rural Northford man arrested on drug charges last week. Walter Miner, 43, of 16187 Vance Road, Northford, is being held on a $5,000 cash bond for allegedly manufacturing and selling methamphetamine and marijuana. Additional charges, including child abuse and reckless endangerment, are expected to be filed as well.*
>
> *Search warrants were served last week at Miner's home, shop, and lab site. Found in the search were a number of firearms, scales, containers of suspected marijuana, and equipment for making meth. No meth was found, although according to a search warrant document filed earlier this week, controlled buys of both drugs took place between*

Miner and a confidential informant in late November and
early December of last year.

According to police, Miner voluntarily turned himself in
and cooperated with authorities during investigation,
apparently citing as his reason for doing so his recent con-
version to Christianity. Miner appeared for a bond hearing
March 18. He is to appear in court May 26.

"At least they didn't say anything about me," I commented. "Did
Tom give in yet?"

Mom made a growling noise. "We're negotiating. I thought
Walter was stubborn, but that guy takes the prize."

I read the article again, trying to imagine what my classmates
would think if they saw it. Would they realize he was my father?
Some of them would. Would they tease me? Shame me?

I slept very little that night. I knew Mom wouldn't let me stay
home, but I dreaded facing everyone. As dawn crept through my
window, the escape plans invented by my sleep-deprived brain
grew crazier. I even contemplated drinking something poisonous
to make myself sick, until it occurred to me that I might die from it.

The dreaded knock on my door eventually came. "Come on,
Tessa. Get up. It's time for breakfast."

"Screw breakfast. I'm not going to school today."

Mom was silent for a minute. "Well, come out anyway. We can
talk about it."

I waited as long as I dared, then wrapped a bathrobe around
myself and shuffled out to the kitchen. "Mom, please. I barely slept
all night. I feel awful. I am not going."

Mom dropped two pieces of bread into the toaster and depressed
the lever. "Tessa, letting you stay home isn't gonna solve a thing. It
might even generate rumors."

"But I can't go. I feel like a convict or something. I wish I could
just disappear until everybody forgets about it."

"I know." Mom emptied a can of frozen juice into a pitcher. "I
feel the same way. But let's look at it. As far as everyone else knows,
you and I had nothing to do with this. There's nothing saying we
even knew about it. Any thinking person would feel sorry for us,
not blame us. When you go out there, you just keep telling yourself
you had nothing to do with it."

"But I did have something to do with it!"

"Don't even think about it. That was Walter's fault. Now I want you to get dressed and try to eat something. I'll drive you to school today."

I tried to take Mom's advice and talk myself out of the shame. And it helped. But I could feel something unpleasant in the atmosphere when I walked into school that morning. All my friends gave me a wide berth. Sandy turned her back and refused to speak to me. Behind my back, I heard snatches of conversation.

"I can't believe she dared to show up."

"I thought it was just that Lorraine. Now we've got two of them."

I felt embarrassed and hurt. I wanted to yell that I had done nothing, and all of this was just a stupid rumor. But I couldn't silence the fear that maybe, somehow, someone had found out I was involved. What would I say to that?

Things worsened during lunch hour.

"So, they let you out of juvi to come to school?" Gary taunted, as he followed me out of algebra class. "How does that work?"

"I'm still living at home, if that answers your question," I snapped.

In the cafeteria, I slipped in line behind Lorraine and Brittney. Although neither of them turned to greet me, I felt relief just being near them. They wouldn't look down on me because of some crazy rumor. If anything, they'd like me more.

I passed over most of the food, taking only a small scoop of corn and a chicken patty. As stressed as I was, I'd be doing well to finish that. I stood a moment holding my tray, scanning the crowded room for Heather's blond head. My heart leaped when I spotted her, but then it fell back. Sitting at the table with her were Lois and Sandy. After some internal debate, I carried my lunch over to Lorraine's table. That's where I got my biggest shock of the day.

"Traitor," Lorraine hissed. "What're you doing here?"

I stared at her. "What?"

She glared back, her eyes dark with anger. "My mom's in jail, that's what. So's her boyfriend. Tell your dad thanks a lot."

"But I–"

"Beat it! You're no friend of mine." She grabbed her carton of milk and threw the contents right in my face. Cold milk poured down my face and soaked the front of my shirt. I stepped back, coughing and wiping my face on my sleeve.

"What's going on here?" said a man's voice. I wiped the milk from my eyes and blinked. My algebra teacher was standing there with his hands on his hips.

"None of your business," Lorraine muttered, then cursed.

Mr. Stone clamped a hand on her shoulder. "All right, young lady. You're going to the principal's office. And Tessa, you're excused to go clean up."

I couldn't wait to get out of there. Grabbing a napkin, I hurried from the room. Milk dripped from my hair and my wet shirt clung to me like shrink wrap. How would I ever get it dry?

Passing the restrooms, I turned right and continued on toward the lockers. I might as well leave. It would be a long walk home, but anything was better than staying here.

"Tessa?" called a familiar voice behind me. "Hey, wait!"

Through the blur of tears, I saw Janet hurrying toward me. She caught up and grabbed my arm. "Good grief, Tess, what happened?"

I tried to shrug her off. "It's too late, Jan. I'm leaving. Nobody wants me here."

"What are you talking about? What's going on?"

"I wish I knew! Everybody hates me." Then I started to cry. "I'm never gonna be good like you and Heather. Why should I even try? I'm just a stupid fool, going to church and thinking I'm a Christian all this time."

"Tess, you're not a fool. Now tell me what's going on."

I wiped my eyes with my damp sleeve and sniffed hard, trying to compose myself. "Well, nobody will talk to me, and . . . they're saying stuff about me being in jail, and using drugs, and…"

Janet put an arm around me and steered me back toward the bathroom. "Listen to me. You are God's beloved child. You are not what any of them say. You never will be. Stop pulling away from me."

"But . . . but I feel so dirty."

"Because you've got milk in your hair?"

"Because I know what everybody's thinking."

"Well, everybody's wrong. Don't you remember what we learned in Sunday school last week?" Janet opened the restroom door for me, then took a paper towel and began wiping the remaining drops of milk out of my hair.

"I don't think it applies to me."

"If it doesn't apply to you, then it doesn't apply to me or Heather or the pastor either, and we'd better all go to jail. Now, do you remember it or not?"

"Uh . . . this sounds kinda stupid, but I'm righteous in God's eyes?"

"It's not stupid at all. It's the truth. Jesus made you holy and righteous and blameless because you belong to him. Even if your dad is in jail, even if everyone is lying about you. Doesn't make the tiniest bit of difference."

I sniffed a couple of times. "Where've you been all day?"

"I had a dentist appointment this morning. I just got back now. Couldn't you hang out with Heather?"

"Lois and Sandy are with her. And Lorraine got mad and threw her milk in my face."

"Oh boy. I'm sorry."

Dabbing my shirt with paper towels did little to make it presentable again. Janet lent me her sweater so I'd have something dry to wear, and then accompanied me back to the cafeteria.

The rest of the day wasn't easy, but I kept reminding myself I belonged to God and I was a good person, regardless of what anyone else thought. Once I met Janet between classes, and she gave me a quick thumbs-up, which I knew meant she was doing her best to counteract the lies. When three thirty came, I latched onto Heather like a piece of Velcro and didn't let go until we were sitting side by side on the bus.

The following day, things were better. Sandy and some of my other friends apologized to me for believing the rumors. Apparently Lois had told them I'd been arrested for selling drugs myself. Her uncle, who worked for the sheriff's department, had supposedly shared this "confidential" tidbit with her dad so he could warn Lois to stay away from me. Yeah, right. The only good part was that it would take Lois a while to live down the reputation she'd gained from this prank. Maybe she'd think twice before spreading such hurtful rumors again.

46

Two weeks after Walter's arrest, Mom returned from another late-night visit to the neighbors with the news that she'd raised the money for Walter's bail.

I was surprised. "You mean Tom agreed to pay it?" I asked.

"More or less. With a few stipulations and things."

"Interesting." I couldn't imagine Tom caving in to her demands. There had to be more to the story.

"They also agreed to let you stay with them again," she continued. "I hope you're okay with that. You'll be moving this weekend."

I stared at her a second. "Great. I don't get any say in it, do I?" I whirled and stomped out of the room. Why should my whole life be uprooted for the benefit of Walter? But I should've known. Mom always did what was most convenient for her. What I wanted didn't matter.

Mom followed me to my bedroom. "I thought you'd like staying with Heather again," she apologized. "But if you really don't want to, we'll think of something else."

I kept my back to her as I pretended to busy myself digging in my top drawer. Since Walter had gone to jail, Mom had started spending time with me. Last weekend, we'd stayed up past midnight, playing Scrabble and Chinese checkers. Mom had assured me we'd do it again soon. Was that just an empty promise? And what about the seeds that had arrived in the mail yesterday? If I wasn't home, how would I ever plant them?

"Why don't you sleep on it, and we'll talk tomorrow," Mom said.

But morning came, and I still didn't know what to say. The week I'd spent with Heather had been enjoyable, but I also remembered how difficult it had been to leave. If it hurt that much to leave after only a week, what would it feel like after several months?

Of course, the circumstances were different this time. Life at home wasn't unbearable, and when I did have to leave, it would be with the promise of seeing them again every Sunday. Maybe it would be all right. They might even have room for me to plant my garden seeds if I stayed into the summer.

Once I'd made up my mind, I couldn't wait to go. Early Saturday morning, Heather came over and helped me pack my clothes and other belongings into a couple of large cardboard boxes. Then Mom drove us and my stuff over to Heather's house and said goodbye.

Patty had already made up my bed in the back room, complete with several hand-crocheted pillows. There was even a mirror and an old dresser for me to use. Once I was settled in, Tom and Patty sat down with me and explained the situation.

"We don't want you to spend the next several months wondering whether we really invited you, or Julie pushed us into this," Tom began. "The truth is, God placed a love and concern for you in our hearts, and that's why we agreed to help in this way. You are as welcome here as any of our grandchildren."

"Thanks," I said.

"Something else you should know," he continued. "We're putting up about half the money to bail Walter out. Our pastor offered to provide the rest. I'll be driving into town this afternoon to post the money and pick Walter up."

So those are the stipulations, I thought. It made sense, considering the amount of money involved. But I could only imagine Mom's embarrassment over not being trusted to handle it herself.

Aloud, I said, "That's awful nice of the pastor. Does Mom know?"

"She was over there with us, talking to him the other night."

"You're kidding." Mom hated preachers almost as much as cops. How had she ever agreed to this?

"You won't believe what Roger had to say about Walter," Tom went on. "Last Monday he went over to the jail to talk with the guys like he does every week. He says typically he'll get one or two of them to pray for salvation, but last week there were about ten. Walter's been preaching to everybody, including the guards, and creating quite a stir."

I snickered. Only Walter would try preaching to the guards. Did he really think they'd listen to him?

That first day at Heather's passed much like usual. I'd spent so many Saturdays visiting that I felt right at home helping out with the chores, playing fetch with Sadie, and watching movies with Heather. After supper, the four of us worked on a puzzle until bedtime.

The next morning, I awoke to the tantalizing aroma of fried sausage. I pulled on my clothes and rapped at Heather's door. "Hey, sleepyhead, I'm gonna beat you to breakfast."

"Yeah, yeah," she mumbled.

Out in the kitchen, Patty was pouring the last of the pancake batter onto the griddle. Tom sat at the table with his laptop, trying to connect to the internet.

"Morning," he greeted me, then added, "Say, do you know what this 'no contact' thing Walter has with you means?"

I frowned. "Not exactly. Why?"

"Because Walter called to ask us to take him to church. He thinks it's okay, but Julie says it's illegal because you're going too."

The internet page finally loaded. Tom typed the term into a search. "All right, here we go."

"Well?" I asked, as he scrolled down the page of some lawyer's website.

"I think it's iffy," he concluded. "It seems they're trying to prevent communication. Sitting in the same room with you is probably not allowed. I guess I'll have to tell him no."

Fair enough, I thought. Walter would be disappointed, but it was his own fault for getting into so much trouble. Still, pity tightened my throat as I imagined the ridicule Mom was heaping on him for wanting to go to church.

"I could stay here," I suggested.

"Yes, I suppose you could," Tom said. "But do you really want to?"

I nodded. "Sure." It wasn't often I got the chance to turn the tables on Mom.

"I'll keep you company," Patty offered.

So it was settled. Tom called Walter back, and after explaining the plan to Mom's satisfaction, he set a time to pick him up.

"I don't think Julie's happy about it," Tom commented afterwards. "But Walter is as eager as a kid on Christmas morning. I hope he's not disappointed."

Just then Heather padded into the kitchen barefoot, carrying her socks. She perched on the kitchen stool and yawned. "Did I miss something?"

"You sure did," I told her. "You've been assigned to take Walter to church."

A look of mock fright crossed her face. "Oh no you don't."

"Not even with a chaperone?" Tom teased her.

She shook her head, laughing. "No thanks. I'll stay here."

"I guess it'll be just you two guys," Patty said. "I think that's more appropriate anyway."

After breakfast, Patty tuned up her guitar and sang with us for a while. Later, we peeled potatoes while she seared the meat for a pot of beef stroganoff. By the time Tom returned around twelve thirty, dinner was ready.

"Well, how did Walter like church?" Patty asked, as she dished up plates.

"He enjoyed it. He'd says he'd like to go back sometime," Tom said. "But I was disturbed how some of the men treated him. You could tell they were only shaking his hand out of duty."

"Did they know who he was?" I asked.

"Most of them did. The story has gotten around. But Walter took everything with a good attitude. He did surprise me after the service though. He wanted to know if Pat was there. I guess he knows her. I pointed her out, and he hobbled all the way across the sanctuary just to apologize for being unkind to her in the past. I don't suppose Pat has that happen very often. She held out her hand, and Walter took it, like he couldn't believe it. He even thanked her. It was the most beautiful thing I've ever seen."

Picturing the scene, I felt tears prick my eyes. This was not the Walter I used to know. Not even close. If only I could have been there to witness it for myself.

***

As the days and weeks passed, good reports about Walter continued to filter back to me. Most of them came from Tom, who visited him every few nights. Mom rarely mentioned him, at least around me, but she couldn't hide the spark in her eyes. At stores she picked up his favorite snacks, and when she drove me up to the park one Sunday to see the spring wildflowers, she brought along her old film camera and snapped pictures of them so he could see them too.

I puzzled how Mom could overlook all the contempt and ill-treatment Walter had given her. Maybe the change in him had affected her more than I realized. Still, her growing fondness for him provoked distrust and even resentment in me. If she really cared about me, like she claimed, how could she ignore all the terrible things he'd done to me? Didn't they upset her even a little?

It helped I knew Walter's time at home was limited. Around the third week of April, I received a letter from the district attorney's office encouraging me to stop by and talk to a victim/witness coordinator about the case. Patty drove me to the courthouse after school the next day and helped me find the right office.

The lady I talked with was very kind. Her name was Brenda. She helped me fill out some forms and explained how the court system worked and what was going to happen next. Brenda told me I had the right to be present at Walter's court dates, and, if I wanted, I would have a chance to speak before the sentencing occurred. Then she gave me her card and told me to call her if I had any more questions or concerns.

I thanked her, then went home with Patty and did my best to forget the whole mess. Every time I thought of Walter standing trial, I felt a vague guilt. I knew he'd done terrible things and deserved to be punished, yet at the same time it felt so wrong to demand he pay for everything he'd done to me. He was my father, after all. And he had said he was sorry. Was I evil to want to see him punished?

Patty told me I didn't have to attend the court sessions unless I wanted to, which made me feel better. But then I remembered what Brenda had said, that I had every right to be there, and the guilt returned. It was Mom who finally set me straight on it.

"You need to be there," she said in her no-nonsense way. "I dare say it'll do you more good than that drug abuse program they want me to put you in. Besides, some of his crimes were against you. Do you really want to hear the outcome of this secondhand?"

I had to admit I didn't. Right then, I promised I'd attend. But I dreaded the date.

47

The twenty-sixth day of May dawned clear and bright. Outside my windows, a robin chirped to his mate in the apple tree. Yellow dandelions strewed the yard, and against the shed pink tulips bloomed. But I scarcely noticed the beauty before me as I stood combing the tangles from my hair. If Walter was sent to prison, would I spend the rest of my life crushed under the guilt that I'd helped send him there?

With a heavy heart, I turned from the window. The other day, I had called Brenda and told her I wanted to speak in court. I had even written out a statement. But now, thinking about it made me feel worse. How could I stand up and accuse my father of hurting me, when I had supposedly forgiven him way back at Christmas time? Maybe I should tell Brenda I had changed my mind. Then no one could say it was my fault if Walter did end up in prison.

Or could they? My heart sank even lower as I remembered the hour and a half I'd spent talking to the police detective. No doubt he'd used my story to further incriminate Walter. Chris had assured me that my anger over Walter's mistreatment of me was normal and healthy. I wished I could believe that. I wished I could somehow silence the voice in my head that kept screaming I was a terrible person because of my "extreme" reactions to Walter's supposedly "reasonable" behavior.

Tom had taken the day off so he could accompany Patty and me to court. After a rather solemn breakfast, Heather left for school.

The rest of us finished the chores and piled into the SUV for the drive to town.

At the courthouse, we took the elevator to the second floor. Brenda met us and escorted us to the courtroom at the end of the hall. Half a dozen people I didn't know were sitting on the rows of wooden benches at the back of the room. Mom was there as well, sitting in the far back next to Walter. She glanced up when we entered and gave me a weak smile.

Brenda guided us to an empty bench and then sat down at one of the tables ahead of us. I huddled on the hard bench next to Patty and glanced around. I'd never been inside a courtroom before.

The judge and the other court officials were already in their places, discussing via microphones whether or not a certain man would make a good replacement judge. Talking softly, Patty pointed out the various officials to me, including the clerk, the court reporter, and the district attorney, who was sitting next to Brenda.

A heavyset man in a suit and tie walked in and sat down at the other table. Patty whispered that he was a lawyer, probably the public defender. The judge ended his conversation, adjusted his glasses, and stated that court would commence.

The public defender began calling cases. One by one, his clients walked up to sit with him at the table while their case was being heard. When it was finished, they left, and the next case was called.

At last the lawyer announced, "State vs. Walter Miner," and it was Walter's turn to walk up and sit at the table. The district attorney handed him some papers, and the judge proceeded to read the charges.

Patty slid an arm around me as the reading continued. I counted ten charges, all of them felonies. For the first time, I glimpsed the enormity of Walter's wrongdoing. The crimes seemed much more shameful when they were read aloud in public.

"Do you plead guilty or not guilty?" asked the judge.

I held my breath.

"Guilty, sir." Walter's voice was low, but clear.

"Mr. Miner, have you made this plea of your own free will?"

"Yes, sir."

MELISSA WILTROUT

"You do realize these charges carry a maximum penalty of eighty-two years in prison, and I could sentence you to that if I feel the offenses warrant it?"

My heart lurched. *Eighty-two years?* That would be like a life sentence.

For a long moment, Walter hesitated. Then, in a strained voice, he said, "Yes, sir. I've thought about that."

"Have you actually committed all the crimes you are being charged with today?"

"I did."

"Walter Miner, if you are not a citizen of the United States, you are advised that a plea of guilty or no contest for the offenses with which you are charged may result in deportation or denial of naturalization, under federal law. Do you still wish to make this plea?"

"Yes, sir."

"The court will accept the plea. You may now proceed with your defense."

Walter's lawyer spoke up. "Thank you. Your Honor, my client deeply regrets his misdeeds and has proven it by his voluntary confession and cooperation with law enforcement. Mr. Miner has led a very difficult life. His father physically abused him as a child. He had little schooling and has only recently learned to read. Under the pressure of trying to earn a living with no education, he made some poor choices which landed him where he is today.

"Mr. Miner is determined to put his evil past behind him and start fresh, beginning with a decent education. I believe he can do this, especially in light of the spiritual awakening he has experienced. Therefore, I request leniency from the court. Although a short period of confinement seems fitting due to the nature of these charges, I believe a harsher punishment will only dampen Mr. Miner's resolve and further alienate him from the society he desperately needs to integrate with. I recommend that counseling and community service requirements be combined with probation to finish out what I would consider an adequate sentence of six or seven years."

The lawyer paused. "Your Honor, my client would like to speak in his own defense."

"He may do so."

After a brief consultation with his lawyer, Walter stood to his feet, steadying himself on the table. Though he still wore his traditional oversized jeans, he had tucked in his flannel shirt and cut his hair. He looked almost respectable.

"I want to explain that I became a Christian about five months ago. I confessed to these things because I saw it was the right thing to do. I couldn't stand them sitting on my conscience anymore. I know I have to pay for what I did, and I'm sure not trying to make excuses or say it wasn't wrong. I want you to know I'm sorry for everything. I'm ashamed, and I wish I hadn't done it. God changed me, and I'm not the same man. I don't even smoke. I hate what I did, and I'm not gonna do any of it again. That's all."

As Walter settled into his chair, his lawyer spoke again. "Your Honor, I would like to call character witnesses for my client."

"You may call them."

"Tom Erickson?" The lawyer craned his neck, scanning the benches on our side of the room.

"Please come up to the clerk and be sworn in. Give your full name and your relation to the defendant, then you may proceed with your statement," the judge instructed.

Tom crossed the room and took the stand with a confidence that suggested he had done such things before.

"I'm Thomas Erickson. I'm a master plumber with P&B Plumbing here in Northford. I've known Walter for the last five months. Being a Christian, I don't generally hang out with people of his sort. It was only through a series of unusual circumstances that I met him.

"It started last December when his teenage daughter showed up at my door, shivering, without a coat, saying her parents were fighting. She ended up staying with us for a week. During that time, Walter was in a bad car accident. Later, while he was at home recuperating, we got a call from his wife asking if we'd come over and keep an eye on him so she could go shopping. She said he was hard to manage, and she didn't want to leave him alone with her daughter.

"This was the first time I'd ever met Walter. When we got there, he was so full of hate and anger toward us that I think he would've thrown us bodily out of the house if he could. Since he was in a wheelchair and couldn't, I sat in his living room and witnessed to him of the saving power of Christ. He didn't like that either, but as I continued talking to him, he saw the truth of the gospel. When he received Jesus, his violent temper and all that hate and anger vanished. It was a miracle.

"Since then, I've visited him at least twice a week, and I know him as a kind and humble man. I trust him enough that I contributed $3,000 of my own money toward his bail."

When Tom finished speaking, the judge asked the district attorney if he wished to cross-examine him.

"Yes, sir." The lawyer rose and positioned himself facing Tom.

"Mr. Erickson, you say Mr. Miner suddenly changed during your talk with him that day."

Tom nodded. "Yes. When he prayed."

"You also imply that you've never seen him angry or hateful since then. I find that hard to believe."

"Sir, I didn't say that. I have seen him angry on a number of occasions. But I believe it has gotten less frequent in the last few months, and he deals with it nonviolently."

"Mr. Erickson, you said you've only known Mr. Miner five months. That's not very long."

"No," Tom admitted.

"And you only see him during brief, scheduled visits, correct?"

"Yes. About twice a week."

"Don't you think there could be aspects of his character that you haven't seen during those brief visits?"

"There could be, although I doubt it."

"No further questions," said the lawyer.

The judge nodded to Tom. "Thank you, sir. You may step down."

"Julie Miner?" Walter's lawyer again scanned the nearly empty benches. "Did you want to speak?"

Mom trembled as she walked to the front. "I'm Julie Miner. I'm Walter's wife. We've been married for twenty-four years. And most of that time, it's been hell. He'd get mad over any little thing. He drank and used drugs, and he was really mean. Most people who knew him were afraid of him. He mistreated me a lot, especially last fall when it got really bad. He'd hit me with his fists or a heavy object. I know he mistreated my daughter too. I never turned him in for domestic abuse, but I should've. He was so horrible to live with that I was seriously looking at divorce. I just couldn't afford it.

"But the day Tom came over, something strange and wonderful happened to him. He says God saved him. I don't know; all I can say is ever since then, he won't get mad even if I yell at him. I haven't seen him drinking or smoking at all in the last couple months. I've actually started to enjoy spending time with him. He's like a new person. I don't see what good would come of sending him to prison."

When she finished, the judge again asked the district attorney whether he wished to cross-examine.

"I'll pass on that. I would like instead to proceed with the victim's statement and my sentencing recommendations."

The judge nodded to Mom. "You may step down." To the attorney, he said, "Go ahead."

"First I would like to give the victim, Tessa Miner, an opportunity to speak," said the lawyer.

My heart began thudding so hard I thought I'd have a heart attack. Brenda turned and smiled at me, nodding for me to go ahead. I tugged the paper containing my statement from my pocket and unfolded it, but I was too nervous to speak. After one or two false starts, I gave up and handed the sweaty, tattered page over to Brenda. She read it aloud.

"I want you to know that my father made my life very miserable for a long time, and it's not like I can just forget it all and it's gone. I still feel I'm a terrible person because of the bad things he made me do. Sometimes I have horrible nightmares. I'm not mad at him, but that doesn't change what happened."

There. It was out. I ducked my head, my face burning as if I had done something very inappropriate. A swarm of accusing thoughts hurled themselves at my mind. *You evil, wicked person! Can't you be more forgiving? You know very well that he's changed!*

Patty reached over and put an arm around me again. "Good job," she whispered, and smiled. "I'm proud of you." I began to breathe easier.

The district attorney took his time detailing the seriousness of Walter's crimes, particularly the ones relating to me. He pointed out that Walter had been convicted of burglary in another state some eighteen years before, and finished by reviewing his more recent rash of convictions for drunken driving, possession, and disorderly conduct.

"Mr. Miner is a chronic criminal and troublemaker," the lawyer concluded. "As you see, he couldn't even keep the conditions of his probation last summer. He is walking with a cane today because six months ago he crashed into a dump truck while high on his own methamphetamine. If it had been any other kind of vehicle, we'd likely have a homicide case on our hands.

"Despite the seemingly positive testimony we heard here today, I believe it's a mistake to think men like Mr. Miner really change. They merely get more skilled at manipulation and deceit. Notice that he didn't turn himself in until the last minute, when law enforcement was already closing in on him. That's not remorse; it's a desperate man's attempt to get off easy. I dare say we'd see a much different attitude in the defendant were he not in the clutches of the law.

"Therefore, in keeping with the severity of these crimes, and for the safety of his daughter and of our entire community, I recommend Mr. Miner be locked up for a considerable length of time. Twenty-five years is the sentence I would like to see him given, and I think that's generous."

As the attorney finished speaking, the room went silent. Then, to my surprise, the judge called a fifteen-minute recess.

"What's happening?" I asked Mom, as we walked out into the hall in search of the restrooms.

"Don't ask me." Mom looked at least as nervous as I felt. "I told him not to plead guilty. It's just plain stupid. But he insisted."

48

ack in the courtroom again, the tension was unbearable. Tom and Walter sat together on the front bench. Mom hunched next to me, her head down. Patty had her eyes closed as if praying. None of us said anything.

When the judge returned, he ordered Walter to stand. "This court cannot pass lightly over such serious crimes," he said. "Mr. Miner, you have done untold damage not only to your daughter, but to many others in the community through your illicit drug business. I concur with the sentencing recommendations of our prosecuting attorney, which I feel are very appropriate for your case. However, in view of the apparent change in your life, Mr. Miner, I have decided to reduce your sentence somewhat."

He paused.

"You are hereby sentenced to five years in the state prisons and eight years of extended supervision. That is a total of thirteen years. You are also ordered to pay a fine of $35,000."

A weight I didn't even know I was carrying lifted from my chest. For the first time in days, I could draw a full breath. I had been vindicated.

Beside me, Mom was fighting back tears. Walter came and gave her a hug. "Hey, Julie, it's over. All done. Could have been worse, hey?"

"You're crazy," she said, sniffing. "You always were." She tried to smile, but it only made her cry harder.

A short time later, I followed Mom down a flight of stairs and out the front doors of the courthouse, leaving Walter behind. Tom and Patty had taken the elevator. We met again on the sidewalk.

"Thanks for coming," Mom said to them. "I appreciate it. And thanks for looking after Tessa all this time."

"Would you two accept an invitation to supper at our place?" Tom asked. "Maybe Tessa could get her things then."

"What time?"

"How about five o'clock?"

"Okay."

The drive home was somber. Mom and I were silent, each occupied with our own thoughts. Personally, I felt satisfied with the outcome. Walter was being punished, but not beyond measure. Hearing the district attorney's viewpoint on the charges cemented things for me, as I grasped for the first time that the way Walter had treated me wasn't just mean, it was a terrible crime. The guilt that had plagued me for months was dissipating like fog on a sunny morning.

At home, Mom sought comfort in cigarettes and soap operas. I went outside and lay down on the grass in the sun. Exhausted from the events of the morning, I fell asleep.

Supper at Tom and Patty's house that evening was uncomfortably quiet. Whatever Mom was thinking, she wasn't telling anyone. After the meal, Tom drew me aside.

"How are you doing? Are you okay with what happened today?"

"Yeah. Mom's unhappy, but I think it's fair, what he got."

"Good."

"I didn't know you were gonna testify for him."

Tom smiled. "I didn't either, until last week. When he said he was going to plead guilty against his lawyer's recommendations, I knew he needed help."

Out in the kitchen, a drawer slammed, and I heard Mom's voice raised in anger. Her words drifted into the living room where we sat.

"He's not, huh? Yeah, I know. God loves me and all that. I've heard it all before. Well, then where was God when they took my kids away?"

Electricity ran through me. *She means my sisters.* Tom half rose, then sat down again.

Patty's reply was soft. "You're carrying a lot of anger. Can I ask what happened?"

"Never mind. I shouldn't have brought it up." Then Mom came into the living room and said it was time to leave.

49

I heard no more about my sisters for some time. I couldn't stop wondering about them, though. Who had taken them away, and why? But I didn't dare ask Mom, and trying to piece together the facts I'd heard over the years yielded no sensible answers. I would have to wait until the subject came up again.

Even so, that summer was the happiest I had known. The first weekend in June, we turned over the soil in Walter's garden and planted my seeds. Everything came up within a week. I liked working in the garden, and as the plants grew, I spent hours pulling weeds and watering

Afternoons often found me over at Patty's, playing with Sadie and helping Patty in her new flowerbeds. She had a gift for growing things and was happy to share her knowledge with me. As the summer progressed, she also began teaching me to cook and play guitar. I missed Heather, who had moved back home with her parents, but we kept in touch by writing. Once in a while she even called me.

Pleasant as my life was, however, there were shadows that friendships and sun-drenched days couldn't dispel. Painful memories resurfaced, eclipsing my joy. Patty encouraged me to talk them out, but I didn't like to. I wanted to forget the past and move on with my life.

The trouble was, I couldn't. I'd have one good day, but then something would trip the switch and plunge me back into the old feelings of guilt and worthlessness. Over and over, Patty reassured me that God loved me and would heal and restore my broken life if I'd give it to him.

I desperately wanted that healing. But entrusting my broken self to God proved incredibly difficult. I hung on, afraid I would lose who I was if I let God take charge.

Patty spent many hours with me, praying, reading Psalms, and teaching me what God was like and what he said about me. As the weeks passed, my guilt and fear gave way to a cautious but growing trust in God. Often when I prayed, he would reassure me of his love. The despair that had threatened to swallow me retreated.

Mom seemed pleased Patty was spending time with me, though I was careful not to let on how much I confided in her. Over supper, I'd recount the latest things I'd learned about growing fuchsias or making white sauce. Mom would listen and ask what we were planning to do the next day. She laughed when she heard I was learning to play guitar.

"It figures. I always said stuff like that was genetic."

"What do you mean, it's genetic? You don't play."

"Want to bet?" Mom laughed again, then got up and disappeared into the bedroom. I could hear her shuffling through the boxes in her closet. When she returned, she laid a small photo album on the table. "Take a look. I don't believe you've seen these before."

Pushing back my now-empty plate, I took the album and eagerly opened it.

The first picture was of a very ancient car. The thing might have been black at one time, but years of rust had rendered it a mottled brown. Light shone through fist-sized holes under the doors. Plastic sheeting and duct tape covered the rear side window. But what captured my attention was the curly-haired teenager leaning against the driver's door. That crooked half grin looked familiar.

I bent for a closer look. Yes, that was Walter. But with his black T-shirt, greasy jeans, long hair, and backwards baseball cap, he looked every bit as disreputable as his car. What had Mom seen in him?

"Pretty, ain't it?" Mom commented from behind me.

It took me a minute to realize she meant the car. "Uh, I don't know about pretty," I said. "Interesting, maybe."

"It's too bad Walter isn't here to scold you," she teased. "That car was his pride and joy for years. The transmission finally died on the thing; otherwise we'd still have it."

The following pages held more pictures of Walter – driving a tractor, bottle-feeding a calf, stacking hay bales, roasting hotdogs over an open campfire, lying barefoot and shirtless in the grass by a muddy stream.

I was halfway through the album before I found the first picture of Mom. She was sitting cross-legged on a shabby, mustard-colored couch, playing a small guitar. I marveled how young and pretty she looked.

"This would be shortly after we were married," Mom said. "Walter took that picture on the sly."

The remainder of the album contained a series of posed shots of the two of them together, several pictures of white ducks on a pond, and a final shot of Walter lying on his back underneath his car. The hood was propped open with a piece of wood, and all that could be seen of Walter were his dirt-caked boots.

"Don't you have any wedding pictures?" I asked.

"We didn't have a wedding," Mom said, reaching for the album. "Neither of us had any money to speak of. We drove to town one day and got married, and that was about it. Anyway, like I said, I did play guitar. I wasn't half bad, either."

"Do you think you could still play?"

"I don't know. It's been like twenty years."

Then she changed the subject. "Say, I wanted to ask you. One of the ladies I work with has a cat she's been trying to find a home for. You're not still interested in a pet, are you?"

Excitement bubbled up in me as I realized what she was saying. "You mean we could get her?"

"If you want. But you'd have to take complete charge of her."

"Don't worry, I'll take care of her. How soon can we get her?"

Mom laughed at my eagerness. "Maybe Saturday. We'll need to pick up a few things first. I'll talk to Kathy tomorrow."

That night I could hardly sleep for excitement. A cat! And it was going to be mine! I would have been content to settle for something small – like a hamster or even a turtle. But this was more than I had dared to hope for.

"Thank you, God," I whispered into my pillow. "I don't know what you did to make this happen, but it's totally awesome."

After our shopping trip that Saturday, we drove over to Kathy's home to pick up the cat. A short, dark-haired lady answered our knock and took us behind the house to the enclosed porch. As she opened the screen door, a sleek black cat with a white face and bib jumped from a wicker chair and greeted us with a series of loud meows. I scratched her head, and she curled around my legs, purring.

"She likes me," I breathed. "What's her name?"

"I call her Nikki, but you can rename her if you like," the lady said. She lifted the cat and gave her an affectionate kiss. Then she handed her to me. "Well, she's all yours. Take good care of her."

"Thanks. I will." I felt overwhelmed. This was the best gift I'd ever had. I hooked a finger under her red collar to prevent a possible escape as we walked to the car, but Nikki seemed content in my arms.

Back home, I set up her cat box at the bottom of the basement stairs and her food dishes in the kitchen next to the pantry. Nikki wandered from room to room, meowing and rubbing against the furniture as she investigated every inch of her new home. At last she sprawled out on the living room carpet for a nap, her black coat gleaming in the sunlight. I stretched out beside her.

"I think she's happy," Mom commented, glancing up from where she sat reading a magazine.

"Oh yeah," I agreed. "She thinks she owns the place. Don't you, Nikki?" I scratched her chin with one finger, and she rolled over and batted at my hand, purring loudly.

"I was wondering though, what made you change your mind?" I asked Mom.

"Change my mind?"

"Yeah. About me having a pet."

"Oh, that." Mom thought a bit. "Lots of things, I guess. We had a dog once, way back, but it didn't get along with Walter. He got rid of it."

"That's too bad."

"Yeah, well, maybe it was for the best. He was getting aggressive. But I've always wanted a cat. I figure it's the best way to deal with the mice in the basement."

"Or in my room?" I added.

She laughed. "You two are gonna make a great pair." Reaching for her camera, she snapped a picture of me and Nikki lying on the carpet.

50

I returned to school in September feeling like a different person. Had it been only a year since I'd run away and sustained myself by stealing from the grocery store? Much as I wanted to forget those dark days, I knew I never would. Nevertheless, seeing how far God had brought me filled me with thankfulness.

It felt good to see my friends. Janet smothered me in a bear hug and asked how my summer had been. Sandy wanted to know how my garden was doing. Even Lois begged to see a picture of Nikki, though she laughed at me when I said she'd have to wait until the pictures were developed.

Lorraine, however, made it clear she wanted nothing to do with me. When we met in the hall that first day, she scowled and turned her back. I shrugged and continued walking. If she didn't want to be friends, that was fine with me. She was kind of strange anyway.

But try as I did, I couldn't blot Lorraine out of my mind. She still had her little gang of followers and acted tougher than ever. But the veneer was wearing thin. She looked sick. Even when she was with her friends, I could see the loneliness in her eyes. Was there nothing I could do? I admired the way Heather had reached out to me, even though I was often rude to her. Maybe someday, I'd have a chance to do the same for Lorraine.

Or maybe not. Two weeks into the school year, Lorraine was caught selling drugs on school property. She was arrested, along with Brittney and another student. I had to admit I was relieved.

At lunch the next day, I noticed Crystal sitting alone at the table Lorraine and Brittney had always claimed. I walked over to her.

"Hey," I said. "Want to come sit with me and Janet?"

She glanced at me, then looked down again and shook her head.

"Okay then. Well, I just wanted to let you know you're welcome to."

Feeling awkward now, I returned to my own table. "She won't even talk to me," I complained to Janet.

"That's okay," Janet said. "Are you trying to change her, or be her friend?"

The question made me think. "Be her friend, I guess."

"Then I'd say you did just fine."

It took a week of invitations before Crystal came to sit with us. She didn't say much the first day, but I trusted she would open up more in time.

I returned home that afternoon feeling particularly good about myself. Stepping off the bus, I got the mail and started up the driveway. The September sun still shone warm on my back, although storm clouds loomed in the western sky and golden leaves drifted from the big silver maple with every whisper of the breeze. I paused under the tree and gazed upward through the branches, feasting my eyes on the color. All too soon, winter would come and lock us into seven months of cold and dreariness. Mom wouldn't mind if I borrowed her camera for just a few pictures.

I pulled a key from my pocket and let myself in the back door. Nikki jumped from a chair and greeted me with loud meows. I stroked her as I flipped through the mail.

"What's this?" I wondered aloud, picking a card-sized blue envelope from the pile. My heart stopped when I saw the return address. *Sarah Miner, Springfield, Missouri.* It was addressed to Mom.

I pressed the envelope to the window, but all I could determine was that it contained a card and a letter. Disappointed, I dropped it back into the pile. Mom would be furious if I opened it. But my mind raced in curious speculation. Why would my sister write to Mom after all these years? Did she perhaps want to visit? The possibility both excited and scared me. What would it be like to meet her? Would she be friendly to me? Or would she act snobbish and grown up?

The hour until Mom came home felt like an eternity. I had plenty of homework to do, but instead I went back outside and used up the film in Mom's camera taking colored leaf shots. I even walked a few hundred feet up the road to capture a particularly colorful hill. If that really was a storm in the west, it might be my last chance. Meanwhile Nikki sniffed the bushes around the shop, hunting crickets and mice before sprawling out on the step for a sunbath.

As the hands on my watch crept toward six o'clock, I called Nikki inside, fed her, and settled at the table with my schoolbooks.

Mom drove in a few minutes after six. She greeted me, then washed her hands and set to work making supper. Unaware of the blue envelope hidden beneath the bills and catalogs, she sliced an onion and fried it with hamburger, then added spaghetti sauce and a can of green beans. By the time she finished and reached for the pile of mail, I was ready to burst.

Her face paled when she saw the blue envelope. In one quick motion, she tucked it in her back pocket. Then she spread out the grocery flyer from Allen's and began marking the coupons she wanted.

"Is that from one of my sisters?" I couldn't hold back the question.

"I don't know anyone else with that name." Mom's answer was matter of fact, but I detected a catch in her voice.

"Could I read it, do you think?"

Mom tried to laugh. "Before I do?"

"Well no, but..."

"Look. Whatever's in there is none of your business."

I felt as if she'd slapped me. "But Mom, she's my sister! How can you say it's not my business!"

"Because that's the way it is." Mom folded the Allen's flyer and shoved it on top of the refrigerator, then strode down the hall to her bedroom and shut the door.

I tried once more during supper. "Can't you at least tell me what the letter says? Please?"

"No! And if you don't quit bugging me about it, you're gonna be sorry!"

It was a sharp disappointment. Why hadn't I gone ahead and read Sarah's letter while I had the chance? Now I might never know what it said, much less solve the mystery of what had happened to my sisters.

***

Mom seemed quieter than usual in the weeks that followed. She made supper, vacuumed the crumbs off the floor, and did the laundry, but she no longer laughed at Nikki's foolish antics or invited me to watch movies with her on Saturday nights. Instead, after the kitchen was cleaned up in the evening, she'd slip off to her bedroom. There she'd remain for hours, with the door closed and only a dim light burning.

I thought she was ill. But one night on my way to bed, I heard muffled sobs behind the closed door. Mom rarely cried, except after one of Walter's beatings. I listened a moment, then crept off to bed with tears in my own eyes. Maybe Mom wasn't as tough as she wanted me to think. Maybe she carried hurts I knew nothing about. Was she lonely? Did she wish she had a friend, or even someone to talk to? I wanted to comfort her, but I did not know how.

Nikki jumped up and nuzzled my face, then curled up against my chest with a purr. I stroked her silky fur and prayed for Mom until I fell asleep.

The next day was a Sunday. As usual, I left for church before Mom got up. When I returned, I found her sitting in Walter's easy chair, smoking and watching television. She glanced up when I walked in.

"How was church?" she asked.

"It was good. I like it a lot now that I know most of the songs."

Mom clicked the TV off. "There's something I wanted to talk to you about. Remember that letter?"

I nodded. How could I forget it?

"Well…" Mom pushed her hair back out of her eyes. "I think it's time I told you a few things. About your sisters, and how things were before you were born." She hesitated, and I could see her hands were trembling. "It's not a pretty story. But I need to tell you. And Ericksons."

"Ericksons? Why?"

She stood up. "Because I'm sick of how they treat me. Are they at home now?"

"Yeah, they should be."

"Then let's go." She went to the back closet and put on her coat, then shouldered her purse. "Come on."

Puzzled, I grabbed my coat and followed her to the car.

51

The ride to the neighbors' was short. "What a surprise," Patty greeted me, as she opened the door. "And Julie, we haven't seen you for a long time. Come in."

Tom sat on the couch in his church clothes, playing catch with Sadie. Seeing me, the dog bounded over and began licking my hands. I laughed and gave her a good scratch on the shoulders.

Mom settled into Tom's armchair. "I need to talk to you guys." She glanced at Tom. "You know Walter's story."

"A good piece of it," he agreed.

"Well, you know what they say. You gotta hear both sides to get the truth. I'm sick of you guys treating me like a crook, based on some half-baked story Walter told. I'd like to give you my side of things."

"Okay. I'm not sure what you're referring to, but go ahead," Tom said.

Patty sat down next to Tom. I settled into the other armchair and pulled my legs up.

"This might surprise you, but I grew up in a religious, church-going family," Mom began. "My parents were respectable people who didn't drink or smoke or even swear. I had two older brothers and a sister five years younger than me who was slightly retarded. I was a pretty good kid. I went to church every week, learned verses for Sunday school, and even sang in the children's choir. But when I got older, things changed.

"I was fifteen when I started drinking with a couple of friends. I never drank a lot, and at first my parents didn't know. But one night, the party got out of hand. The cops busted us, and Dad had to come get me. After that, I had to stay home in the evening. It was probably a good thing, though I didn't see it that way. It just made me mad.

"I didn't get along at all with my mom. She was always busy with my sister and never had time for me. One day we were having this big fight, and I yelled that God didn't exist. She totally flipped. When Dad heard about it, he claimed it was blasphemy and gave me a whipping. I tried to be more careful after that, but nothing changed. I fought constantly with both of them. My dad said if I kept on like I was, I'd go to hell. That scared me, until I decided it wasn't true. I decided nothing they'd told me was true.

"I was seventeen when I met the boy who worked on the neighbor's farm. The two of us hit it off right from the start. I'd sneak out at night and even Sunday mornings to see him. We'd go sit by the creek, or tramp through the hayfields together in the moonlight." She smiled, remembering.

"He was bold and daring and fun to be with. I knew right away I wanted to marry him. One day he showed up in his rusty beater of a car, looking for me. He was a bit of a character even back then, with his long hair and all. Mom was furious. She said if I went and married somebody like that, I was going to hell for sure.

"I was so sick of them trying to scare me into being good that I said some pretty mean things to her. She started crying. When Dad came home, he said he'd whip me, so I slipped out and ran to Walter. He promised to protect me if my dad showed up. We sat up in the haymow for hours, talking and smoking cigarettes. I sneaked home about three in the morning, and I never did get a whipping.

"We eloped a short time later. I had just turned eighteen. Walter was nineteen. For a while, we lived in a trailer on the farm. Later we moved to town, and he got a job driving a truck. By then we had two little girls. Walter was gone a lot with his job, and he started to change. He was drinking a lot more, and who knows what else he was into. He was always experimenting. But anyway, he wasn't all that nice to us when he came home. He'd get mad at the girls, yell, and slap them. I tried to keep them out of his way.

"A couple years went by, and Walter got into an accident with his truck. He lost his license and his job. After that, he couldn't stay out of trouble. I pushed him to get another job, but he never did. He kept saying there were easier ways to make money.

"One night he got this idea. He wanted me to help. It sounded kind of interesting, so after the girls went to sleep, we took off. Everything went smoothly until the cops pulled out behind us on the way home. Walter tried to outrun them, but it was a pretty stupid idea. We slid into the ditch and got arrested.

"We both ended up in jail. I did nine months, and he did a year. During this time, my parents took care of the girls. When we got out, I took a job, since I was the only one who still had a driver's license. Walter stayed home with the girls. Things went okay for a couple of weeks, until my boss found out I had a record and fired me. She didn't even ask me to explain, just handed me my check and told me to beat it."

Mom paused, and for a moment she looked like she was going to cry. But she composed herself and continued.

"About this time Walter discovered we could make lots of money selling drugs, and it was safer than burglary. Pretty soon he had quite a business going. I got used to it, but I never could get used to his temper. It didn't take much to set him off. One day, the girls were playing tag, and they knocked a lamp over and broke it. Walter went into a rage and beat both of them. It was horrible. I was so mad I could've killed him. But Walter said he was sorry and he hadn't meant to do it.

"I believed him, until it happened again about a month later. As the summer wore on, it became a regular thing. Every couple of weeks, he'd find some reason to beat up the girls. It got to where I was afraid to leave them home with him.

"Sometimes I let the girls stay overnight or even all weekend with my parents. They had a good time there, and I liked being free of them now and then. But you know little kids. They talk about everything. I guess my mother noticed some bruises and asked them about it. Next thing I knew, Dad was at the door chewing me out. He says to me, 'This is terrible. Why don't you stop him? Don't you even care about your own kids?' Well, of course I did, but what was I supposed to do? Walter was a lot bigger and stronger than me.

"I said, 'Look. I'm doing the best I can.'

"He said, 'Well, it's not good enough. We know what you guys are doing over here. Either you straighten out and make a decent home for your kids, or we're keeping them. And if you raise a fuss, I'll just see to it that everything comes out.'

"I didn't know what to do. When I told Walter, he was really mad. He went over and started threatening my dad, and I guess things got pretty ugly. Somebody called the police, and Walter spent a couple days in jail. Disorderly conduct, they called it. Meanwhile, I could not get my parents to let me take my girls home, and when Walter got out, we had a big fight. I wanted him to get his act together so we could get the girls back, but he said it was no use."

Mom's voice choked. She tugged a handkerchief from her pocket and wiped her eyes. With difficulty, she continued.

"Several months passed, and we had another baby. I was afraid my parents would find out and take her too. Walter tried to convince them we had changed, but my dad wouldn't listen. He wouldn't even let us see the girls.

"We couldn't do a thing. It was terrible. When Tess was a few weeks old, we packed up and left. We moved around quite a bit, afraid the police were after us, but we finally settled down here so Tess wouldn't have to keep changing schools. So, that's what happened." She stopped, and dropped her gaze to her lap.

An awkward silence followed. I sat quietly, fitting the pieces of the story together. Things that had puzzled me for years finally made sense. I had never dreamed Mom was carrying this much pain.

At last Tom spoke. "So you were both selling back then?"

Mom's face flushed, and she nodded without looking up. "If it hadn't been that way, I think I would have left Walter and gotten my girls back."

"Walter confessed to dealing drugs in the past," Tom recalled.

"I know. I don't see why he had to bring it up. For a while there, I thought I was done for. But I guess it happened too long ago for them to do anything about it."

"Why did you tell us this, Julie?" Tom asked. "It can't be to clear your character, as you said in the beginning, because it turns out you're an even worse character than we thought."

Mom tried to laugh. "I don't know. Guess I just had to get it off my chest. I blamed Walter for the trouble in our family, and I blamed God too, but I guess I'm as much to blame as him." She bowed her head in an attempt to hide the tears that slipped down her cheek. "I'm sorry. I shouldn't have come here."

"Jesus wants to forgive you," Patty said. "All you have to do is ask."

"I don't know," Mom said, but more tears ran down her face. She buried her face in her hands.

"Nobody is too bad," Tom said. "The more sins you have, the more love and forgiveness he offers. You can't do a single thing to clean yourself up. All you can do is accept what Jesus has done and ask him to save you. Wouldn't you like to do that?"

Mom was sobbing now. "Yes. Yes, I would. I don't wanna be like this anymore." Amid the sobs, she prayed. "Jesus, I'm so sorry."

She lifted her face with a look of astonishment. "He's in me! I can feel him!"

"Thank you, Jesus!" Patty exclaimed.

Mom was smiling and crying at the same time. "Wait til Walter hears about this. He's not gonna believe it!"

I almost couldn't believe it myself. With her pride and her cynical attitude toward what she called "religion," Mom was the last person I expected to see praying for salvation. Especially with others present. Only God could have brought it about.

***

The next morning, I awoke to Mom singing in her bedroom. How long had it been since I'd heard her sing? I lay still and listened as the words floated out.

> *My Jesus, I thank you,*
> *My sins are gone, my life you made new*
> *Now I can sing, I feel so free*
> *My Jesus, I thank you.*

It sounded like a hymn, except the words and tune kept changing. Over breakfast, I inquired about it. "What's that song you were singing this morning? Something about 'Jesus I thank you.'"

Mom smiled. "It just came to me."

"I like it," I said.

Mom poured milk into her bowl of cornflakes, then leaned forward and tugged an envelope from her back pocket. "I guess there's no reason why you can't read this now," she said, and passed it to me.

I slid the card from the envelope and unfolded the paper inside. The letter was written in red ink with a neat hand.

Dear Mom,

I hope this letter finds you. I did a search on the internet only to discover that you aren't the only person with your name. For a long time I've wanted to write and let you know how Megan and I are doing. I guess you've probably wondered about us all these years. I sure did about you. Why didn't you ever come back for us? Grandma said you wouldn't, but we kept hoping anyway. I know Dad was mean sometimes, and you were always so busy, but I still wish we could've stayed together.

I found an article about Dad and his trouble last spring while I was looking for you. How awful! I didn't know he was into stuff like that. I am curious, did he really become a Christian? How did it all turn out?

Things are going okay for me. I have a job as a salesperson at a furniture store here in Springfield, and Saturday nights I'm usually over at the theater selling tickets. I'm making my way in the world, I guess. Megan is still living at home and helps out there a lot. Grandma has had some health problems and can't handle all the housework on her own.

I can write more if you like, but I will wait for your reply. I hope I haven't bothered you with this letter.

Sincerely, Sarah

I folded the letter back into the card. "You wrote back to her, didn't you?"

Mom shook her head. "I wanted to, but…" Tears fell into her cereal. "I don't know how to say this. I guess I knew I'd have to tell her the truth, and it just scared me. I mean, what's she supposed to think? Chances are she'll hate me."

She reached for the card and held it in her hands for a long moment. "I guess all I can do is try."

52

*C*ome on, Tess, sit still." Janet was trying to French braid my hair so I would look elegant for the evening. I was rebelling.

"It's just a movie," I grumbled. "Nobody's gonna see me in there anyway."

Ignoring my protests, Janet worked in more layers of hair, then braided it down my back and secured everything with an elastic band.

"There, take a look."

I stepped to the mirror and studied my reflection. "Hey, not bad. Thanks."

"You're welcome." Janet reached for the purse she'd left on my bed. "Ready to go now?"

I dabbed a bit of powder on my wrists, grabbed a sweater, and said, "Yup."

"Have fun, girls," Mom called as we hurried toward the door.

I slipped into the passenger seat of Janet's car and settled in for the long drive to town. Tomorrow was my sixteenth birthday, and Janet was taking me to see a movie with a few other young people from church. To them it was a simple outing, but for me, it was a dream come true. For the first time in my life, I was going out with friends on a Saturday night. Mom's only stipulation was that I be home by eleven.

I cracked my window and inhaled the fresh, moist air. Nothing smelled as good as rain and wet earth at the end of a long winter. In a few weeks, I'd be able to plant my garden. I had already ordered the seeds, sneaking in a packet of nasturtiums along with the beans, corn, and squash Mom had authorized. If everything went right, I'd have a garden of little seedlings to show Sarah when she came.

I smiled to myself. Sarah had corresponded with us for some time now. With each letter she opened up more, telling us details about her boyfriend, her new apartment, and her two black Pomeranian puppies she hoped to breed someday. In Mom's last reply, she had invited her to come up and visit us. The meeting was set for Memorial Day.

"How's your dad doing? Have you heard from him at all?" Janet's question broke into my thoughts.

"Yeah, he writes to Mom once in a while. His spelling is atrocious, but otherwise he's doing okay, I guess."

"How much longer before he gets out?"

"Three years, maybe three and a half. I don't know exactly." I leaned back in the seat and closed my eyes. I did not want to think about Walter. Not tonight.

Janet seemed to understand, for she asked no further questions, but instead slipped a tape into the player. Soon the mellow voice of Don Williams filled the little car.

At the theater, Janet's sister and half a dozen other girls joined us.

"Hey Tess, aren't you gonna say hi?" asked a voice behind me. I whirled to find myself face to face with Heather. How had she gotten here? We embraced, laughing.

"You should have let me know you were coming," I said. "You practically scared me to death!"

"I wanted to surprise you. After all, it's not every day a girl turns sixteen." She hugged me again. "Come on, let's get in line."

After buying tickets and a giant bag of popcorn to share, we all trooped down the hallway to the theater.

"I wish Crystal would've come," I said to Janet as we took our seats. We had both invited her.

Janet shrugged. "Maybe she will next time. I'm just glad you could come."

I took a handful of popcorn and said, "Me too."

The movie turned out to be a Christian film about extending forgiveness and grace to those around you, whether or not they deserved it. Although quite entertaining, it also challenged me to consider my own life and relationships. And I realized there was something I needed to do.

As the credits rolled across the screen at the end, I followed Janet and the others down the carpeted ramp to the hallway.

"Hey, anybody wanna go out for ice cream?" suggested one of the girls.

"That sounds fun," Janet said. "Tess? You in?"

I agreed.

At the ice cream shop, I ordered a chocolate sundae, then sat at the table nibbling and listening to the conversation. Now and then I interjected a comment, but mostly I kept my thoughts to myself. I needed to finish thinking over what I'd learned from the film.

In many ways, the past year had been much more pleasant without Walter. I could go on shutting him out of my life, and no one, not even Walter, would say I was wrong. In fact, the law dictated he had to keep his distance from me until his sentence was served.

Yet I knew the change in him was genuine. Everyone who had dealt with him in the last sixteen months could attest to his good character and Christian testimony. Though I could never completely forget the past, maybe God wanted me to offer him a measure of friendship as a gift.

"Would you mind stopping by the grocery store on the way home?" I asked Janet, as we walked out to her car afterwards. "There's something I need to pick up."

"No problem. I need some batteries for my camera anyway."

While Janet debated between the eight pack and the sixteen pack, I headed for the candy aisle. There in the corner of the bottom shelf, I found what I was looking for – a box of Andes mints. Mom had told me once that it was Walter's favorite kind of candy.

On impulse, I bent and picked up a second box. I'd ask Mom to include them, along with a short note, in the next care package she sent Walter.

Resources

If you have suffered abuse and would like help or counseling, here are a few resources to get you started.

National Child Abuse Hotline (ChildHelp USA)

1-800-422-4453

http://www.childhelp.org/pages/hotline-home

Provides crisis intervention, information, literature, and referrals to other resources. Calls are anonymous and confidential.

Christian Survivors

www.christiansurvivors.com

Provides support forums and links to resources for survivors of all types of abuse.

Christian books dedicated to healing the wounds in the heart:

For women: *Captivating* by John and Stasi Eldredge

For men: *Wild at Heart* by John Eldredge

Connect with the authors at http://www.ransomedheart.com

About the Author

Melissa Wiltrout lives in west-central Wisconsin with her two dogs, an energetic terrier named Daisy and a Sheltie named Chester. During the summer months she keeps busy at the family nursery and landscaping business. Writing is her favorite activity, but she also enjoys relaxing with a good book, playing guitar, breeding goldfish, and gardening.

Connect with Melissa
Blogspot: www.mychroniclesofhope.blogspot.com
Facebook: www.facebook.com/authormelissawiltrout
Review this book on Amazon:

Made in the USA
Charleston, SC
20 September 2013